Earther 27

A Fragments novel

Kell Willsen

For Mrs. Lovegrove
and Mr. Smith

Chapter One

'The walls are going again, Earther 27,' bellowed the warden. 'Don't just stand there you useless mud-rat! Do your job!'

Kerrig, Earther 27, rolled his eyes but otherwise ignored the younger man. He was already channelling his Elemental ability into the brittle rock of the tunnel walls and he wondered, not for the first time, why someone with a Talent like Sound Projection had been assigned as a warden to the prison mines. The man's inability to restrain his voice had the entire sector on the verge of collapse. The big Earther sighed and shrugged. Who knew why the Avlem did anything?

The light shower of rock dust stopped falling, and Kerrig turned his attention to firming up the rest of the tunnel. With another two Earthers and a couple of Marshlanders he thought that this stretch could be stabilised for a couple of weeks - long enough to empty the seam of the ore that had tempted them to dig into this shale in the first place. Then it would be back to the main seam for all of them.

Even as he assured himself of this, Kerrig doubted it would be that simple. The warden had been gone for some time, counting by the steady pulse of Earther power coming in through his bare feet and out through his calloused hands. It shouldn't take this long to fetch help, even from another sector.

His muscles burned with the effort of holding off the collapse. Kerrig forced himself to ignore the pain. *Just a little while*, he thought to himself. *Just hold firm; it will all be back to normal soon.*

'Normal' for Kerrig meant being back in the main body of sector 27, not up in this cramped side-seam. It meant trusty duty with the pit donkeys morning and evening, away from the other prisoners. It meant using his innate Earther abilities to monitor his sector for potential problems, not being called in at the last minute to keep the roof from collapsing on stupid wardens' stupid heads.

Normal wasn't perfect, but it was reliable. You knew where you were with normal. And there was always that dream, in the back of his mind, of the day when things would *really* get back to normal; with the People free, the Outsiders gone, and the Shanzir avenged. He might not live to see it, but he knew it must come. Time healed everything.

Kerrig had sunk himself so firmly into the walls that he felt the warden's return before he heard it - and his heart sank. A heavy cart and a half-dozen workers carrying tools were *not* what he needed. He only hoped that some of the workers were Earthers or Marshlanders, and not Fire Breathers like the poor child who'd discovered this dangerous branch in the first place. The boy who was crouched in the corner even now; though he was bright enough to have stopped digging as soon as the warden left.

The only other person there (not counting the ever-present guards) was an Avlem prisoner. Kerrig ignored her. When she'd first been transferred into his sector, Kerrig had been curious to know what crime would cause the Avlem to shut up one of their own with the 'native scum'. After a week, he thought he knew: the crime of being a sludging nuisance. She had *fussed* over the Fire Breather boy, bringing him to the notice of the warden and his guards. If not for her, Kerrig thought, they wouldn't even be in this area and the boy wouldn't be in danger of drowning in shale.

The warden barked at the guards on the tunnel entrance to stand aside; and Kerrig braced himself for further shouting. He couldn't maintain this level of output for long, even with his legs buried in his Element up to his knees, and he hoped the warden wouldn't insist on staying to oversee the whole operation.

A small, copper-coloured donkey came into view hauling a cart laden with wooden pit props. Two of the workers were pushing from behind and Kerrig looked at them with approval. As a rule, he didn't take notice of individual prisoners but anyone who helped his animals surely deserved some consideration.

The warden, meanwhile, started directing the workers to get the props into position. Simple shoring up would be useless but harmless, so Kerrig let them work. But when the warden ordered the prisoners to make holes and hammer the props into them, the Earther knew he had to object.

The warden didn't take it well. He accused Kerrig of exaggerating the danger in an attempt to score a few days' light work for himself and his 'native pals'. He raged when Kerrig flatly contradicted his orders to the workers, and was practically apoplectic when the Earther's instructions were obeyed. With every shout more dust and loose rock fell until everyone was grey with the stuff. Kerrig felt his strength running out, and knew he had to make a decision. The Fire

Breather child was to his left and the pit donkey stood in front of him. He looked at the prisoners who had helped push the cart and said just one word.

'Run.'

Earther 27 let the walls fall, using the dregs of his power to throw the debris to his right. The last thing he heard were the panicked cries of the warden and his guards as they fled the tidal wave of rock.

◆

Kerrig flickered back to consciousness through a series of troubled dreams.

Memories of being carried from his mother's deathbed by the old chief; hanging face down across the man's arms, and limp with grief and fury.

Of beatings when he was sent away to be the Earther of sector 27 for the first time, both when he protested the move and when he tried to escape it.

Of cold nights, before he learnt how to wrap himself in a blanket of stone. And finally of his first soil bed, warm and snug in Earth's embrace.

He smiled in his sleep, and resisted the urge to wake. This one was a *good* dream.

◆

Kerrig registered various things as he clung to sleep. The scent of smoke, thin and sharp. Not quite the same as the torches that lit the tunnels, nor the cooking fires that filled the ovens. The covering of real soil, so rare in the rocky confines of sector 27. Perhaps the Mines had an infirmary of sorts, where someone knew enough to let an Earther heal in his own Element?

But it was the voices that eventually persuaded Kerrig to wake up. One adult and two children. The boy's voice sounded like the Fire

8

Breather's - good to know the child was safe. The adult was, unfortunately, the Avlem prisoner. Eh, at least she wasn't dead. The third voice, a little girl's, was unfamiliar. It was also the closest, and sounded worried.

'Why won't he wake up? He's always wake up before breakfast, and it's more than breakfast. It's nearly time to go back home. Does he need to be back home to wake up?'

Kerrig heard the Avlem woman murmur something soothing, but it didn't seem to placate the child. In fact, the girl sounded close to tears. Curious, Kerrig opened his eyes and started to sit up.

He was almost knocked down again by a small body smacking into his chest, head first. He felt arms squeezing his ribs, reaching only halfway around his bulky frame. The girl's voice became a muffled, happy babbling.

'He's awake and alright and awake and he's going to take me home!' There was more in the same vein, but it was absorbed by the rough fabric of his tunic. Kerrig steadied himself with one hand, and awkwardly patted the small coppery head with the other.

'There now, little one, it's alright. No need to-'

The little arms squeezed him harder than ever, then the child stepped back and danced on the spot, her red-brown face swallowed up by a huge grin.

'You *see*?' she said to the Avlem woman. 'He *does* knows me! Knows my name, says, "Little One" - that's me! My Stony-Man is ever so clever and he knows me like I know him!' The girl rounded on Kerrig again, pushing her face at his chest. Suddenly, she wasn't a girl at all, and Kerrig was unconsciously petting the mane of a small, copper-coloured donkey. Orange eyes looked trustingly into his, and Kerrig froze.

It's a Shifter, he thought, panic making his mind race. All this time, I had a sludging Shifter in the stables and never even knew it. Ugh! Shifters, sneaking around in disguise like criminals. The big Earther shuddered, and tried to push the animal away. He saw the Avlem woman approach, but barely spared her a glance. The Avlem were rude and cruel, but they were nothing compared to the lurking horror of their allies. With Shifters around, you couldn't trust anyone or anything.

The Avlem laid a hand on the creature's shoulder, and it took child-shape again.

'That's nice, dear,' she said, as if the last five seconds had never happened. 'Now that you know your friend is alright, why don't you go and find a nice place to graze?'

The Shifter smiled brightly at the two adults, and scrambled through a hole halfway up the low wall of earth. Kerrig saw long strands of grass around the outside, and thought they must be under the slope of a hill. For the first time, Kerrig took stock of his surroundings.

A roughly spherical space, with a flattened floor. The Avlem woman had to duck her head to avoid the ceiling, and Kerrig could tell that he would be in the same position when he got up. A small fire burned on a double-handful of twigs, tended by the Fire Breather boy. The Avlem crossed the room in a couple of awkward steps and spoke to him.

'Go and keep an eye on Maddie, Volnar,' she said. 'We're hidden well enough here, but make sure she doesn't go too far.'

'Can I take the fire with me?'

'No. You don't need it - the sun hasn't set yet.'

The boy made for the entrance, and Kerrig called after him.

'What are you thinking, going out alone after that thing? It's a Shifter!'

The boy stared at the Earther.

'She's a little kid,' he said, heatedly. 'You don't leave little kids out on their own.' And he was gone before Kerrig could say another word, or move to close the entrance.

'Shifters aren't children, they just look like them sometimes,' he said, but the young Fire Breather was apparently out of earshot.

The woman wasn't. Before he could blink, Kerrig was face-to-face with an angry Avlem.

'Madrigal is a *child*, and one who's devoted to you - though Life alone knows why. You don't have to like her, but if you hurt her then I swear by my Talent that I will hurt you.'

She sounded so sincere that Kerrig tried not to smile at the idea of the slightly-built woman being able to do anything to him. Her expression hardened, and Kerrig's confidence faltered. Resentment, usually a slow-burning fire banked carefully in his heart, suddenly sent forth a jet of flame.

'Oh, how original, he sneered. 'Avlem gentry threatening a common Earther. What're you going to do? Take away my land? My family? My freedom? No, because you've already done all that. What's left, Avlem? What's left for you and your pet Shifter to steal?'

She stared at him for a moment, as if in shock. Then she gave him a look of contempt. It should have suited her, being the default expression of all Avlem in Kerrig's experience, but somehow it didn't. The lines of her face were at odds with the curled lip and the pinched nostrils.

'And I thought my eyes were bad,' she told him. 'Yours can't see anything closer than a hundred years ago. For the love of... it's all in the past! Things might not be perfect, but we're at peace now - the Avlem, the Sidrax, and you Elementals. The wars are over, and have been for decades. Don't take out your grandparents' quarrels on a child.'

There was so much Kerrig wanted to say to this that the words choked him. A strangled laugh came out, hitching like a sob.

'You know nothing,' he said at last. 'You're ignorant, like all your kind, and you destroy everything with your ignorance. You talk of forgetting the wars - easy to do when you're the winner. Not so easy when there are losses in the past it would kill you to forget.

'Shifters are soldiers and assassins by nature, vicious and deceptive, but you Avlem - you go one better. You deceive yourselves! Wiping out whole cultures to make more room for yours, then expecting the survivors to be grateful to you. It's almost funny, so long as you can forget the past.'

Kerrig glanced at the fire, which was starting to fade without the boy's careful tending. 'Are you even aware of how much harm you've done to that young Fire Breather you pretend to be so fond of?' he asked, bluntly. 'Getting him noticed, begging the warden to show him mercy? The best mercy in the mines is to be invisible, and you sabotaged that. You caused all this trouble, and when it's over the warden will take his displeasure out on all of us. You and I will probably survive his idea of a suitable punishment, but it will kill the boy.

'Stupid, arrogant Avlem. Why couldn't you leave well enough alone?'

'She couldn't do that! It was the plan, weren't it?'

Chapter Two

Both adults turned to see the Fire Breather boy standing in front of the entrance hole.

'Tell him, Nesh. Me bein' a brat, and you bein' all stroppy at the warden, and me pretending to be ill an' all: it was the plan.'

Nesh started to say something, but Kerrig cut her off.

'The plan', he said, flatly. 'You mean to tell me that all this was part of a *plan?* Raining down death and destruction? Planting a Shifter in the stables? Disrupting what little stability we had left? You *planned* it?'

'Yeah,' said the boy, sounding proud. Then, grudgingly, 'Well, not all of it. Nesh helped. But all the really cool stuff was my idea. Like making the warden mad, an' gettin' sent to the edge of the Mines, an'..., yeah, that was me. Nesh jus' found us the right place to get sent.'

He beamed at them, and Nesh quickly put herself between Kerrig and the boy. The Earther bristled at the implication he would hurt a child, especially a child of the People, but before he could say anything else, the Avlem sent the boy back outside 'to watch Maddie'. Then she turned back to face Kerrig. They were both standing slightly stooped, to avoid hitting their heads on the ceiling, and Kerrig noticed that he and the Avlem were much of a height.

He also noticed that it's hard to glare at someone the same height as you when your head is tilted forwards. He tried it anyway.

'What exactly was this plan of yours meant to accomplish?' he asked, through beetled eyebrows. 'Apart from chaos, that is?'

The Avlem eyed him for a moment, then gracefully stepped back and sank down into a sitting position. This made it easier to glare at her, but also left him looking and feeling rather foolish, with his head jammed against the ceiling. After a moment he followed her example and knelt down, sitting on his heels.

'You may or may not know,' said the Avlem, 'That I have spent more than half my life as a prisoner; some two and a half decades in various sectors of the Mines. I am well aware of the mercy of invisibility, and have spent many years mastering the art.'

She spoke as though she had been trained in storytelling, Kerrig noticed with surprise. He didn't know the Avlem had any sort of storytelling traditions in their culture.

'Despite my efforts, I was often subject to the ire of my fellow Avlem. Those in authority objected to my very presence, finding reasons to transfer me from sector to sector. Two months ago, I was transferred to Sector 27, where I discovered a child of the Fire Breathers who was similarly rejected by his own people. You must have noticed them yourself: Three angry young men, sleeping close to the brazier every night?'

The Earther nodded. 'Yes, I saw them. Full of fighting talk and revolutionary fervour. The boy was better off away from them.'

'But he was not better off away from the fire. He was missing his friends, and suffering without his Element. He told me that sunlight was the best cure, so between us we devised a plan that would allow us to break a window in the cliff-face wall.

'I knew the layout of the Mines well, after travelling around them so widely; and I soon Found a place that would allow us to dig a path to the cliff face from within. Then it was simply a matter of baiting the warden until he assigned Volnar and me to the cramped little seam as punishment. It was going perfectly well until we hit that spot of trouble. You know, we were worried that you might catch on and report us.' She looked at him thoughtfully for a moment, then continued her story.

'You know most of the rest: the warden started throwing his Voice around, and we got rather more than just a window. We emerged from the cliff just out of sight of the perimeter guard tower, and made our way into the woods. As the sun came up, we discovered this hollow in a bank. Young Volnar got a fire going, and you settled into the ground to recharge. We all slept for several hours, and then you woke up and started exploding at people.'

Kerrig listened without reacting until Nesh had finished speaking.

'I see,' he said. 'And how did the Shifter fit into this plan of yours?'

The Avlem chuckled. 'The Sidrax child? She didn't. Maddie's true nature was a surprise to us as well. Apparently she's been living as a donkey ever since her parents hid her there a few years ago. Don't ask me what happened to the parents - and don't ask her, either. No need to distress the child.'

Nesh looked at him, her expression completely serious. 'Understand this: I wasn't going to bring you along with us,' she told him. 'It was

Maddie who refused to leave you to be discovered by the warden. It was Maddie who carried you, all night, until we could find a place to sleep safely. And it was Volnar who explained about your Elemental needs. You should be grateful to those children, but instead you seem intent on rejecting and scaring them.'

'That's not fair; when I was talking about the warden's reaction, I didn't know the boy was there,' Kerrig said. 'And I won't let harm come to him as a result of your foolishness.'

'Really? And how about when you accused Volnar of his plan causing death and destruction? Did you still not know he was there?' She rolled her eyes at him and sighed. 'You Elementals have certainly got a flair for the dramatic, haven't you? Alright, I'll give you "destruction", at a stretch, because cutting a hole in the cliff-face was always going to make a bit of a mess, but "death"? Come on now, nobody died!'

Kerrig levelled a serious look at the Avlem. 'You *hope* nobody died,' he said. 'I hope so too, but I can't be sure. A tunnel collapsed. You say you've lived in those mines for years, and yet you think that a tunnel can collapse with no harm done but "a bit of a mess"? I've been protecting people in those Mines my whole life, and yesterday I had to choose who to save. I can *hope* nobody died, but I can't know. I can't even help dig out survivors, because you and your screeding Shifter screeding *kidnapped* me!'

◆

'So it's true then,' she said, in a voice cooler than wet slate. 'The Earthers in the Mines aren't prisoners at all. No prisoner would describe being given his freedom as a kidnapping. You, with your high-and-mighty attitude about the Avlem and the

Sidrax taking over your precious land, when all the time you've been working for them. Do the wardens know? Do they know that the only thing stopping the Earthers in each sector from ripping that place wide open is that you're all on the Citadel's payroll?'

Kerrig slapped the sneer off the Avlem's face. 'I say again, Avlem, you know nothing. But hear this: No Earther would ever take a penny from your foul Citadel, just as no Earther would destroy the Great Sanctuary. We wait, and we protect, until you Outsiders are removed and the Land is free again. Somewhere, beyond your reach, the People of the Land are working against the Citadel.'

'Of course they are' said the Avlem, unimpressed. 'Where do you think half the prisoners come from? There will always be some who refuse to accept reality.'

There was a lot that Kerrig wanted to say to that, but the light from the entrance hole was growing dim. It was time to fix this.

'It's getting dark,' he said. 'No doubt you and your Shifter will want to be moving along. I'll take the boy back with me.'

The Avlem stared at him like he'd gone mad. 'After all the trouble we went to getting him out in the sunlight, do you think Volnar would willingly go back there? I can hardly understand your wanting to return, but I can't even *imagine* his wanting to. You can do what you like, but don't bring the boy into it.'

'I can hardly leave him with you, can I? A child of the People in the company of a Shifter, and with an Avlem so bad that even her own people take against her? The Earthers and Fire Breathers were always on good terms, I won't abandon one of theirs to you.'

Kerrig turned away without another word, and pulled himself through the entrance hole. The earth smelled fresh and cool, and the last light of the sun lingered in the western sky. He quickly located the Fire Breather and approached him, ignoring the donkey who was nosing at a clump of mushrooms.

'Come along lad, we're going home' he said, without preamble. The donkey pricked up its ears, abandoned the mushrooms and came trotting over to join them. Kerrig frowned and shooed the animal away.

'Not you,' he said. 'You're going with the Avlem. I'm going home, and taking the boy under my protection.'

'You ain't taking me nowhere,' insisted the boy. 'I'm going home too, and my home ain't that miserable pit.'

The Shifter became girl-shaped again and latched herself onto Kerrig's arm. 'Go home now?' she asked, sounding hopeful. Kerrig stiffened, and he looked at Volnar to avoid having to meet her pleading eyes. It was disturbing how well Shifters could imitate real people.

He put his hand out to the young Fire Breather, but the boy danced away out of reach. Kerrig tried to follow, but was hampered by the creature on his arm.

'Boy! Volnar! Get back here!' Kerrig called after him, but the Fire child simply moved further away. Kerrig stomped his bare foot into the ground, but soil moved differently from rock. Instead of the long crack he'd been trying for he simply made a shallow ditch, which was quickly filled up again by the loose dirt. The child was now beyond his reach, and disappearing into the distance.

The Avlem climbed out onto the bank to join them. Through the hole, Kerrig could see the dim flickering of a dying fire. He tapped his foot again, more gently this time, and made the opening collapse.

'There,' he said. 'Once the fire burns itself out, no-one will be able to tell you were ever here. Take your Shifter and go; I'll catch up with the boy and head home.'

The Avlem laughed. 'You let him run off? Ha, and you think *I'm* an unsuitable guardian for the children.'

'Just go,' growled the Earther. 'And take her with you.'

◆◆◆

Nesh pried the tearful Maddie away from Kerrig and the big man set off at once. He could faintly feel the tread of the Fire Breather's feet, heading eastwards. Kerrig's longer strides soon ate up the distance between them, especially as it was now dark and the boy had to slow down to avoid tripping on tree roots. Kerrig, meanwhile, followed the path easily with his Earther senses. The moons rose, but only one of them was even half-full. The boy made a torch out of a fallen branch, which only made it easier for Kerrig to catch up with him.

As soon as he was in range, the Earther stomped his foot again, this time adjusting for the movement of the soil. The torch wobbled wildly back and forth as the Fire Breather struggled to keep his footing, then boy and torch both sank into a patch of loose earth. Kerrig came along to find the child trapped up to his waist, the torch still burning. Volnar swung the torch like a weapon, fending Kerrig off. The Earther doused the flames with a double-handful of dirt, blinking the spots out of his eyes. The pair were plunged into darkness, the moonlight barely strong enough to define the tops of the trees against the sky.

The Fire Breather child tried to slip out of the trap, but Kerrig stopped him easily. He caught hold of the youngster's shoulders, and hauled him free of the ground. The boy squirmed and kicked, so Kerrig tucked him under one arm and began walking north. He was too far away to get a feel for the mines yet, but the Great Cliffs that defined the north-western border of the Land could be felt for miles. The Mines only took up a part of the huge range, but it would be easy enough to pick which part when they got closer.

The Fire Breather kept on struggling, and occasionally trying to burn Kerrig. The Earther was glad of his thick skin, and that the child had run down his energy reserves on sustaining other fires before the sun had set.

When fighting proved a failure, Volnar turned to pleading.

'Don't take me back underground, mister. I'll die down there without the sun, I know I will.'

'No, you won't,' Kerrig replied. 'In all my fifty years there I've never seen a single Fire Breather die from lack of sunlight. The wardens aren't so stupid as to kill off their workforce. There's plenty of Fire, Water and Air in there, as well as Earth. I didn't tell the Avlem about your little trick, because if you want to lie to Outsiders then that's your own business, but you don't fool me.'

The Fire Breather whimpered for a moment, then sighed.

'Fair enough,' he said, with a lop-sided shrug. 'Had to try, though. I really *do* want to go home, you know. I'd've thought you'd understand that.'

'And you will go home,' Kerrig assured him. 'After you finish your sentence. Be released, all proper and correct, and it's over. Run away, and you're running for the rest of your life.' Kerrig paused for a moment, testing the direction through the ground. When he set off again, it was with renewed purpose, heading directly for the entrance to the Great Sanctuary-turned-Prison Mines.

'Now listen, young Volnar, because we are going to have to tell a good story when we get back. Here it is then: The Avlem woke up first, and stole the donkey to escape on. She took you along against your will, and you didn't get away until sunset. I was tracking you down, and we met up here. Then I carried you back, because you were worn out from your long run. Agreed?'

'Why should I back you up?' said the boy. 'Too proud to say it was you what got took?'

'You'll back me up because if you do, I'll make sure you don't get into trouble for this little adventure. And I'll request your assistance with the pit donkeys. It means time out in the sunlight with them twice a week.'

'You can do that? But what about what you said to Nesh about the warden being out for our blood?'

Kerrig smirked. 'Seems like you're not the only one who's been lying to the Outsiders,' he said. 'Turnabout is fair play, after all the lies they've told us over the years.'

The boy seemed to think about it for a while. In the end, though, he nodded.

'Alright, it's a deal. Let me ride on your back, then. Looks better'n you carrying me under your arm like this. People might think I didn't want to come.'

Kerrig agreed, and the child clambered around the Earther's stocky frame until he was clinging to his back, hands gripping shoulders, and feet barely meeting around Kerrig's waist.

They walked on like this as the sun rose, Kerrig drawing strength from the ground to push himself on when he began to tire. They cleared the tree line, and only a gentle rise now stood between the Earther and his ancestral home. He smiled, then stopped short and frowned.

The guard post was a hive of frantic activity, soldiers bustling like beetles. Looking to the left, Kerrig could see the dark mark, about three feet above the ground, that showed where the cave-in had opened the cliff to allow the prisoners to make their escape. He hoped that he would be able to get to the repair work before some heavy-handed idiot got there and made it worse. Such a scar on the face of the Great Sanctuary would be a tragedy.

He was about to start forward again when he heard the warden's voice booming out. He was surprised to see the man still in his job after causing so much trouble. But he soon forgot about such minor concerns when he heard what the warden's Talent-boosted voice had to say.

◆

'Listen up, troops, listen up! You are going in pursuit of one Earther 27 and his gang. Do not underestimate him. Earther 27 is powerful, and clever. He'll drop you down a hundred-stride pit soon as look at you. He'll crush you under a mountain with a wave of his hand. He'll turn your bones to mud. This is a dangerous, desperate criminal. Your only hope is to shoot him before he sees you.'

Kerrig stood still, unable to see the commotion over the crest of the rise, but well able to hear and feel the state of panic spreading amongst the soldiers. Some of them were even of the People, to Kerrig's disgust. Not only were they traitors for working with the enemy, they were idiots too. Everyone knew that Earther abilities didn't work like that. Even the legendary Shanzir didn't have those kind of powers. He turned to share the joke with Volnar, but the boy was nowhere to be seen.

Kerrig cursed under his breath as he caught sight of a small figure moving between the trees. He set off toward it, heedless of the continued ranting coming from the guard towers.

As he drew nearer, Kerrig realised that the small figure was not running away, it was approaching. He slowed down, relieved. The child had simply been frightened, and was now coming back to keep his promise.

But it wasn't Volnar at all. It was the Shifter.

The figure of a little girl waved cheerfully at Kerrig as she jogged towards him. Then it became a donkey, running flat out as if its tail were on fire. It charged at Kerrig, head down and hooves pounding. Kerrig stumbled and fell backwards as the creature thundered towards him.

A crossbow bolt skimmed over his head, passing through the space his chest had occupied only a moment before. The donkey came to a halt in front of him, and a second bolt drew a line of blood across her flank. The animal screamed and collapsed on top of Kerrig, red blood running down her copper-coloured leg.

Chapter Three

Kerrig didn't hesitate. In one movement, he sank the two of them into a pit, and threw up the excess soil as a protective wall.

Cradling the injured animal's head in his lap, Kerrig reached over and began gently drawing the dirt out of the wound. The cut was shallow but painful, to judge from the way Maddie twitched and whimpered.

'Little One,' he whispered, aware of the soldiers overhead. 'Little One, you need to be a girl now. I can't move you like this, I'll hurt you.'

Kerrig winced inwardly at the thought of trying to get a Shifter to change right in front of him. He cursed his weakness, but it went against all his instincts to leave an animal or a child to suffer. And this Shifter did look horribly like a suffering animal.

She stirred and blinked one eye up at him. He patted her neck, and repeated his request. The eye closed again, and then Maddie was girl-shaped.

Kerrig frowned. He'd tried to watch for the moment of change, but it was as if he'd blinked and missed it.

The wound on the Shifter's leg looked larger now, but only because the leg was so much smaller. Kerrig cleaned it again, and ripped a sleeve from his tunic to serve as a bandage. The child in his arms didn't so much as flinch while he worked. She was unconscious, but whether from shock, exhaustion or blood loss the Earther couldn't tell.

Carrying the injured girl in his arms, he sank them down further into the ground then forced a tunnel to appear ahead of them. He deliberately let his head and shoulders brush the undisturbed earth, drawing power from it to offset the energy used by his feet and arms. In this way, they moved secretly through the ground until Kerrig felt tree roots in the soil.

Cautiously, the Earther pushed towards the surface, and emerged in the shadow of a particularly large tree. He laid the sleeping Sidrax on a bed of roots then, still half-buried in earth, he closed his eyes and focused on the sensations coming from the ground. The heavy tread of running soldiers, getting fainter. Good. He only hoped that the Fire Breather boy didn't meet them.

He reached out the other way next, looking for the heavy, saturated clay that would mean a river or a stream. To his relief, he found one almost due south of their current position, and underground, too. An underground river, if it was a river, meant natural caves. Natural caves could be home to those of the People who had stayed loyal to the Land, living in the old ways, and not in artificial, Avlem-style buildings. It was a slim hope, but slim hope was better than none.

Kerrig looked at the Shifter (the Sidrax, he corrected himself) and grimaced. It was undoubtedly his enemy, and had deceived him for years about its true nature; and yet it - *she* - had thrown herself in harm's way to save him. An Earther always recognised and repaid a debt. If nothing else, Kerrig held that he had a responsibility to this creature, to care for it while she could not care for herself.

The Sidrax slept, and Kerrig rested, drawing strength from the rich soil around the tree roots. He was no stranger to hardship, but his reserves were low after the events of the last two days. He wondered how long it would be until this silly misunderstanding was settled, and he could get back to his normal life.

Kerrig pulled himself to his feet and replaced the disturbed soil around the base of the tree. Then he gathered the child in his arms, and started walking towards what he hoped would be civilization.

◆

They walked for hours, and Kerrig was becoming painfully aware of how long it had been since he last slept, ate, or even had a drink of water. The child in his arms was heavy, and seemed unnaturally hot. Kerrig supposed this might be normal for Shift-, Sidrax, but he had his doubts.

The Earther let his feet guide him towards the pull of wet clay. He hoped for a river, but even clean clay would be better than nothing. The bleeding appeared to have stopped, but the little creature was still unconscious. Why had she jumped in front of him like that? The bolt *might* have missed him anyway, she hadn't needed to make herself a target. Had it been a trick? A clever ploy to win his trust? Everything he knew about Shifters told him that this was the only explanation, but it didn't sit well with him.

This creature had been in his care for the past three or four years, unless it had somehow replaced the real donkey during that time. Again, Kerrig knew that this was how Shifters operated; they mimicked a trusted form in order to get access to places, people, and information. But Kerrig also knew the donkeys of the Mines. He knew their personalities and their habits. He was sure that the donkey who had greeted him so enthusiastically when he woke up last night was the same one as had listened to his stories in the stables every night. It would take a very clever Shifter to be such a good mimic, and a clever Shifter would surely have been able to come up with a better plan than getting itself shot.

It was a puzzle, and one that would have to wait. They were over the underground river now: it was time to open a path downward. The big man sat down and eased himself into the ground, carefully moving the soil around himself and the child. As he closed off the space overhead, he was once more in total darkness. His eyes told him nothing, but his Earther senses were flooding him with information. There was a layer of stone coming up to meet them, and Kerrig concentrated on making a way through it. Stone and soil behaved very differently, but living inside a cliff for fifty years had made him familiar with rock of all kinds. The stone beneath his feet thinned, and he concentrated on pushing it out and down, making a pathway from the cavern roof to the floor. It was tiring, forcing the Earth to obey him in such an unnatural way, but once they were down, Kerrig was able to relax. The cave was large, and the floor was smooth. And there, bubbling in the darkness, was water.

Kerrig tasted it and found it clean enough. He formed a section of the riverbed into a smooth platform, only a couple of hand-breadths below the surface, and lowered the injured child onto it. He built up a headrest of rock for the little creature, and unwrapped the makeshift bandage from her leg.

At first, she didn't seem to react at all. Kerrig felt a coldness that had nothing to do with the icy water. Then, to his relief, he felt her shiver and try to sit up. He reached for her shoulders and supported her carefully.

'Easy, Little One,' he said. 'You've been hurt. Sit in the water for as long as you can bear it, it will help.'

'My Stony-Man,' she said, happily. 'Did my eyes get hurt? I can't see you.'

'No, your eyes are fine. There's no light here. But we're safe, for now.'

Maddie seemed to accept this without hesitation. Kerrig felt her relax against his arm; and her complete trust in him was slightly worrying. He'd been prepared for her being frightened, sad, even angry; he hadn't expected calm. It was so simple, so... well, *childlike*, that he started doubting himself again. Could anyone really be such a good actor? Either this Shifter was diabolically clever, or else she was exactly what she seemed: a little girl. A child, all alone and injured.

That thought cut through all notions of rights and wrongs. Whatever she was, and whatever she may go on to become, at this moment she was his responsibility and he would look after her.

Kerrig pulled Maddie from the water after a while, and held her while she shivered. He wished he had something dry to wrap her in, but the child said she was fine. She wanted to walk by herself, but Kerrig insisted on carrying her.

'You can't see where you're going, it's not safe,' he said.

'Can you see?' she asked. 'Can you see this?' Her voice sounded strange, and Kerrig wondered if she was pulling faces at him. He also wondered what sort of faces a Sidrax child could pull. In that moment Kerrig was glad of the darkness.

As he walked through the cave, Kerrig tried to explain what it meant to see with this Earther sense. Maddie grew so quiet that he might have thought her asleep, except for feeling her so bright and alert in his arms. At one point she put her hands - nearly dry - over his eyes, as if wanting to make sure he really was as blind as she. When he trudged on without hesitation she laughed with delight and told him with undisguised pride that he was her 'very clever Stony-Man'. After that she let her hands fall from his face, and settled her arms comfortably around his neck instead.

The light started so faintly and grew so gradually that Kerrig didn't notice it at first. It wasn't until he blinked that he realised his eyes were picking up anything at all. A soft, blue light ahead of them was getting bigger with every step. Kerrig could feel a network of tunnels there too, linking many caves and caverns. A few paces more brought them into a tunnel lined with translucent crystals. Although completely underground, the polished surfaces channelled sunlight, reflected and refracted down multiple tiny vents. These, Kerrig realised, were not a purely natural formation. Someone had crafted this place as a home. It could only be the work of Earthers.

Kerrig pressed on eagerly. When Maddie asked to walk now that she could see again, Kerrig let her down without a murmur. The prospect of meeting other Earthers, and not just for brief moments during cross-sector emergencies, filled him with an unfamiliar excitement. He marvelled at the skill of the creators of these tunnels and his mind was buzzing with questions for these artisans. Surely there must be many Earthers here, because the tunnels were too extensive and too intricate to have been the work of any one person.

He walked faster, and Maddie changed to her donkey form to keep up with him. The change caught his attention and he forced himself to slow down. Even with three good legs, the Sidrax child was in danger of re-opening her wound if she pushed herself too hard. The Earther took advantage of the gentle pace to reach out with his Earther sense. Distantly, he registered the presence of other people, and he set out in that direction.

Maddie heard them before he did, to judge by the pricking of her ears and the change in her pace. Kerrig moved to keep up with her, too happy at the prospect of new friends to worry about what they would think of the Sidrax at his side.

It wasn't until the owners of the voices came into view that Kerrig realised he already knew them. Kerrig and Maddie stood face to face with Volnar and the Avlem.

◆◆◆

Kerrig shot a hostile look at the new arrivals, and received two in return. Maddie, seemingly unaware of the invisible ordnance above her head, switched forms in order to properly greet her friends.

'Did you getted here in the dark like us? My Stony-Man can see in the dark, you know. He's very clever. Can you see in the dark?'

'We, uh, came another way,' said Volnar, awkwardly.

Nesh, meanwhile, was staring at the angry wound on Maddie's leg.

'What did you do to her?' Nesh demanded. 'I meant what I said about that, you know.'

Kerrig glowered at her. 'You're the one who let her run off,' he countered. 'And you're the one who stirred up the guards so much that they were out looking for escaped prisoners to shoot on sight.'

'Oi, it was you they was all scared of, not her!' Volnar pushed forward, craning his neck to meet Kerrig's eyes. 'That warden didn't say nothing about Nesh, but he had a lot to say about the "*dangerous criminal, Earther 27*". Don't talk like this is all her fault.'

The boy backed up to take a swing at the Earther, but was caught off-guard by the irregularly-shaped rocks, worn smooth by the water. Volnar landed on his back with a thud, missing the river itself by inches.

Avlem and Earther were at the boy's side in a moment.

'Are you alright?'

'You need to be more careful, lad.'

'Don't get up too quickly, you might be hurt.'

The Fire Breather's face burned deep red and he brushed off the adults' concern. He scrambled to his feet, but couldn't hide the wince of pain. His hand went to his side, and he paled.

'Ribs,' said Kerrig, with the confidence of long experience. 'Probably just bruised, that fall wasn't hard enough to crack the bone.'

Volnar looked like he wanted to argue about that, but decided to accept a fuss from Nesh instead. The Avlem alternated between looks of concern for the boy, and looks promising pain at Kerrig.

'Well done, Earther,' she said. 'That's two injured children now; Volnar *and* Ma-- wait, where's Maddie?'

Three sets of eyes scanned the cavern for any trace of girl or donkey.

'Maddie! Madrigal, where are you?'

'Volnar, be careful!'

'How can anyone hide in here? It's empty! There aren't even any big rocks.'

'Madrigal! Maddie!'

There was a splash in the water and a flash of copper scales. The next moment, there was Maddie sitting in the water up to her chest.

'I founded swimming things,' she announced. 'And they can hold their breaths for a long long long long time.'

Any other observations she had to make were cut short by Nesh sweeping her up into a hug, and rubbing the girl's arms vigorously.

'You're so cold, Maddie! What were you doing in the water?'

'When my leg hurted before, he putted he in the water and it helped. And then there was swimming things, so I maked a shape like them, but I don't think I did it right because I can't stay down like they do.'

Nesh pulled the girl in for another hug. 'Maddie, I don't think you should try to turn into any animal you've only just seen. You might get hurt.'

Volnar took off his shoes and waded into the river. After a moment he pulled out a silvery fish, holding it tightly with both hands.

'See, Mads?' He said, pushing the creature under her nose. 'They don't hold their breath at all - they can breathe the water.'

The gills on the fish's neck gaped wide, and Maddie looked on in fascination.

'I think you tried to be a fish on the outside and a person on the inside. That's why it didn't work. You gotta be one thing, all the way through.'

Both children watched as the fish wriggled in Volnar's grip. Maddie touched it gently.

'It's cold,' she said. 'Poor swimming fish thing.' She rubbed its scales, but that only made the fish flap more.

'I'd better put it back now,' said Volnar. 'They don't like to be out of the water too long.'

But when the boy returned the animal to the clear water, it didn't move. The children poked at it, but it didn't respond.

'Swim, fish, swim,' said Maddie. She looked to Kerrig and Nesh, standing on the other side of the stream. 'Is it asleep?' she asked.

'I think it's dead,' said Volnar. 'How can it be dead? I only had it out for a minute.'

Maddie changed to her donkey shape and nosed helplessly at the lifeless animal. Kerrig crossed the stream, put his hand in her mane as he had done so often in the past, and guided her away from the water. Out of the corner of his eye, he saw Nesh and Volnar carry the fish away.

Chapter Four

Kerrig took Maddie hunting for mushrooms and moss, which she seemed to like no matter what shape she was in. He carefully kept her away from the sight and smell of Nesh and Volnar cooking and eating the fish. He would have joined them, but didn't think that Maddie would understand. He could go without food for a few days more if needed, and there was plenty of water.

Something about water was niggling at his mind, but he couldn't place it. Meanwhile, he sacrificed his other sleeve to make a clean bandage for Maddie's leg, and soaked the bloodied one in the water to make a cold relief for Volnar's ribs. There was a faint but distinct current flowing in the stream, and Nesh said they should follow it towards an exit. Volnar suggested that they rest first. A safe, comfortable area with clean water was not an opportunity to be wasted.

Kerrig wondered what sort of experiences gave a boy not yet in his adolescence that kind of tactical mind. Then he wondered if he really wanted to know.

After making Maddie promise not to go into the water again without supervision, everyone settled down to sleep. It wasn't easy; in the Mines there were blankets and mattresses - thin and threadbare, but better than nothing. Kerrig drew out a layer of stone to cover himself, and made the ground as smooth as possible for the others, but it was a hard and cold bed compared to the soft soil of the hollow. The light faded away when the sun set and, with nothing to burn, Volnar could only create lingering sparks that drained his energy.

Kerrig was sure that people lived in these tunnels, and that meant food, and clothing, and warmth were to be had. But where?

The moons rose, one a slim crescent and the other just past half full. The silvery light filtered down through the crystals, and the stream glinted for a moment.

Water, said his mind again. Water is important. Anyone living here needs a steady supply of water; coming to this stream at least once a day. A path that well-travelled would show wear. To find the People, find the worn path.

Kerrig thought he would get up at once - his Earther sense was better than sight for finding this sort of path anyway - but he suddenly felt overwhelmingly tired. He could almost feel his mind relax, like muscles after a hard day's work, as if to say, *Well done, you've worked out the answer. Now rest.*

◆◆◆

Kerrig woke in the soft glow of crystal-filtered sunlight, and for a moment he thought he was back in the Sanctuary. When he remembered where he was, and why, Kerrig felt the rage of the previous day swell up again. Silently, mindful of the children, Kerrig cursed all Avlem for their idiocy and selfishness. He cursed the soldiers guarding the mine, and the Sidrax for bringing their violent culture into every part of the Land. If not for those 'shoot first' fools, and the Avlem warden's paranoia, he'd be back home now.

Kerrig sighed and gave himself a mental shake. The past was unchangeable, the future was out of his hands, and that was that. He couldn't go back yet, not until the fuss died down, so he could best use his time finding a safe place for the children to live.

He got up, crumbling his rock blanket back into the ground, and noticed that the Fire Breather boy was awake and watching him without blinking. Volnar was sitting directly under a shaft of sunlight that lit up his hair and threw his face into shadow. He seemed to be drinking in the light as dry ground drinks up rain. *Maybe there wasn't quite enough fire in the Mines after all*, thought Kerrig. *Or maybe he's just enjoying being in his Element.*

The Earther looked around at the carved walls and smooth crystals. Yes, it was good to be immersed in your own Element. Each breath was a banquet for the spirit. He settled himself opposite the Fire Breather and they sat quietly until the others woke up.

After a long drink of cool water in place of breakfast, the four set off at a gentle pace. The stream flowed out through an ornate archway and along more crystal-lit corridors. The channel was neither wide nor deep, so the adults walked on opposite banks and watched as Volnar pushed ahead to explore. Maddie wanted to explore too, but Kerrig carried her. The cut on her leg was scabbed over and didn't seem to be causing much pain but he wasn't taking any chances.

The light brightened with the day, and the workings became more and more elaborate as they went on. Kerrig thought that this must have been a great centre of Earther culture before the invaders arrived. His thoughts soured as he watched the Avlem stroll through this artwork without giving it a glance. He was glad to notice a side path soon after that, shiny with use, leading away to the left.

'Wait here a moment,' he said to the others. 'There's a side path over there; I'm going to see where it leads.' He set Maddie down, and moved towards the shadowed opening in the left-hand wall.

'We shouldn't split up,' the Avlem said. 'We'll come with you.'

'No. There's no light down there; you'd be walking blind. As soon as I know where it leads, I'll come back for you.'

'But why do you want to follow that path in the first place?'

Kerrig ignored the question and stepped into the gloomy passage. Before he had taken a dozen steps the light from behind him had faded to nothing. For a moment it was pitch black, then he saw a light ahead. Feeling forward through the stone, he identified a series of linked caverns. One nearby was warm, and had someone walking about in it. Here were the People he'd been looking for!

Kerrig felt suddenly shy. His Earther abilities were largely self-taught and functional. He vaguely remembered the old men of his youth, who talked about 'elegance' and 'style', urging him to practice on pebbles and mould them into tiny figurines. At the time he'd been more concerned with power and speed; now he wished he'd paid more attention to his pebbles. These Earthers, growing up in this splendid place, would surely be artists and crafters. What would they think of him?

Kerrig would have turned back but for his duty to the children. He had to get help for them, no matter what. The big man, feeling more like fifteen than fifty, forced himself towards the light.

◆

Kerrig could feel someone moving in the cavern as he approached it, but he couldn't hear any sound from them. Even when he was close enough to see shadows from their fire flickering on the walls it remained eerily quiet. He approached the doorway and saw an old, old woman sitting alone beside a fire. She beckoned him to enter. As Kerrig stepped across the threshold he felt a strange heaviness in the air, and sound suddenly returned to the world. He started at the roar of the little cooking fire, and the woman laughed.

'Come in, dear, and sit by the fire. There's a bench for you, and there's a broth on the boil if you're hungry.'

The pot over the fire was giving off a mouth-watering smell that might have tempted anyone, even if they hadn't been without food for the better part of three days. The benches were covered in thick, woollen blankets and the air itself was warm compared to the dark tunnels. Kerrig's stomach clenched painfully tight, and he struggled to stay focused.

'If you please Lady, and no offence,' he said, dredging up long-lost memories of manners from his childhood, 'But are you this hospitable to all strangers who pass by your door?'

The woman smiled at him. 'And who would be passing by this door?' she said. 'But yes, worthy visitors are always welcome here. Come in, and rest your bones.'

Kerrig stepped back, and felt the strange firmness in the air again. It seemed to bend around his back and shoulders. 'Then, Lady, if you'll excuse me, I have others with me who need your welcome more than I.'

The woman smiled in a way that might have meant any number of things, and bad him fetch his friends. The Earther began to retrace his steps, and found that the others had followed him after all. Kerrig scowled at Nesh for bringing the children into what could have been danger, but decided not to waste time on further reprimand. The Avlem would probably just blame it on Maddie, anyway. The Earther led them back to the old lady's cavern, and the travellers were soon seated around the fire. Nesh and the children were each given a bowl of hot broth, while Kerrig and their host used wooden cups. The benches were raised stone, and when Kerrig lifted a corner of one of the blankets, he saw carvings that matched those in the crystal-lined tunnels. This, then, certainly was an Earther refuge - so where were they all?

Kerrig was still trying to think of a polite way to ask about this when the meal ended. The pot had been emptied and removed from the fire, and the used cups and bowls piled up next to it. The old lady had done the clearing up herself, refusing all offers of help. Kerrig noticed that she was not bent or hobbled by her age, but rather moved with a marvellous efficiency around her small living space.

Volnar lay stretched out full length on the floor between the benches and the cooking fire, basking in the warmth and light. Maddie, still in her girl-form, watched him carefully for a long moment, then lay down on top of the bench in an exact imitation of the Fire Breather's posture. Kerrig's lips quirked into a small smile at the sight, until he looked up and noticed the Avlem watching the pair with the same expression on her face. He sobered quickly, unwilling to have even that much in common with an Outsider.

'Well then,' said the old lady, disrupting Kerrig's musings, 'Now that we're all fed and resting, shall we start the introductions? You may call me Zirpa, and I've lived in these Caverns longer than I care to remember.'

Kerrig bit back his flood of questions, and the Avlem got to her feet to make the introductions.

'It is good of you to make us so welcome in your home,' she said. 'The boy beside the fire is Volnar, and the girl is Madrigal, or Maddie. This is Kerrig, and I am known as Nesh. We have been travelling south for two days, and both the children have injuries. Good food and a warm place to rest is exactly what they - and we - needed. Thank you for your generous hospitality, Madam Zirpa.'

She bowed to their host before sitting back down on her bench. Kerrig gaped at her. What sort of an introduction was that? He moved to quickly fill in the most important information.

'Yes, and the boy is a Fire Breather, although I don't know where he's from. The girl is actually Sidrax, so don't be too surprised if she suddenly becomes a donkey. So far as I can tell she really is a child, even so. Nesh is an Avlem, and I'm one of the last Earthers of the Great Sanctuary, before it fell to the invaders.'

He waited for Zirpa to reciprocate with her heritage, but she simply smiled and said that it was nice to meet them all. Kerrig frowned. Zirpa was of the People, he was sure; and she was old enough to have been brought up properly. It was a mystery. *Another* one. Kerrig didn't like mysteries, they made his head ache. First Maddie, the mysteriously selfless Shifter; and now Zirpa, the strangely-mannered... what? Earther? Marshlander? She hadn't demonstrated any Elemental ability yet, and neither had she identified her tribe. Unless... perhaps she took it as understood that she had been born in this place, which would make her an Earther of... whatever this place was called. Well, that was an inoffensive enough question at least.

'Forgive my ignorance, Lady Zirpa,' Kerrig said, determined to use his own manners perfectly even if no-one else did, 'But what is the name of this place? We are isolated in the remains of the Great Sanctuary, and I am not familiar with other Earther strongholds.'

Zirpa chuckled. 'I don't think this was ever much of a stronghold, dear,' she said. 'For the Earthers or anyone else. When we moved in there was no-one left to ask, so I call it the Crystal Caverns, because of those beautiful tunnels out there. You don't get the effect in here - I think maybe they were still building this part when they left.'

Chapter Five

Kerrig sat staring into the fire. The Earthers had left before Zirpa even arrived. Gone to the Great Sanctuary more than likely. As the lady had said, this place was not designed as a stronghold. There would have been no need of defences and vantage points when these tunnels were laid; the People had been at peace, only needing protection from wild animals and bad weather. Not from killers, and liars, and thieves.

The Earther was dimly aware of the others moving around, but paid no attention to them until someone touched his arm. It was the Avlem.

'What do you want?' he snarled, unwilling to brook any interruption, much less one from the very race to have destroyed his latest hopes.

'Charmed, I'm sure. And *I* don't want anything; you could sulk there forever as far as I'm concerned. Madam Zirpa, however, wants to talk to you. Through there.'

Kerrig looked where she was pointing and saw a thin, ragged curtain hanging across the entrance to an alcove. He went over to it without another word, and found the Lady Zirpa waiting for him in a room full of colour. High shelves held strangely shaped jars, with tiny leather bags dotted around between them. From the lowest shelf, which was set just too high for a child to reach, there hung woven blankets like the ones covering the benches in the main area. On the floor, more blankets, covering seats and a low table. Kerrig's Earther sense could tell that there was good, solid stone underneath the abundance of fabric, but his eyes were struggling to make out shapes against the mash of colours.

Two things stood out clearly. One was Zirpa herself, white hair vivid against the dyed cloth. The other was Maddie, curled up in a corner. Her wound was freshly bandaged with a strip of bright cloth, which stood out strangely against her copper-coloured dress and skin. She didn't look up when Kerrig came in, intent on examining some sort of toy that Zirpa must have given her to play with.

'You wished to speak to me, Lady?' he said.

The old woman smiled, and gestured for him to take a seat. Kerrig felt for it carefully, still too dazzled by the colours to trust his eyes.

'Yes, Kerrig, I did. I've spoken to each of the others in here, privately, and now it's your turn.'

The Earther raised an eyebrow at this remark. When had she taken...? He must have been lost in thought longer than he'd realised. With no ringing bells or screaming wardens to mark the passage of time, it could slip by remarkably smoothly.

But all he said was, 'Privately?' with a significant look towards the child playing in the corner.

Zirpa laughed. It wasn't an altogether pleasant sound. 'Oh, don't worry about the little pitcher, she's occupied. You did the right thing, bringing her to me; I've seen to her injury, so your debt to her is paid.'

Kerrig hesitated, unsure of how she knew about such a private matter. Surely Maddie was too young to have understood the situation, so who had talked? Probably the Avlem.

'And my debt to you?' he asked. 'For taking care of her?'

'You'll pay that now, by sharing your story with me. That has always been the way of the Shanzir: information and entertainment trade just as well as goods or services.'

Kerrig was glad he was already sitting down.

'The Shanzir?' he said, in a reverent whisper. 'You are of the Shanzir? Why didn't you say so?' Kerrig asked, with delighted incredulity.

'Your story first,' said Zirpa. She didn't seem best pleased by Kerrig's enthusiasm, and listened without comment as he told his tale.

He expressed himself awkwardly, working backwards from current events in fits and starts. First Maddie's injury, and the journey to the Crystal Caverns. Then their reason for being outside the Sanctuary in the first place, which in turn led to an explanation of the Mines, and how the Outsiders had laid siege to the Sanctuary for three years, finally taking possession of it when Kerrig himself was a baby. How, since then, the surviving Earthers had been put to work turning the great halls into mines, charged with protecting the prisoners brought to work there, to expand the tunnels further and further in search of minerals and ores for the invaders to use.

'So the Sidrax army took the Northern Border Cliffs at last, did they?' said Zirpa. 'That *is* a surprise. All those Earthers, literally surrounded by their Element, and still defeated. What a shame.'

She spoke lightly, as of a minor disappointment. Kerrig felt his temper rise like lava.

'We were only defeated because we were betrayed!' he said. 'The Air Crawlers sold out to the invaders and joined their side. We held off the army, even with their destructive Talents and their Shifter spies, but once the Air tribes got involved we were lost.'

'Air Walkers?' said Zirpa. 'Are you sure?'

'Of course I'm sure,' he said. 'I had the story directly from my great-uncle and he was there. "The Flying Filth", he called them. When we sealed ourselves in, they drew out the air from our chambers and choked us; when we fought in the open they picked us up off the ground like rag dolls, or pulled the air directly out of our lungs. After they'd killed all our fighters they gave the elderly chieftains an ultimatum: surrender, or watch the invaders murder the young mothers and their children in the nursery. My great-uncle wanted to fight on, but the others counselled surrender. They knew that so long as my generation still lived there was a hope for the future. We would know the old ways, and keep the culture alive. The alternative was to let the Earther tribes die, there and then. To be completely destroyed, like the Shanzi-'

◆

Kerrig stopped, the present slamming into the past like an earthquake. He blinked, then smiled hugely at the Lady Zirpa, who was still sitting impassively before him.

'It's incredible,' he said. 'I thought the Shanzir were wiped out at the very start of the invasion. You were the tribe of legends, attuned to all the Elements at once, the greatest of all the People. And to find survivors, after all this time...'

'A survivor,' Zirpa corrected him. 'I am the last, as far as I know. In all the time I spent travelling the Land, and all the years since I retired to this place, I have had no word of any others.'

Kerrig closed his eyes and tried not to take it personally. After all, if the last of the Shanzir could talk so calmly about the death of her own people, then he ought to be able to hear the news without pain. But it was hard; twice today he had been sure he was going to find People, Earthers or otherwise, and twice he had been disappointed. The Earthers who had created these marvellous caves were dead and gone. Maybe they had retreated to the Great Sanctuary and been killed defending it, just like his parents. And now he was sitting across from the last Shanzir. It was tragic. An entire culture reduced to one person, living out her days in the abandoned halls of another dead tribe. It was a painful reminder of just how badly the Outsiders had hurt the People, and Kerrig was learning that he wasn't as hardened to that sort of pain as he'd thought.

'Why are they so... *evil?*' he said at last, whether to himself or his host he neither knew nor cared. 'Coming here, destroying everything they touch, they just...'

Kerrig flinched as a small hand patted him on the knee. He looked down to see Maddie beside him, and he forced his temper down. He tried to smile at the child, but it felt more like a grimace.

'Why don't you go and see how young Volnar is getting along?' said Zirpa, seeming to take pity on Kerrig.

The little Sidrax nodded and started for the door curtain.

The adults watched in silence as the curtain swished behind her. It was the Shanzir who broke it at last.

'So, Kerrig of the Earthers, what will you do now? Go back, stay here, or go on?'

Kerrig sighed. 'Go on, I suppose. I need to find a Fire Breather family for the boy, and we all need to get away from-' He stopped himself, but Zirpa finished the sentence for him.

'From the soldiers who are trying to kill you, yes. I heard all about that from young Volnar. You're a desperate criminal, he tells me.'

'What?! No! I don't even know why they're after me. It was Volnar and the Avlem who broke out. I just got dragged along with them. Literally. I was out cold the whole time.'

'Yes, according to Nesh the only thing you did was attempt to bury the warden and his guards in rubble, and then evade an armed pursuit while carrying an injured ally. You're just an innocent victim in all this, I'm sure.'

'That was... I didn't have any choice! It's not as if I...' Kerrig floundered for words, hating the helpless feeling that was welling up inside him. 'Whose side are you on, anyway?' he demanded.

'Whose side are *you* on, Earther? You could have left that place at any time, or overwhelmed the guards and freed the prisoners. You were in your Element in a way second only to an Air Walker, and yet you chose to obey your Outsider masters. You get sad and angry about the changes to the Land, but what have you ever *done* about it?'

Kerrig sat perfectly still, shocked by the accusation. He struggled to find a place to begin explaining to this clueless, ignorant, insensitive... *Shanzir*, said his mind. *Show some respect. Greatest of the People.* The Earther tried to moderate his thoughts towards the old woman but failed. How *dare* she imply that Earthers, that *he* collaborated with...

'Well, what have *you* done about it?' he countered. 'If I with my one Element should have been able to drive out an army, what excuse is there for a Shanzir? You control all the Elements!'

To his surprise, Zirpa laughed. 'It's remarkable how quickly legends can grow, isn't it, Earther 27? There's never been anyone who had an affinity with more than one Element, even children born of two Elements only command one of them. I have one Element, Kerrig, just like you, and Volnar, and any other of the People.'

Kerrig frowned. 'But all the stories say that the Shanzir had all the Elements. Was that just invented, to make your tribe seem more powerful than you really were?'

'We did have all the Elements,' Zirpa said. For the first time, she sounded sad. 'We were the Shan Zir - the People in Unity. Did you not learn the Old Words from that uncle of yours?'

'We never... the Old Words were forbidden,' Kerrig said. 'Not that there was anyone to speak them with once I was sent out to my own sector. What does this have to do with the Shanzir's mythical powers?'

'The Shanzir were a tribe of individuals from all over the Land. We had all the Elements in our tribe, not in ourselves. Earther, Air Walker, Fire Breather, Marshlander - once you were Shanzir, those distinctions didn't matter so much. We travelled from place to place, taking along any who wanted to come. Not every Marshlander wants to spend her life growing plants, you know.' It sounded like she was quoting, but whether from her younger self or from someone else she'd once known Kerrig had no idea.

'Well,' he said, 'If you call the Earthers collaborators for being conquered despite our strength, what do you call the Shanzir? All the Elements at once? You should have been able to drive the Outsiders away easily! How did they manage to defeat you? I say again, Shanzir, whose side are you on?'

Kerrig was on his feet, unconsciously bunching his hands into fists. He clenched his toes, but the thick carpet of blankets and rugs muted his connection to the ground. The silence felt like it lasted for a long time, roaring in Kerrig's ears like the rush of pebbles in a scree. When Zirpa's answer came, he almost didn't hear it.

'I don't know how we were defeated,' she said. 'My parents were there, although they were not much older than Madrigal and Volnar at the time, and they never spoke of what they saw. I only know that the survivors of that encounter took the ways of the Shanzir into hiding with them. My generation, few in number, learned of the Shanzir way by our parents' stories, not by our own experience. But I know this: We didn't start the war. The Avlem and the Sidrax came to the Land, and the People of the Land made them welcome. And they killed us.' The old woman's voice was brittle with old fury, and Kerrig shrank from her.

'Whose side are you on, Earther? Why did you serve them without revolt? Why have you let them live?'

He froze, struggling to form words. 'I... what do you want from me? Do you mean to say that I, and all my peers, should have been raised to be murderers? To pull the Sanctuary down around our own ears, for the sake of killing a few Outsiders? We were the last of the Earthers, and there will always be more soldiers. The Sidrax are born to it, and there are plenty of Avlem who take pleasure in bloodshed. Tell me, what else could we have done? What else could your parents have done? The Outsiders won. Once upon a time the Land belonged to the People and we to it, but now the Land belongs to the Outsiders, and all we can do is wait for Time to send them away.'

Zirpa shook her head, as at a fanciful child.

'You're waiting on Time?' she said. 'Young man, don't you know that Time only ever moves forward? Things never go back to how they were, they can only go around. So why didn't you try to bring them around more quickly? Why didn't you and those of your generation start up a resistance force?'

Kerrig glowered. 'No-one wanted to "undermine the truce",' he said. 'We were too young, and the elders overruled us, and then most were too busy settling down and having children, and it was never quite the right time to make our move, and we were split up across the sectors, and *yes*, alright, we let it go on. The way we were brought up, living in the Mines like that was just... normal. And now there's another generation that thinks living like that is normal too! Great strata, how did it come to this?'

Zirpa nodded, and seemed satisfied. 'You'll be heading out to join one of the rebellions, then?' she said. 'You and the boy. The Shifter can go off with the Avlem, unless you intend making them into a good-faith gift for the bandits. You might need that, come to think of it. Most of the new recruits are younger than you - they'll ask you what you've been up to all these years. A couple of prisoners might weigh in your favour.'

'Wait, wait - bandits? Prisoners? What are you talking about?' Kerrig stopped pacing and sat down. 'Why would I join up with bandits?'

'Because they're the only revolutionaries left,' Zirpa told him, bluntly. 'All the rest are either waiting on someone else to make the first move, or not interested in changing things at all.'

Kerrig dismissed these last as an impossibility. All right-thinking People wanted the Outsiders gone, it was obvious. But the idea that all the tribes might be frozen in the same sort of indecision that had existed in the Mines... was it possible?

'I don't believe you,' he declared. 'There must be People out there who can act against the Avlem without becoming bandits! Why - wait. Of course, they're not really bandits. That's just what the Outsiders call them, to discredit them. Right?'

'Wrong!' said Zirpa, cheerfully. 'They call themselves bandits, and they don't really care what they do so long as they kill plenty of Outsiders while doing it. And they define "Outsider" as "anyone not fighting with us". And if the bandits help themselves to the loot afterwards, it's the spoils of war.'

Kerrig went grey. 'If they... no, that's not right. I want the Outsiders gone, not killed. Stealing, killing... it's not right. If that's all you've got to tell me, then I think it's time for us to move along.'

He stood up to leave, but Zirpa called him back.

'That's far from all I have to tell you, Kerrig of the Northern Border Cliffs. If you had been willing to join the bandits you'd be leaving my home now, promptly and alone. As it is, I'm inclined to offer you some help. For a favour in return, of course.'

'Of course,' Kerrig replied, dryly. He was beginning to think that 'the Way of the Shanzir' was not so much about wisdom and harmony as it was about being very shrewd merchants.

'Aren't you going to ask what the favour is first?'

'It will involve something that I am willing and able to do,' Kerrig said. 'Unless the old tales were wrong, the Shanzir have always given what was needed, and only taken what could be spared. You won't betray your ways now, at the end of your days.'

'Are you so sure?'

'If you do, you're no Shanzir. And if I tried to cheat you, I'd be no Earther. And I'd say we're both too fond of our identities to give them up so easily.'

The old woman smiled, and this time it was warm and genuine. 'I think you might just do, Kerrig,' she told him.

Chapter Six

Zirpa led Kerrig out into the main living area, and the Earther was embarrassed to see that the others were close enough to have heard him shouting at their host. He braced himself for the looks of scorn, but none came. This so wrong-footed Kerrig that he missed what Zirpa was saying at first. Only when she had gathered everyone around the fire did he become aware of his surroundings again.

'You all seem determined to press on with your journey, even though you have no provisions, or any experience of surviving on the road,' Zirpa was saying. 'Do you at least have a destination in mind?'

'Somewhere quiet, safe for the children,' said Nesh.

'Anywhere we can lay low, until the patrols give up looking for us,' agreed Kerrig.

Zirpa shook her head. 'Quiet and safe are not directions,' she said. 'Which way will you go when you leave here? South? East? West? Not north I assume, since you came from there. That still leaves three choices. Where are you going?'

Volnar spoke up then. 'Which way is the City Dell from here?'

The Avlem frowned. 'The City De- do you mean the Citadel?' she said. 'That's away to the south-east, no need to worry about it.'

'I've heard of that place,' said Kerrig. 'Some kind of large army base. Lots of officers and officials, sending out orders and suchlike. I should think we can avoid that easily enough.'

'It's a bit more than an army base,' said Nesh. 'It's a stone tower, surrounded by layers of thick wooden walls. It was built when the Sidrax arrived, so they say, and the Avlem expanded it into a city. *The* city, the largest on this continent. The army presence is mostly ceremonial these days, and the stone tower has been converted into the governors' residence.' Nesh's expression grew wistful as she gazed into the past.

'It's a marvellous structure, like the rings of a tree. The large stone tower in the centre, then the official buildings inside the first wall, and then a bustling market town all around that, with a second wall around it. Huge gates that never close, and brilliant colours on every market stall. I was only there once, many years ago, but I remember it vividly. So bright and clean, and everyone at peace.'

The Fire Breather laughed. 'Clean? That place? Maybe inside the posh houses, up by where the inner walls used to be, before they tore 'em down to make more room. Did you have your eyes shut on the way in - an' your nose? The Scrums is filthy, and the Market Ring ain't much better. And peace? I s'pose it's not too bad if you keep to the right paths, and stay clear of the guards. Still not clean, though.' He smirked at the older woman.

The adults stared at Volnar. Even Maddie seemed to notice that something was wrong; she put down the bowl she was playing with and looked at the group.

'You seem to know the Citadel well, young Volnar,' said Zirpa at last.

'Course I do. I was born there, weren't I? You lot can do what you like,' said Volnar. 'I'm going home.'

Everyone found their voice at once.

'You've been arrested, Volnar! You're meant to be hiding, not going right to the heart of the governors' stronghold.' That was the Avlem woman.

'I'm not taking you within a day's journey of that Outsiders' pit.' That was Kerrig.

'Going home? Can we go home now?' This was the little Sidrax, sounding pathetically hopeful.

Volnar loudly protested that he didn't need to be 'taken' anywhere, and that Nesh needn't worry because he wasn't stupid enough to get caught twice. He was absolutely determined to go 'home' - as if that den of Outsiders could be a home for a child of the People! Strangely enough, Madrigal seemed equally determined to go 'home', which turned out to mean going back to the Sanctuary-cum-Mines. He was looking forward to going back there himself, but tried to explain to the little Sidrax that they couldn't return just yet.

'The soldiers who hurt you are still upset, so we have to wait for them to calm down,' Kerrig told her. 'And we have to help Volnar, too. We need to find a nice family for him, somewhere safe.'

'I don't care,' said Maddie, mulishly. 'He's going to his home, and I want to go home too! We can go there in the dark, like before, and then the soldiers don't see us and we can stay there and they won't find me.'

'I think they will find you, Little One, and me too. That's why we can't go back yet. I want to go home as well, but we have to go to other places first.' Kerrig took in the girl's stubborn expression and made her promise not to go back without him. She pleaded with him a while longer, but eventually gave her promise in return for one from him: that they would both go back home one day. This promise the Earther made easily. He was certainly going to return to his home once this madness was over, and he found that he didn't mind taking the little Sidrax with him. She was so innocent and charming; perhaps if he brought her up away from others of her race she might become as honest and trustworthy as any natural-born child of the People.

If he was careful, she might not grow up to be a shifty Shifter after all.

◆

Zirpa took them aside again, one at a time. When Nesh emerged from the small room she was wearing a multicoloured bag across her body. Then Volnar was called in, leaving the two adults stood looking at each other for a long, awkward moment.

'OK, how much did you hear?' Kerrig asked eventually. There was only so much silent judgement he could take, especially after Zirpa's more direct criticisms.

The Avlem only frowned. 'How much of what? Your conversation with Maddie? Hardly anything; young Volnar was giving me an impassioned argument in favour of our leaving him to make his way across the country by himself. Why, what were the two of you talking about?'

'Not with Maddie,' said Kerrig impatiently. 'With Zirpa. We were shouting at each other loud enough, people could probably hear us on the surface. I want to know your position, especially if we're travelling further together. Anything you have to say, say it now. Let's get this over.'

She merely blinked, still frowning slightly. 'Kerrig, I give you my word that not one sound came from that room the whole time you were in there. Even when Madrigal pushed aside the curtain to come out, I couldn't hear anything.'

Kerrig wanted to call her on this obvious lie, but she interrupted him before he could marshal his thoughts into the right order for a really searing put-down.

'Listen,' she said. 'Volnar's in there now - can you hear him? Voices? Movement? Anything?'

Kerrig had to admit that he couldn't. It was fascinating, and more than a little disturbing. But before he could think on it too deeply, Volnar emerged from behind the amazing soundproof curtain and sent Kerrig in. Maddie followed 'her Stony-man' as if it were the most natural thing in the world. The Earther saw her but didn't try to send the girl back. When they entered the room together, Zirpa seemed unsurprised to see the little Sidrax.

'Well, Kerrig, it's time for that help I promised you. Here.' She handed him a bag larger than Volnar's and Nesh's put together. 'Dried food, a blanket roll, two skins of water and a some medical supplies. Nothing fancy - you wouldn't know how to use most of the things I keep in here anyway - but any fool can tie cleansing moss to a wound, or strap up a sore muscle. The dried food will cook up into a decent broth with hot water. You're carrying the cooking pot, and you've a fire expert with you already. When the food runs out you'll have to start hunting. You and the Avlem both have a small knife and trap wire in your packs.'

Kerrig objected that he had never hunted in his life, and that he didn't know how to set a trap, but the old woman waved off his concerns.

'You'll figure it out when you get hungry enough. And, of course, there's always the Shifter.'

Kerrig nodded. 'She seems to be able to get by on a diet of grass and mushrooms, so even if we get low on food she will be provided for. That's one less thing to worry about, I suppose.'

Zirpa nodded. 'Yes, yes,' she said, dismissively, 'Shifters hardly ever starve, that's one of the interesting things about them. Shall I tell you another interesting thing I've learned about them? They have no true form, either at birth or at death. They are born in a shape that matches the mother's at the moment of birth, and after they die they keep the shape they had last. From what you told me, it was lucky that the creature was able to change shape when you asked her. Carrying a couple of hundred pounds of donkey all that way wouldn't have been nearly so easy as carrying a slip of a child. Then again,' she added, in the tones of a careless afterthought, 'It might have made it easier for you to leave it behind. Why didn't you?'

'What? I would never...! What sort of... She was...' Kerrig struggled to put words around the thoughts and feelings he'd had while carrying a helpless Maddie in his arms.

'She was my responsibility,' he said at last. 'She still is.'

The elderly Shanzir smiled and nodded. 'I was right about you, Kerrig. You'll do very nicely indeed. And so, I have two important tasks for you.' She walked to the curtain and held it open. 'Come on. The first is through here.'

She led him back into the main area, where he found the Fire Breather boy digging through the pack he'd been given and showing the contents to Nesh. Zirpa walked over to the far wall, took hold of one of the many woven wall hangings, and twitched it aside to reveal another room.

'Wait here. I won't be a moment.'

The room beyond was as dark and subdued as the other alcove had been bright and colourful. Zirpa disappeared into the darkness and emerged a short time later with a thick bolt of cloth that was almost as tall as she was. The whole thing was wrapped in canvas and tied with string.

'In return for my aid, you will keep this safe and deliver it to those who will value it.'

Kerrig knew better than to argue with that tone of voice. It wasn't a question, or even a request; it was a statement of fact. Still, he had to ask,

'What is it?'

'My life,' said Zirpa. 'And as much of other people's as I could remember. I've recorded the history of the Shanzir, as far as I know it.'

She loosened one of the ties that held the heavy canvas closed, and pealed back a corner to reveal the cloth beneath. It was a crazy pattern of twists and colours, and Kerrig found that he couldn't look at it for long without his eyes watering. He blinked and looked away.

'How is this a record of anything?' he said. 'There are no words or even pictures, just... I don't even know what it is.'

Just then, Nesh came over and peered closely at the weaving. She frowned for a moment, then her eyes went wide.

'This is a history blanket, isn't it?' she said. 'I haven't seen one of these since I was a girl. Did you make all this yourself?'

'Most of it is mine,' Zirpa said. 'Though I've included some blankets made by my father; he was the one who taught me to weave.'

'This is beautiful,' Nesh said, pouring over the outermost layer. 'You're very skilled, Zirpa.'

'You could learn to be just as skilled, if you want. Carrying these history blankets safely is your payment to me for the supplies, but handing them over to someone who can read them is another transaction altogether. Ask for some lessons in return for the blankets, and you'll surely learn enough to read them. Maybe even to make them, if you're a quick study.'

Nesh looked uncomfortable. 'I know it's normal for Elementals to trade Talents like that, but I don't think I could bring myself to ask for any such thing. I was just admiring your skill, not trying to get it for myself.'

'Well do as you please, I'm sure. Makes no difference to me,' said Zirpa, sounding quite unconcerned. Kerrig gave the Avlem woman a disapproving Look, but Zirpa called him back into her alcove to 'fetch more supplies.'

◆◆◆

As he pushed through the curtain, Kerrig hesitated.

'Er... Lady, I don't wish to sound ungrateful, but, well...'

'Spit it out, lad,' said Zirpa. 'Never mind the fancy talk; what's bothering you?'

'It's just that, what with carrying that big bolt of cloth and all, I don't see how we *can* take any more than you've already given us. And it's very good of you to be so generous, but...'

'Generous nothing,' interrupted Zirpa. 'It's a fair price for the service you're doing me. That's how much I value the story of my life; do you understand?'

Kerrig frowned. 'I think so,' he said at last. 'Although I'm a bit worried that you won't have enough food left for yourself.'

The Shanzir sighed and sat down. 'Do you know how old I am, Kerrig of the Great Border Cliffs?' When he shook his head she said, 'Neither do I, exactly. But I remember the Proclamation of the Citadel, so that gives us a clue.'

Kerrig stared at her while he tried to calculate the time between then and now. 'But that was over eighty years ago! If you're old enough to remember that, then... Well, I must say that you are remarkably healthy for your age, Lady Zirpa.'

The lady laughed, and it was bitter. 'I'm not though,' she said. 'That's the problem.'

She fixed the Earther with a steady gaze. 'I'm dying, Kerrig,' she said. 'I've known for a year, and my time is almost up. If you hadn't come along when you did, I'd have sealed my history in wax before many more days were done. Though it would have been pure chance who would have found it then.'

Kerrig sank down into a chair himself. 'But you've been acting as though you intend us to leave today. If you're dying, we should stay with you.'

'You should do nothing of the sort. You and the others will leave here today, just as planned.'

'You're asking me to let you die alone? To leave you here with no comfort at the end? You think me so cruel, Lady?'

'It would be more cruel to do otherwise,' she said. 'To have you hovering over me, waiting for my death? All the while knowing that you could be tracked here, and that by delaying you risk everything? You would, all of you, be wishing for me to hurry up and die before two days were out. No, you will show me respect and kindness by leaving today.'

'I...' Kerrig felt as though he ought to argue this further, but felt just as sure that doing so would accomplish nothing. 'Very well,' he said. 'You are not depriving yourself by giving us so much. Thank you for the reassurance. But even so there is no more room in our packs, so I must respectfully decline your offer of further supplies.'

Zirpa smiled. 'Have you ever noticed that your speech gets more formal when you're anxious? It rather makes me look forward to this evening. I'm sure you'll be quite hilariously stuffy.'

'This evening? But didn't you just say that you wanted us gone today?'

'Yes. And then this evening, when the others are safely bedded down for the night, you're going to come back here and fulfil the last part of your bargain. I did say there were two things I wanted you to do for me. Carrying my life-story is the first, and you'll hear the second when you come back this evening.'

Kerrig sighed. 'Can't you just tell me, or have me do it now? Why do I have to come back? If I do, I'll be leaving the children, not to mention your precious weaving, to be watched over by a single Avlem. What if something happens, and I'm not there to protect them?'

Zirpa didn't blink. 'I'm trusting you to get them safely through these tunnels and settled for the night. Nesh is perfectly capable of looking after things for a few hours while you come and pay your debt to me.'

Kerrig had the same feeling of mutinous helplessness as before. Arguing would make things worse; it always did against those with the upper hand. So he smothered the impulse and simply nodded.

'You have my word,' he said, with deliberate formality. 'And if that's all, my Lady of the Shanzir, I think we'd better get started. The children will be getting impatient.'

Kerrig left the alcove and walked directly to the main door, stopping only to pick up the large bundle of cloth that contained the Shanzir's life story. Volnar, eager to get back out into the sunlight, followed at his heels.

The Avlem was with the Sidrax, who was still in her child-form.

'Remember, Maddie, no making shapes until your leg is healed properly,' said Nesh.

Maddie scowled. 'But being a donkey is better for walking. I *like* being a donkey.'

'I'll carry you, or Kerrig will,' Nesh countered. 'Walking in any shape is bad for hurt legs.'

Kerrig tuned out the argument. Maddie didn't want to be carried, Nesh wasn't going to let her walk. In the end, Maddie glommed onto Kerrig's arm and insisted that either she walked or her 'Stony-man' be the one to carry her. Kerrig put down the bundle of weaving, shifted his pack round onto one side of his body and invited Maddie to sit on the other. Nesh similarly balanced her own pack, and reached for the bundle.

'We'll carry the weaving between us,' the Avlem declared. 'It's a good thing you and I are much the same height, Kerrig. That makes things much easier.'

They said their goodbyes to Zirpa, and set off, Kerrig and Nesh walking a little awkwardly at first until they found their rhythm. Maddie seemed content to sit quietly on Kerrig's arm, but Volnar kept darting ahead.

Kerrig focused his attention on his Earther sense as he formed a mental map of the Crystal Caverns, and selected a suitable exit. He didn't want to make a new one if he didn't have to; apart from the damage it could do to these beautiful tunnels, it would also take a lot of energy. He was already facing a sleepless night in order to keep his promise to Zirpa, and he wanted to conserve his strength where possible.

They picked up the stream again and decided to follow it to the surface. After a while they stopped to rest, refill their bottles, and bathe their tired feet in the cool water. Kerrig closed his eyes, and let his Earther sense rest as well. The path was safe and simple enough, and Kerrig was confident that he'd be able to get back to Zirpa's home quickly that night.

Maddie was sitting beside Nesh, and Kerrig heard her talking with the Avlem and the Fire Breather. The chatter washed over him as he rested, and for a moment he allowed himself to revisit an old daydream: himself, a wife and children, in a traditional Earther home, sharing the old stories and their deep connection to the Land.

He wondered what sort of family the Avlem had come from, before she'd been sent to the Mines. It was strange to think of 'Avlem' and 'family' together when he was so used to seeing them only as officials and tyrants. But for once Kerrig didn't dismiss the idea out of hand. Considered as a whole the Avlem and the Sidrax were, of course, bad news; but that didn't mean that you couldn't find the occasional decent individual amongst them. Kerrig thought that he was very lucky to have fallen in with two such remarkable exceptions.

Chapter Seven

They followed the stream for about half a day altogether, until it rounded a final bend and revealed daylight. The path sloped ever so slightly downward, and a quick scan with his Earther sense showed Kerrig that they would be emerging from the side of a hill, facing south-east. It also revealed that there were people around.

Volnar had perked up at the sight of sunlight, and now he started to run towards it. As soon as Kerrig realised that they were not alone, he called for the boy to stop, but Volnar pushed ahead.

Kerrig put Maddie down and stamped his foot to raise a ridge at Volnar's feet. The boy hopped over it with a laugh.

'You'll need to do better than that, old man. I'm on to your tricks, you can't stop me!'

'Come back here, it's dangerous! You'll get...'

Before he could even say the word, a hand caught Volnar by the shoulder. Kerrig saw a glint of sunlight on the blade at the boy's throat.

'Let go! I'll burn you!' Volnar said; but the blade didn't falter.

Kerrig raised a shield of rock from the floor, just in time to block the arrows that came from either side of the entrance.

'Come on out from those shadows, Earther 27,' said the figure holding Volnar. 'I know you're there. You can't hide forever, criminal. Surrender while you still can.'

Kerrig put down his pack and his end of the roll of cloth. Then he deliberately stepped out from behind the wall and moved towards the light.

'I'm here,' he said. 'Let the boy go.'

In answer, she pressed the flat of the blade more firmly against Volnar's collarbone. There was no blood yet, but from where he stood Kerrig could see the boy struggling to hold absolutely still. The Earther's own blood raged at the sight.

'Come out, Avlem,' called the captain. 'And bring the animal you stole. I'm tasked with catching your whole gang, and I don't fail.'

There was a noise behind him, but Kerrig didn't dare turn to look. He could feel the shape of the two bodies behind the protective wall, and that was reassurance enough. Then he heard the Avlem woman say, 'No, Maddie, stay down.'

A small, copper coloured head peeked out from the edge of the wall, changing from girl to donkey in an instant. Kerrig quickly extended the defence to block her, but he heard her cry out all the same - in pain or surprise, he couldn't tell. Furious, he rounded on the archers and advanced, pulling power from the ground as he walked.

The captain continued to demand a full surrender, and hadn't acknowledged the Earther yet. Kerrig wondered if she could see him, coming in as she had from full sunlight.

He was about to call out again when he heard a voice say, 'Captain, there's another child...'

'There are no children here, soldier, only criminals. And silence in the ranks.'

As he got closer, he took in more details. The soldier holding Volnar was taller than Kerrig, her armour highly decorated but sparse. Shoulder plates and a single strip of mail down her front, connected by loose straps. Underneath that she wore a simple tunic as white as her hair and skin. On her helmet was her badge of rank. Kerrig didn't recognise the insignia, but she was clearly a leader of some sort. His Earther sense identified nine others, presumably her soldiers.

Kerrig noticed all this while calculating his chances of getting Volnar away from her. Something of his intentions must have shown on his face, because the captain laughed.

'Are you going to try and fight me, Earther 27? They told me you were desperate, but I didn't think you were stupid.' She sighed, theatrically. 'Well let's at least make it fair. You're unarmed, so I'll drop my knife. See?'

The hand holding the weapon flashed out to the side, throwing the shining blade to the floor. Kerrig saw Volnar move, wriggling like a fish. He got about two steps before a huge white paw knocked him to the floor. Where the captain had been now stood a large white bear. The shoulder pads and mail snug against the thick fur, leather straps at full stretch.

Kerrig recoiled from the massive Shifter, and she sent him a look of malice that had no place on any animal's face.

The bear threw back its head and roared. Kerrig took advantage of the distraction to make his move. He'd been slowly feeding power into the ground, prying open weaknesses where he found them. Now he pushed hard along these tiny faults, channelling energy through them to break out under the Shifter's feet. She staggered for a moment, and Volnar shot away from the sharp teeth and lethal claws.

The white bear dropped to all fours to regain her balance, her front paws landing heavily and speeding up the fragmentation of the ground underneath her. Kerrig let the stone floor turn to sand, and the Sidrax officer quickly sank up to her knees. Before she could pull herself out, the enraged Earther reached up to place his hand on the low ceiling. At his touch, a chunk of the overhanging hillside came down and crushed the white bear. When the rocks stopped falling and the air cleared, all the soldiers had gone. Volnar was before him, gazing up at the Earther with awe.

Kerrig stood rooted to the spot, unable to take his eyes from the sight of the pile of rocks before him. As his anger drained away, all he could hear was the roar of his own blood pulsing in his ears. One clawed paw stuck out, red stains stark against the white fur. Earther 27 wanted to be sick, but even his stomach felt rigid with the shock. He was a murderer.

◆

The next few hours passed in a blur. Someone was speaking to him. Maddie was climbing back into her position at his side. Volnar was talking with Nesh, and being scolded. Maddie's bandages were ripped, and her leg looked sore. The entrance was crumbling at the edges, and the rockfall loomed.

With the way ahead unsafe, Kerrig made a new exit facing south, further up and around the hill. He checked that this exit was clear of people, and the Avlem agreed with him. They made camp, and dinner, and then Kerrig turned to go. The Avlem called after him to be back before dawn.

There was a sleepy protest from Maddie, and a curious noise from Volnar, but he heard Nesh tell them to leave him be, and that it was time for them to be asleep.

◆

Kerrig retraced his steps, even though it meant passing uncomfortably close to the...

He closed his eyes, shut off his Earther sense, and walked forwards until he was sure that it was out of sight. He cautiously opened his eyes and saw the stream ahead. He made the journey at a fast walking pace, unencumbered by provisions or passengers, and was soon back at the entrance to Zirpa's home. He stepped in, expecting the change in the air that had marked the warm and welcoming home the day before. But the air felt no different in the tunnels than in the cavern. The fire in the pit had burned low, and the only other light came from a torch burning in a bracket beside an uncovered door that Kerrig knew he hadn't seen on his last visit.

As he crossed the floor, he noticed that the colourful rugs and blankets had been cleared away, even from the stone benches. Some of the wall hangings were still there, but others had been taken down. He glanced into the room where they had talked before, and saw that the blankets were gone from there as well. The shelves were full, each one covered over with a thin sheet. The place had the air of being packed up against a long journey. Kerrig's heart ached. The longest journey, with no return.

Kerrig found the Shanzir in the room marked by the torch. She was lying on a bed of stone, set into an alcove of its own. She was on a thick mattress of folded blankets, with more covering her. At her side, a stack of water skins and a bag of the same sort of dried food she had supplied them with.

The Shanzir's face was worn and grey, and she seemed so helpless lying in her colourful bed, that Kerrig faltered. He let out a relieved sigh when he saw her open her eyes. Not dead then. Not yet.

'Hello, Kerrig. You've come to keep your promise? Good. How are Nesh and the children? Is everyone tucked up safely, waiting for your return?'

'Everyone's fine; but I'm not sure I ought to be allowed around children anymore. Perhaps I should go back to the Mines like the criminal I am.'

Zirpa gave him a Look. 'Wherefore this sudden attack of conscience, young man? When you left here you were running away from that place. Why go back now?'

Kerrig's face fell even further. 'Because now I really am the dangerous criminal they called me. When I left I wasn't a prisoner, not really. Volnar and Nesh were, but Maddie and I were just living there. We'd never committed any crime. Maddie's still innocent, but I'm a...'

He couldn't bring himself to say it. The word echoed in his mind louder than the beating of his own heart, but he hadn't yet spoken it aloud.

The Shanzir smiled gently. 'Come now, you can tell me. I'm an old woman, and have had an adventurous life. You'll find me pretty hard to shock. Tell Auntie Zirpa all about it.'

When he still hesitated, she chuckled softly. 'What did you do - kill someone?'

Kerrig looked at her, then looked away. He steeled himself for scorn, anger, even disgust. He was not prepared for gentleness.

'Tell me about it,' she said again, so gently that Kerrig could hardly bear it. 'You have to talk to someone, and I promise to take your confidences to the grave.'

Slowly, painfully, she coaxed the story out of him. When she had finally heard as many details as Kerrig could bring himself to give her, she reached out to pat his hand.

'No wonder you're shaken,' she said. 'You just faced down armed warriors and walked away without a scratch. That's the sort of luck I like to see in someone who is carrying my life to its new home.'

'But I... I *killed* that soldier. There were so many other things I could have done, other ways I could have defeated them. I could've dropped a few stones to knock the soldiers out, or sunk us all into the ground, or wrapped the captain in rock from her feet to her neck. Instead, I panicked and brought a hillside down on her. I had so many choices, and I chose to be a killer.'

'You said that she had a knife to young Volnar's throat. That limited your choices rather drastically.'

'But she threw it away! I had time to drop a mountain on her head, I could have - *should* have - done something else. Something better.'

'Well, what does it matter? It was just a Shifter, after all.' Zirpa's voice was harsh, and cold. The abrupt mood shift caught Kerrig by surprise, and he gaped at her.

'You don't... you can't mean that. This is another test,' he said. 'And it's in poor taste.'

The old Shanzir laughed, weakly. 'You're learning, Kerrig. That's good.' Her tone grew serious again as she added, 'And now for something that is not a test: My final request. Are you ready?'

Kerrig nodded. He wanted this night to be over, and was not about to argue with a dying woman's last wish.

'I want you to seal up my tomb,' she said.

Anything but that.

'You want me to do *what?*'

'To wall over this alcove, and seal me in here. I have more than enough food and water to last me the rest of my life.' She spoke lightly, as if asking him to fetch her a cup of water.

Kerrig laughed, without a trace of humour. 'Oh, why not? After all, I've used my Earther abilities to kill one person today, might as well round things off by *walling you up alive!*' He glowered at the woman on the bed. 'What kind of maniac do you take me for?'

'Oh don't be so dramatic, child,' she said. 'You're not walling me up alive; I've already told you, I'm dying. I am old and tired, and all my responsibilities are fulfilled. I don't expect to wake up again when I fall asleep tonight, but even if I do it will be for a day or two, no more. If you had come here to find me already dead you wouldn't hesitate to bury me, would you? Don't let my corpse rot in the open like an animal's, Kerrig, please.'

'A tomb would have to be airtight,' said the Earther. 'You might suffocate in there, I won't risk it.'

'No need to worry on that score,' she told him. 'I'm an Air Walker, I can keep my air fresh until I don't need it anymore.' She watched him carefully. 'Do you feel better about burying me now, Earther of the Last Sanctuary? Now that you know I'm an enemy of your people?'

Kerrig blinked, and raised a seat from the ground before his knees gave out.

'No,' he said. 'No, you're Shanzir, not... it's not the same.' His expression hardened. 'I know what you're doing,' he said. 'You're trying to make me hate you enough to kill you, but won't work. You didn't even know the story when I told it to you. You weren't one of the Flying- the ones who betrayed us.'

'Neither are most of the Air Walkers alive today,' said Zirpa, mildly. 'It was fifty years ago, you told me. Even the youngest soldiers from that battle would be old by now, and the leaders are almost certainly dead. And yet you still can't bring yourself to say the words "Air Walker" without cursing.'

She sighed, and reached out her hand to him. Kerrig got up and sat beside her on the thick blankets. She patted his knee, and spoke to him as though he were her own child.

'Kerrig, you must find your own reasons for granting my request. Whether you shut me away because I'm a hated Air Walker, or obey my orders because I'm the last of the Shanzir, or simply because you want to honour the dying wish of an old woman, you must seal my tomb.'

Kerrig didn't realise he was crying until a tear splashed onto the back of the hand that now covered hers.

'It's not right,' he said again. 'You're dying, and a whole way of life is dying with you. It's... I... It's not right.'

'No, it's not right,' Zirpa agreed. 'It just *is*. My parents told me that the Shanzir had a saying, back when we travelled the Land freely: "In life we live on the roads of the Land; in death we live in the memories of our children." I have lived a long time in the Land, and I will live on in the stories I have woven. And in your memories too, perhaps?'

Kerrig nodded, wordlessly, then he stood up. 'I'll never forget you, Zirpa,' he promised. 'And I will do as you ask.'

The Shanzir gave a contented sigh, and closed her eyes. 'Thank you, Kerrig.'

He stood and watched her until he was sure she was asleep, then the Earther drew his hand across the wall, teasing the stone out over the open space between the bed and the room. It took several passes, but eventually there was a thin sheet of rock hiding the old Shanzir's final resting place. Kerrig spent time carefully thickening and smoothing out the new wall until it was sturdy enough to take an inscription without cracking. It wasn't enough, but it was all he had. Then he left.

The fire in the pit was nothing but ashes now, and the single torch in its stone bracket would burn itself out eventually. But until then the flames illuminated the words:

Here lies ZIRPA

Shanzir
Air Walker
Friend

She lives on in our memories

Chapter Eight

Kerrig stumbled back towards the camp on memory and the bare minimum of passive Earther awareness. He was exhausted, and the faint glow of the crystals in the walls told him that the sun was already rising. He was, Kerrig decided, getting too old for this. It was one thing to have the occasional sleepless night when he was a younger man, but at fifty his body was starting to get vocal when he pushed it too hard.

He refilled his water bottle at the stream before he left the caverns. He then drank most of it down on the spot, and had to fill it again before he moved on. Passing the dead Captain was still not a pleasant experience, but Kerrig forced himself to bury the exposed paw and make sure that the area was safe from further rockfall. Even with his new-found resolve and perspective, the Earther struggled to subdue his churning stomach.

Kerrig arrived back in the camp hoping for an hour's sleep before facing the day, but his hopes were dashed by the bustle of breakfast being prepared around a cooking fire. The woman and the boy were working together, and the Avlem looked up as Kerrig approached.

'Good morning,' she said. 'Where have you been?'

Kerrig waved the water skin and shrugged. 'I brought more water,' he said, unwilling to go into detail.

Oh, good. I'm using the last of mine to make breakfast,' she replied. 'It's not a huge improvement over what they'd serve us in the mines, but at least we don't have to fight for it.'

Kerrig made a non-committal sound that blended with a gruff thanks when she handed him a small bowl of thick broth. He'd rarely had to fight over the food in the mines, and ate his meals apart from the guards and prisoners alike. It had never struck him as a privilege before, but maybe it was. Or maybe nobody was stupid enough to pick a fight with a large Earther in his Element.

◆

Breakfast was a leisurely affair, as was clearing away their camp. By the time everything was packed away, the fire doused, and the ground smoothed out, the sun was high overhead.

'There's some woodland ahead, to the south,' said the Avlem woman. 'We'll reach it easily before dark, and then we can start heading west. Maddie, don't scratch at your bandages. Volnar, have you got your bag?'

'Wait just a minute,' said Kerrig. 'How do you know what's ahead? Why go west? We ought to find a way back underground, that would be safest. And then we need to find someone of the People who can take charge of Zirpa's great weaving.'

'I'm not going back underground,' said Volnar, 'And you can't make me. Anyway, we're not going to find anyone down there. All the Earthers are either back at that prison pit, or living in houses like normal people.'

'Like Outsiders, you mean,' said Kerrig, dismissively. 'There must be some People left who still honour the ways of the Land.'

'Of course there are,' said a new voice. 'Fusty old codgers with no appreciation for modern life. You'd like them.' A young woman came towards them, with the voice of a Marshlander and the uniform of a...

'Soldier!' Kerrig threw up a wall of dirt to shield the children, and dropped the stranger neck-deep into the ground. The soil was feeble compared to his native stone, but it served to at least confuse and halt the soldier's advance.

'Wait, no! Not soldiers!' said another voice - a man this time. He wore a similar uniform but Kerrig couldn't place his accent. Outsider, then. 'Sorry! This is all a big misunderstanding, honest. We'll laugh about it one day - please? I can explain. Or we can go our own way and not bother you anymore if you like. That works t-oof. O-kay. I'm trapped. You've got me, us, trapped in the ground. No threat, not dangerous at all, nope. No sir. *Pleasedon'tkillus.*'

Kerrig was so absorbed in watching the two strangers that he didn't notice Nesh approach.

'Is he always this incoherent?' she asked the woman.

'Only when he's nervous. Ash, breathe. We're not going to die.'

'That's what you think,' muttered Ash. He had his head tipped back, and seemed to be searching for something in the skies. 'Flying mountain to the head - *boom*. We'll never see it coming.'

'Don't mind him,' said the woman. 'We're not soldiers, not anymore, and we can explain everything. We might even be able to help you.'

'But would you mind setting us free first?' said the young man - Ash. 'It's awfully uncomfortable down here.'

'Good.' snapped Kerrig. 'First things first: Who are you, and why are you here?'

'Well, I'm Ash, and this is Tray, er, that is, Try-gull, and we're-'

'It's Traegl, you fumble-tongued foreigner,' said the woman, without malice. 'I'm Traegl, Marshlander of Westhaven, and this is Ash, Sidrax of nowhere in particular.'

'Hey! I have a home,' protested Ash. Then, to Kerrig, he said, 'When you buried our captain, the squad scattered. Some of them might head for the nearest outpost and get reassigned, but we've had enough. Honestly, the captain was crazy. We're not all like her, I promise.'

'And we can help you,' added the Marshlander. 'You hadn't even set a guard - look how close we got before you noticed us.'

'And how far would we get before you changed sides again and turned us in?' Kerrig retorted. 'I don't trust traitors.'

Traegl went red, though out of shame or anger Kerrig couldn't tell. Ash, took up the argument in her place.

'Ironically, that's exactly why you *can* trust us,' he said. 'We're deserters, on the run every bit as much as you are. And we know the land - or at least, Trae does. The Western Marshes are not too far ahead, and she can lead you through them. Trust me, you do *not* want to go near that place without a Marshlander - and Trae's the best.'

'The best? Really?' said Nesh.

In answer, Traegl turned the earth trapping her body into mud, and lifted herself out of the trap.

'Yes, really. And, please notice,' she said, turning to Kerrig, 'I could have done that at any time. I'm not here to hurt you, and neither is Ash.'

She laid a hand on her dirty clothes and pulled the water from them. Then she started to dust off the dried earth that remained. Kerrig watched, interested. It was not unlike the way he used his Earther abilities to draw dirt from things.

'Hey, Ash,' said the Marshlander, once she was as clean as she could get, 'Should I let you out, or do you want to do it yourself?'

'Let me out, please,' said Ash, 'I don't have your showmanship.

◆

Kerrig sank down to sit on the ground, too tired to even make himself a seat, while the Marshlander pulled the Sidrax to his feet and cleaned him off. Nesh rolled her eyes at the youngsters' antics. She shared a wry look with Kerrig, which he returned before he remembered that they weren't friends.

'We're about ready to go,' she said. 'Kerrig, bring our new friends along won't you?'

The Earther wanted to protest this on many levels, but instead simply hauled himself to his feet and herded the soldiers ahead of him towards the others.

'Any funny business, and I'll drop you down a pit so deep you'll be seeing stars,' he warned them.

They took the southward road without any more discussion. While they walked, Nesh interrogated the soldiers.

'Why don't you start at the beginning?' she suggested. 'Unlike some people, I'm a very good listener.'

Kerrig tried to ignore the subtle dig and pay attention to the soldiers. It was harder to ignore the Avlem woman's cool, hard tone. She'd promised to listen, but Kerrig thought that the newcomers should be hoping she liked what they had to say.

It was Ash who answered first. 'They told us we were tracking a dangerous criminal gang who had kidnapped a child and stolen a donkey belonging to the Mines. But that's not true, is it? The kid was running free yesterday, and not treating you like his captors, and the donkey was actually a Sidrax child. I'd had my suspicions about this assignment ever since we were given it, but that was the last straw. I quit.'

'You quit,' said Nesh. 'That's a bit drastic, isn't it? For one bad order?'

The Marshlander soldier gave a snort that might have been a laugh. 'One? More like a hundred. I've been thinking about deserting ever since I got assigned to that...' she glanced toward Maddie and Volnar, 'Captain. She was a nightmare!'

'Tell me about it,' agreed Ash.

'And what was a Marshlander doing in the army in the first place?' Kerrig said. 'Aren't you ashamed to be supporting the Outsiders like that?'

'Clouds above, you really *are* a traditionalist, aren't you grandpa? You think I should spend my life living in a house of reeds and tending my vegetable garden? Forget that! Five years in the army gets me enough gold to set my parents up with a comfortable retirement, and myself with a decent, civilian job.'

'Of course, they'll have to make do with three-and-a-half years' wages now. Still, it's more than I could give them otherwise. And I'll have to resign myself to a bit of vegetable gardening until all this blows over. I can't imagine my grandparents will let me get away with less than six months.'

Ash chuckled. 'You make it sound like a prison sentence,' he said, then slapped a hand over his mouth.

'I'm sorry, I didn't mean... Obviously, prison's not a joke, and that was really insensitive of me, I'm sorry.'

Nesh's expression softened, and she nodded at them encouragingly. 'So, you're off to see your grandparents then. That's nice.'

The Marshlander grimaced. 'Don't get me wrong,' she said, 'I love my family. But they're a bit much sometimes. You'll like them, I guess,' she said, with a nod to Kerrig. 'Though I'm not sure how much Grandfather will like you; he doesn't trust Earthers.'

'What? Why?' said Kerrig. 'And, wait, are we coming with you now?'

'Grandfather will explain it all in detail when you meet him,' said Traegl. 'If you're not properly respectful about listening, he'll explain it to you all over again. I'd apologise for him in advance but I expect you can be just as bad, in your own way.'

'You don't have to come with us if you don't want to,' Ash said. 'But a Marshlander village is probably the safest place for any of us right now. A real piece of the Old World, so Trae tells me. I'm looking forward to it.'

Kerrig glanced at the heavy roll slung between him and Nesh, and the Avlem caught his eye. Maybe this 'Old World' village had someone who could be trusted with Zirpa's life-story.

Kerrig flopped onto his back with a groan. After two days without sleep he was exhausted, and the energy flowing into him from his Element was barely enough to keep him awake. The sun was still a finger's breadth above the western horizon, but they'd found a good place to make camp amid the trees and Kerrig was hoping for a few minutes' rest before he had to go and make a shelter.

No such luck.

'Hey there, sleepyhead!' A chirpy, unfamiliar voice sounded right in his ear, and Kerrig would have jumped to his feet if he'd had any energy at all. Instead, he simply opened his eyes to see a young woman's face upside down and above him. He forced himself to sit up, and heard the voice giggle. Where had she come from? The Earther hadn't felt anyone approach.

He saw that the Sidrax soldier was on his feet, and had taken on a strange, mixed sort of shape. His feet and hands were paws, and his skin was covered in thick black fur, but his face and body still seemed mostly man-like.

'What do you want, Falerian?' he said, through a mouth that seemed to have more teeth than it should.

The young woman, apparently called Falerian, laughed delightedly. She was floating, hanging in the air as though she were lying on an invisible bed. She flipped onto her back and let her head hang back, looking at Ash upside down.

'Still playing dress-up, Ashie?' she said. 'Silly boy, as if I would ever hurt you.'

A jet of water landed on the girl's face, and she spun around to face the Marshlander soldier. Kerrig noticed, absently, that her face was entirely dry. The water hung in the air, hovering in front of its target and then suddenly dropped. Straight onto Ash's head.

The Sidrax became completely man-shaped again, and pushed his wet hair out of his eyes.

'No-one likes you, Falerian,' he said. It sounded like a well-worn phrase, but Kerrig was more interested in Falerian herself. An Air Walker, obviously, but the contrast with Zirpa could not have been greater. This one flaunted her abilities, and seemed tireless. The sheer amount of power she must be using, just to float like that! Where was it coming from?

Then he realised: she was surrounded by her Element in its natural state. Even if she was working every hair's-breadth of air beneath her body, she still had all the air above her from which to soak up power. Kerrig himself rarely had more than the soles of his feet available for taking power in, and sometimes he was using them to send power out as well. No wonder the Air Walkers were considered the strongest of the People. Not only did they never run dry of strength, they never *could* run dry, short of being drowned. If only they'd used this near limitless power against the Outsiders!

'We're not going back with you, Falerian,' said the Marshlander soldier. 'None of us are.' Kerrig saw that she had taken up a defensive stance that put her between the Air Walker and the others. Maddie was awake, and seemed confused. Kerrig moved closer to the fire, where he saw Volnar holding a burning branch. The Earther wondered what good any of these measures would be against an enemy who could attack from above.

The Sidrax Ash must have had the same thought, because he hadn't bothered to take another battle-ready form. He was standing beside Nesh, and behind Maddie. Well, good. They would see to it that the girl was safe, even if they were Outsiders.

'What do you want?' Kerrig called up to the floating Air Walker. 'Are there any more of you out there?'

'Oh, there's no-one quite like me,' she replied. 'As for why I'm here, well...' She dangled upside-down in front of Ash, so that her face was level with his. 'I just couldn't bear to be away from my darling Ashie.'

The Sidrax growled. 'Shut up, Falerian. We're tired of your jokes.'

She spun around, contriving a look of hurt and confusion. 'Jokes? Me? Yeah, you got me. I'm actually in love with Trae-Trae here.'

The Marshlander soldier threw water in Falerian's eyes and grabbed at the floating ankle. The move gave her enough of an advantage to pull the Air Walker down towards the ground. Falerian recovered in less than a second, and took to the air again with a laugh. Then she looked at her ankle where Traegl had held her. The muddy hand-print showed up starkly against the crisp white trousers of Falerian's uniform. Her expression became furious.

'You. Got. Me. *Dirty!*' she howled. 'How *dare* you!'

The Marshlander was suddenly in the air, her head thrown back and her arms flailing.

Kerrig reached up to pull Traegl back to earth, boosting himself on a pillar of soil to do so. She was jerked out of his reach, and he drew on his power in readiness for a fight, even though he was aware that Earther-Air Walker battles did not have a good record. Suddenly, the roaring wind stopped, and Falerian deposited the Marshlander in a heap on the ground. The Air Walker drifted back over to them with an embarrassed little giggle.

'Oh dear, what must you think of me? That was rather an over-reaction, wasn't it? I simply can't bear dirt, though.' A puff of air seemed to push the dirt off her clothes from the inside out. All that remained was a faint discolouration, but from the look in Falerian's eyes Kerrig didn't think she'd be happy until even that was washed out.

'So, where are we going next?' said Falerian, lightly. 'Ooh, is that dinner?'

She drifted over to inspect the pot, which Nesh had topped up with more water. The Avlem sounded calm and composed as she offered a bowlful to the Air Walker. She shooed the children over towards Kerrig while she served Falerian, and the Earther watched in disbelief as the Avlem made polite conversation with the whirlwind.

Ash took a look at the Earther's expression and gave a sympathetic chuckle.

'Nobles, eh?' he said. 'That sort never lose their cool, no matter what. You've got to hand it to them, even though it is irritating at times.'

Kerrig frowned. 'What do you mean, "nobles"? Nesh has been a prisoner for most of her life. That's about as *ig*noble as you can get, I'd say. Unless you mean being stuck-up; I think that's just normal for an Avlem.'

The Sidrax laughed. 'They're certainly full of themselves,' Ash agreed. 'Especially the ones who came here, and could pretend to be important land-owners. I reckon her family's been that sort of noble for a couple of generations. But to Sidria, Avlenia's the back-end of nowhere. It's not even a fully-integrated part of the Empire, not yet. Just somewhere worth a trading run every so often, and even then only for the minerals. Just goes to show how cut off *this* place is, if you don't even know that. What do you make of the Sidrax, in that case? We must seem pretty mysterious and exotic, right?'

Ash seemed to find the whole idea very funny. He stopped laughing when the Earther scowled. 'Sidrax are killers, everyone knows that. Liars, thieves, and murderers.'

Kerrig stepped forward, and the Sidrax backed away.

'Young Maddie is an innocent, and I intend to keep it that way. Help her if you want, but if I catch you teaching her anything inappropriate, I'll...' Kerrig hesitated. He didn't like violence, even as a threat, but wasn't sure what else this soldier would understand. 'Well, just don't make me find out what I'd do,' he said.

It seemed to work, if the Sidrax's expression was anything to go by. 'I wouldn't... I mean, we're not... I mean, no sir, Mister... um... Sir?'

'Glad to hear it,' said the Earther, a little taken aback by how effective his vague, half-formed threat had been. 'And the name's Kerrig,' he added.

'Yes sir, Mr. Kerrig, sir.'

◆◆

Raised voices caught Kerrig's attention, and he went over to where Volnar and the Marshlander soldier were arguing. The Earther smiled to himself when he heard the boy vehemently denying that he needed anything from the soldiers. He remembered his own independent phase, and how miserably alone he'd felt when the Avlem warden had taken him at his word and sent him off to his own sector. However much Volnar might insist that he didn't need any support, Kerrig knew that support would still be there.

'You need us,' the Marshlander soldier said, firmly. 'You all do. You're on the run from the law, yet you sleep in the open with no lookout. You've left tracks that a child could follow, and you have no clue what's out here. And that's before you get to the fact that you haven't had any training in using your Element.'

'I don't need training in nothing,' Volnar insisted. 'I ain't gonna be no soldier.'

Just then, Kerrig's attention was caught by Maddie, hopping around below the Air Walker, while Falerian teased the girl with little breezes that lifted her hair. The vigorous movements threatened to work her bandages loose, and might even re-open the wound, not that the Air Walker could be expected to know that. It took Kerrig a while to catch the child and calm her down, but when he got back the soldier was still trying to persuade Volnar that there was more to Elemental training than learning to fight. Kerrig thought that argument might have been more convincing coming from someone not wearing an army uniform.

Kerrig went to help set up the camp. Bowls and blankets were shared out, and the fire built up. Mindful of the Marshlander's warning, Kerrig was careful to mask all tracks from the path to their campsite.

The Air Walker drifted overhead, eating a bowl of broth and watching the various conversations going on below as if they were plays put on for her amusement. Kerrig saw her but didn't comment. In honour of Zirpa, he had decided to give this Air Walker a chance. Even if she did have a bit of a temper, and didn't seem to get on well with people. It would be unreasonable to do otherwise, and Kerrig prided himself on always being reasonable.

Chapter Nine

Getting started the next morning was rather more difficult than it had been the day before. For one thing, although they had a destination in the form of the Marshlander village, there was no clear and direct route to follow. For another, everyone had their own ideas about how to stay safe and hidden. Maddie thought that they should travel underground the whole way, with Kerrig to make the path, lead the way, and look after everything. The Earther was touched by this absolute faith in his powers but had to explain that being underground all the time wouldn't suit everyone.

Falerian, Ash and Traegl went off to have a furious argument that was strangely impossible to overhear. Kerrig could see angry gesticulation and red faces, but heard not a word despite being only a few strides away. He eyed the Air Walker with interest, and wondered if Zirpa had used the same trick to keep their conversations so private.

He must have been staring too hard, because Nesh came over and poked him in the shoulder.

'Don't look so angry, you'll frighten the children,' she told him. 'I don't understand why you're so down on Air Walkers anyway. You seem more comfortable with the Sidrax boy than this new girl, though you know nothing about either of them. Why such hatred?'

Kerrig glowered, but not at Nesh for once. Memories of Zirpa warred with older, deeper memories of living under siege.

'They sold us all out, that's what,' he said. 'It was Air Walkers who helped the Sidrax army kill my parents along with hundreds of other Earthers. Marshlanders and Fire Breathers too, according to what I hear. The Sidrax army came rolling in and the Air Walkers, instead of driving them back into the sea like they should, decided to join forces with our enemy to conquer the rest of the Land. And you wonder why no-one likes them?'

Before Nesh could answer him though, Maddie came over, pulling at the bandage on her leg and begging Nesh to let her take it off. Grateful for the distraction, Kerrig offered to carry Maddie again.

'One more day,' he said, 'And then we can take another look at that leg of yours and make sure it's healed up properly.'

'It doesn't hurt now, honest,' Maddie told him. 'And I can't make my donkey shape with it all wrapped up.'

Kerrig smiled at her and said, 'You can be a donkey tomorrow, if your leg is better. It's not so bad to be this shape, is it? I can't carry you when you're a donkey.'

Maddie laughed, and Kerrig was pleased to hear it even if she was high and loud and close to his ear.

'Silly!' she said. 'When I'm a donkey, I carry you!' She giggled, apparently overcome by the ridiculous mental image of Kerrig walking along with a donkey on his back. She was still letting out little hiccoughs of laughter an hour later when they were finally trudging along the road towards the Marshes.

◆◆◆

The three ex-soldiers had come out of their argument in agreement about one thing: the group should head south-west to begin with, into the damp, unkempt wilderness that separated the Western Marshes from the Fire Plains. It was apparently a popular place to send raw recruits on survival training, so the three knew it well. And, they assured the others, it was entirely the wrong time of year for any training to be carried out there. Far too clement according to the Marshlander.

The party of travellers even got into a sort of formation, with Traegl and Ash taking the front and back respectively, Falerian above, and Nesh with Volnar in the middle. Kerrig was at the back with Ash to remove their footprints from the path.

Maddie, perched on Kerrig's arm, had struck up a conversation with Ash in the easy, comfortable way that belongs to the truly unselfconscious. She told him about her 'shapes', including her attempt at becoming a fish.

'An' Volnar says I got the insides wrong, a'cos fish-things breathe water, so I don't be a fish now.'

'That's probably for the best,' Ash said. 'Fish and birds are hard to do because the insides are so different. You need to learn all about an animal before you can begin to take its form. Er, make its shape,' Ash said, mindful of his audience. 'I've only got a few forms - shapes - myself, and I've been studying - learning about them for years.'

'Can you be a donkey?' asked Maddie.

The older Sidrax shook his head. 'I have a wolf form, and a hawk form, and a mongoose form,' he said. 'And of course this one. I used to be able to become a turtle when I was a kid, but I wouldn't like to try it these days. I'm out of practice.'

Maddie's eyes lit up, and she squeezed Kerrig's neck in a tight hug.

'You were right,' she told him. 'When you showed me I had to practice my shapes so I didn't forget. My clever, clever Stony-Man!'

Kerrig frowned. 'Maddie,' he said, gently, 'I only found out about your "shapes" a few days ago. When did I tell you to practice?'

'When we was at home, and you was telling stories to me and all the donkeys. One time, the guard said "Why you always talking to those dumb animals?" and you said "I'm telling the stories of the People so I don't forget," and I thought that if you could forget stories maybe I could forget shapes so I maked my shapes in the night and practised talking to the donkeys just like you!'

Kerrig didn't know what to say to this, so he simply patted Maddie's back and smiled at her. But Ash seemed very interested.

'Do you tell stories, Kerrig?' he asked. 'I'd love to hear some. There was a storyteller who used to visit the town where I grew up, and we'd go and hear her sometimes. I remember she had a great voice, and bright clothes, but I can't remember the stories very well. There was one about the man who carried the sun in a basket, I think, and lots of stories that started "Long ago when the world was new".' Ash spoke with an animation that belied his adult stature and sombre uniform; and Kerrig was reminded that the young Sidrax was closer to Maddie's age than his own.

'My Stony-Man knows ever so lots of stories,' Maddie said, confidentially. 'My favourite is about the boy who finded mushrooms, but I like the one about the girl who went to the edge of the world, too. And the one about the...'

Kerrig sighed, but not unhappily. 'And which story shall I tell you next, Little One?' he said. Although he was careful not to show it, Maddie's open and vocal admiration was flattering.

'Tell the one about how we got the Land made for us,' said Volnar. Kerrig hadn't realised the young Fire Breather had been listening, but he nodded at the request.

'Very well,' he said. 'In that case, I give you "The Making of the Land".'

◆

'Long ago when the world was new, there were four children of Time: Earth, Water, Fire, and Air. They were great friends, and were always together.

'One day they decided to leave home and make their own way in the world.

'"Let us find a place where we can all be happy," said Water, "So that we may have our own homes and still enjoy each other's company."

'And so the Children of Time travelled through all creation. They went to the frozen South, where Water and Air were happy, but Fire was miserable, and Earth weighed down under heavy ice. They went to the deserts of the North, but that only suited Fire. Even Air was too hot to move freely there. The high mountains of the far East pleased them all except Fire, and the dense forests of the West only appealed to Earth and Water.

'At last they had searched the whole world and not found anywhere they could call home. They considered dividing their time between the various regions, but none could bear to see their siblings unhappy and would rather sacrifice their own comfort than the comfort of the others, so strong was the bond between the Children of Time.

'Rather than part, they appealed to Time for aid. And Time was pleased with their loyalty to one another. So Time fashioned the Land, the world in miniature, for Earth and Air and Fire and Water to live as neighbours and in comfort.

'And the Children of Time gave rise to the People, who hold the Land forever as a gift from Time itself.'

Chapter Ten

It was raining when they made camp that night. Kerrig managed to scoop out a shelter from a steep, loamy bank beside the road. The steadily dampening soil was hard to work with at first, but with Traegl's help Kerrig was able to make an impromptu cave that was big enough for a tiny campfire and a few people.

Rain was a rare experience for the Earther, and he never enjoyed it. Kerrig shored up their improvised shelter and retreated to the back of it with Volnar and Maddie. Ash took his smallest form and curled up to one side of the fire, while Nesh took the other. The Marshlander sat in the mouth of the cave, seeming to enjoy the cold water at her back, while Falerian refused to come in at all and volunteered to take the first watch.

'Don't be too impressed,' said Traegl. 'She never lets the rain touch her and hardly ever sleeps. I'll take over the watch in a couple of hours, though; that airhead can't be trusted to concentrate for long.'

Kerrig prepared dinner while Volnar stabilised their small fire, and Nesh got out blankets for bedrolls and covers. They ate in silence listening to the increasingly heavy rain outside. When the food was eaten, and the pots left outside to be washed by the rain, everyone settled down to sleep.

The rain passed over in the night, but left mud in its wake. The road became boggy, and Traegl switched places with Kerrig in the marching order. Now the Earther firmed up the road ahead and the Marshlander restored the muddiness in the path behind them. Even so it was impossible not to mark the path. Volnar noticed this, and anxiously brought it to Traegl's attention.

'I shouldn't worry about it too much, kid,' she told him. 'The army's been stretched thin recently - that's one of the reasons they were offering such a good recruitment package. They could only spare one squad to go after a supposedly dangerous criminal gang, and they won't notice we failed until the report floats to the top of some over-worked adjutant's "to-do" pile. Even then they probably won't be able to get another force together in a hurry. This footprints stuff is mostly just to be extra-safe. We're small potatoes compared to the bandit raids.'

'Bandits?' Nesh turned to the Marshlander with an expression of alarm. 'Are they still around?'

The uniformed woman nodded. 'And that's another reason for hiding ourselves. We don't leave wheel tracks, so our trail won't be mistaken for a merchant caravan, but there are enough small raiding parties that might think we were carrying something worth stealing.'

'But we're not!'

'Aren't we? Dried food enough for weeks, strong water skins and good blankets? Those would be better than gold to some of these bandit tribes. Not to mention that the three of us still have our short swords and good boots.'

'Come to think of it,' Ash added, 'Little Maddie should probably stay the shape she is for a bit longer.' He smiled at the child when she started to protest that she was much better now and could she please be a donkey again. 'Hoof prints will make it look like we have enough cargo to justify using a beast of burden. Sorry Maddie - you can't be a donkey again until we're out of the mud.'

They walked on, and Ash showed Maddie how to forage for berries. They found a few good bushes along the road and picked enough that no-one had to stop for a meal during the day. In the late afternoon they picked up a small stream which was home to some frogs and newts. Volnar had fun catching them, but Maddie wanted to be sure they wouldn't, in her words, 'go dead'.

'You won't hurt those animals, Maddie, as long as you hold them gently. They breathe air, like us,' Kerrig assured her.

Ash added, 'See if you can catch one and bring it to me. I'll show you something interesting.'

The Earther raised an enquiring eyebrow at the younger man, but Ash only smiled, nervously. 'Nothing bad, I swear,' he said. 'But she's got to start her training sometime.'

'Just you watch out for what you teach her,' Kerrig said. 'She's a good girl, and I won't have you teaching her to be any different.'

The Sidrax blushed. 'Of course not!' he spluttered. 'She's a little kid! I wouldn't... Why would you even think...? I mean, no way!'

'No teaching her how to sneak into places, or to pretend to be someone she isn't, and absolutely *no* fighting. Is that clear?'

'Uh, yeah. Yes. Perfectly. Sir.'

◆

They stayed near the stream that night. Volnar and Kerrig cooked up their catch of frogs and newts on a heated stone slab. Ash took Maddie and her freshly-caught (live) newt off to one side, and they sat in deep and serious conversation for an hour. When they were done, Maddie came running over to show Kerrig how she could turn the skin on the back of her hand into scales. She was so proud of the achievement that Kerrig tried very hard to be pleased for her. Even if the sight made him more than a bit queasy.

After Nesh had inspected her leg and declared the wound safely closed, Maddie begged for permission to be a donkey again 'just for a bit'. Moments later, a copper-coloured donkey was grazing beside the stream, flicking her ears and tail in contentment. Ash became a jet-black mongoose and scurried off after a scent. When he returned, he was carrying two eggs.

'I found these for the pot,' he said. 'Abandoned, but fresh.'

'Great!' said Volnar, enthusiastically. 'Crack them into the stew, add the cooked meat, and our dried food will go that much further.'

'Wait - can I have some of the stew before you put the meat in?' said Ash.

Traegl rolled her eyes, but poured him a bowlful anyway.

'I nearly forgot about you being a picky plant-eater for a moment there,' she said. 'You wouldn't think someone who can hunt in two different forms would be so hard to feed.'

'Sidrax don't eat meat,' Ash said, simply. 'We study animals, we imitate them, we even live as them, but we don't eat them.'

Nesh frowned. 'But you're OK with eggs?' she said, sceptically.

'Abandoned eggs, yes. And we'll take milk if there's extra after the young are fed,' Ash said. He sounded as if he'd had to give this explanation several times before. 'We make leather from the hides of animals who have died naturally, and use their bones. We sheer fleece, and even use horns that've been shed. But we don't kill animals.'

Kerrig didn't look impressed. 'You're happy enough to kill People,' he said.

Ash sighed. 'We're not thugs, Sir,' he said. 'The Sidrax Empire stands for peace, law, and the pursuit of knowledge. I've been in the army for more than two years now, and the only time I've used force has been against bandits and other violent types.'

'Criminals, in other words.'

Ash smiled. 'Exactly,' he said.

'Criminals like us?'

His face fell again. 'No. And if you hadn't taken down my captain I'd be facing a court martial right now for disobeying orders.'

'That captain of yours was happy enough to go up against a group of children though, wasn't she? Your *Sidrax* captain. Don't pretend you're a race of saints, youngster. You don't get an Empire by asking nicely.'

'The captain was mad,' said Traegl. 'You can't judge all Sidrax by her behaviour. And yeah, the Sidrax Empire has got a murky past, but you haven't even considered the benefits of being involved with it. The army does good work; I wouldn't be part of it if we were just going around oppressing people.'

'Wouldn't you?' Kerrig asked, bitterly. He looked at the two female soldiers and shook his head. 'Two of the People taking the uniform of the Outsiders,' he said, feeling tired and old. 'That's how you kill a nation; not with swords and arrows but with pretty clothes and fancy houses. Pull in the youngsters before they know better and flush away everything that makes the People unique. Before you know it there are no more Earthers, no more Marshlanders, just Sidrax citizens with Elemental abilities instead of shape-changing.'

He was speaking low now, unaware of his audience. 'They did it to the Shanzir, and they're doing it to the rest of us as we watch, and we're supposed to "consider the benefits". It's obscene.'

Ash shifted uncomfortably in his seat, but the Air Walker just laughed.

'Oh, you are going to *love* Trae's village,' she said. 'If it's anything like mine, there'll be a whole gaggle of grandparents for you to moan with. You can all get together and talk about how much better everything was a hundred years ago.'

'Ugh, don't even joke about that,' groaned Traegl. 'I know it's the safest place for us, but I am *not* looking forward to my welcome.'

'Are you worried about your family condemning you for bringing Evil Outsiders to the village, or about them swamping you with embarrassing displays of affection?' asked Nesh, unsympathetically. The Marshlander didn't react to her tone, but simply dropped her head in her hands and sighed.

'Both,' she said. 'And probably at the same time.'

The Marshlander soldier gained a reprieve on the teasing once they entered the Marshlands proper. The Air Walker kept herself off the ground entirely, flying high to dodge the splashes thrown up by the others.

Kerrig, Nesh, and Volnar, meanwhile, struggled to get through the damp terrain without losing either the dried food, or the precious history weaving. Maddie and Ash experimented with their 'shapes', but as the ground changed every dozen strides they couldn't fix on anything. In the end, Kerrig carried Maddie and one end of the weaving as before, with either Nesh or Ash on the other end as they navigated uneven ground.

They were almost on top of the village before Kerrig saw it; the huts were made of reeds that blended perfectly with the surrounding wetlands, and the village centre was kept moderately dry and firm by sinking it down into the wet, and pushing the water back behind Marshlander-maintained dams. Three Marshlanders stood around the edge with their backs to the dry space, buried up to their elbows and knees in the water they were keeping back.

The nearest such living dam saw their approach and called for help.

'Outsiders! Evacuation orders, Chief? Releasing the wall in ten-'

The Air Walker raised a hand, but Traegl got there first. Sinking one arm into the dam, she used her other hand to smack the guard lightly on the back of the head.

'Honestly, Ifyn,' she said, 'Is that any way to greet your cousin?'

◆◆◆

While Traegl was swept away on a sea of relatives, being simultaneously welcomed and scolded, Kerrig and the others were left in the middle of the village, surrounded by hostile stares. Then one of the starers noticed the bundle balanced carefully between Kerrig and Nesh.

Once the history blanket was revealed some of the Marshlanders became a little friendlier, but not much. An older couple were summoned away from Traegl's extended family reunion to read a piece of the weaving and verify its value.

Then Kerrig and Nesh had to tell their stories, with interjections from Maddie and Volnar. When it became Ash and Falerian's turn to be interrogated, only Ash was still in the circle. Falerian had found herself a group of young friends, and was amusing both herself and them by making bubbles appear in the water. Ash himself was quickly vouched for by Traegl, and the visitors were offered fresh water to drink and the chance to sit down.

'This history weaving is a valuable find, and you were right to bring it to us,' said one of the oldest men Kerrig had ever seen. He wore the mark of a chief, and bore a faint resemblance to Traegl. 'Of course, if the Earthers had come to our aid back when we needed it, that history might have been very different. Not to mention there would be more people able to read it. But the less said about that the better. By bringing us this treasure, you have gone some way towards offsetting the failings of your parents.'

Kerrig felt the ground tremble under him with his own anger.

'How dare you?' he said. 'My parents *died* trying to keep the invaders from our home.'

'And they failed. As did my sisters, my brother, and three of my children. But my family died first, because yours chose to die later. The Earthers ignored our cry for aid, so it's hardly surprising that there was no-one left to help you in your turn. But that is the past, and best left to the history blankets. Although there are few left who can read such things, and fewer still with the skill to make them. If only more young people were like Ifyn; that young man at least has devoted himself to the study of the old ways. Unlike *some* people.'

Traegl tried to smile, but it withered under the old man's glare. Ash seemed ready to argue on her behalf, but she shook her head at him.

'My parents moved to Westhaven when I was a baby, but Grandfather still thinks I ought to stay here and tend reeds for a living,' she said. Then added, in a lower voice, 'This is why I don't like visiting.'

'You don't like visiting this lovely village, Traegl?' cried Falerian, in feigned shock. 'But whyever not? The people are so nice! There's this one girl - a bit like you, only much better looking. Another cousin, maybe? Or a niece?. Anyway, she was telling me there are other places like this, little islands of the old ways hidden from the Outsiders. So nice, don't you think? To get away from all the stresses of modern life, and have it be like the invasion never happened. Just blissful!'

'Are there other survivors?' Kerrig asked Traegl's grandfather. 'Are any of them Earthers?'

'I'm sure I don't know, and I don't care,' snapped the old man. 'Idle gossip for young ears. As if we need anything beyond what the Marshes give us. Be off with you. But you can leave that weaving; I'm sure we have the only People for weeks around who know how to appreciate it.'

Traegl's grandfather stormed away and disappeared inside the largest of the surrounding huts.

'I'm sorry about that,' said Traegl. 'But he'll cool off soon. I'm sure we'll be able to stay here at least until the start of the next dry season.'

'I'm sorry, but you can't,' said one of the women. 'Traegl, I love you like a sister but it's not safe for you, or for any of us, if you stay here. You know this is where the army will come looking for you once you're known to be a deserter.'

'No, they'll only go to Westhaven, surely?' said Traegl. 'And how would they even get here? That's the whole point of this place, isn't it?'

'You're not the only Marshlander in uniform, Trae,' said the other woman. 'You can't stay, it's that simple. When the scouts come looking, we'll tell them we sent you away into the Deep West.'

'You're going to banish me?' Traegl cried. 'Send me off to die? That's insane! And what about my friends? They don't deserve that!'

'Don't be ridiculous, Traegl! I said that's what we'd tell the scouts. You can go wherever you want, so long as it's not here.'

'So you *are* banishing me,' said Traegl, flat and sad. 'Where will we go? I told Ash we'd be safe here, and now we've got to keep on running? How is that fair?'

'We could go to one of those islands Falerian mentioned,' said Kerrig, trying not to sound too eager. *Surely one of them will have Earthers*, he thought.

'What a great idea!' said the Air Walker, who had drifted over to join them. 'I'll get Golwik to come over and tell you all about them.'

'Golwik?' said Traegl. '*That's* who you were talking to? There's no way she's better looking than me!'

◆

As it happened, Golwik did have some ideas about where they could go - but they weren't particularly helpful. She said that 'someone had mentioned something somewhere in the Peaks', but that it might have been the Border Cliffs after all, and anyway, it hadn't been her they talked to, it was her brother.

Then she shouted over to her brother at the top of her lungs, saying something in the old words that Kerrig couldn't understand. Traegl frowned at Golwik.

'Did she say something rude?' asked Ash.

'I don't know, I'm sure,' Traegl said, dismissively. 'She's just showing off. Golwik was brought up speaking Sidrean just like me, and then she made a big fuss about moving out here, and learning the old words, and making out like that made her better than m- than the rest of us.'

Golwik turned an impish smile in Traegl's direction.

'I can hear just fine in both languages, cousin dearest,' she said. 'And Bren's too busy to come over, but he says it *was* the Peaks as has the hideaway in it. Though it might be Earthers, or it might be Air Walkers, so he doesn't know if you should look on the mountains or inside them.'

'Do you have any idea how massive the Peaks are?' said Ash. 'That range is almost completely unexplored. There might be a hundred hidden communities in there, but we'd die of exposure and starvation before we found one. Haven't you heard of anything closer?'

'How about something defended, rather than hidden?' suggested Falerian. 'Like how this place is defended by the Marshes. Something surrounded by Fire, perhaps? We've got a talented Fire Breather with us who I'm sure could get us through anything.'

But Golwik came up blank on this suggestion, as did everyone else they asked. Then, as the sun was going down, Traegl begged leave for them to sleep in the village square overnight. They were given permission, provided that Traegl took first watch on the dam while the others slept. Kerrig had a nagging suspicion that the second watch would mysteriously fail to show up, and wondered if it was worth getting into another fight with the Chief over it.

◆◆◆

He woke in the middle of the night to a whispered argument between Ash and Traegl.

'He's half a watch late,' said Ash, in the sort of furious whisper that carries so well on a still night. 'That's not oversleeping, that's an insult! We should just pack up and go. We've got torches. It would serve them right if you pulled out and left them to drown. Ignorant louts!'

'Those "ignorant louts" are my family, Ash! I've let them down enough, I can hold the dam for one night. Go to sleep, I'll need your help in the morning.'

'And how are you going to find a safe path through the marsh when you're drained from doing this all night? No, I say we go now. Find a dryish spot of our own, and let you have some proper rest.'

'And I say I'm not leaving my family to drown!' hissed Traegl. 'I swear, I'd smack you if I had a limb to spare.'

'Who's drowning?' mumbled Falerian. 'What're you talk- hey, wait! Drowning! Now that's a sort of a defence, right? Wait, I'm remembering something... an island in the Great River. Yes! I'm sure of it - there's an island that no-one goes to, because it's protected by the Elements. It must be a hidden village, like this one! Come on, let's go find it!'

'Falerian, it's the middle of the night,' said Kerrig. 'Go back to sleep; we'll move in the morning.' He felt through the ground to check on Maddie and Volnar, and was relieved to find both children still sound asleep.

'I'll go to sleep when Trae does,' insisted Ash.

Kerrig sighed, walked over to Traegl, and threw up a thick wall of dirt. He extended it as far as he could reach in both directions, until he felt resistance that might have come from the other Marshlander 'living dams'.

'Pull the water out of this, would you?' he said to Traegl. 'There. Now wrap yourself in a waterbed, or however you like to recharge your Element. I'm going to sleep here, against this nice, dried-out wall. That way, I'll notice if anything starts to give.

Everyone's perfectly safe now, so we can all get some rest. Alright?'

The ex-soldiers shuffled off like sleepy children, and Kerrig smiled as he let himself drift into a light doze.

Chapter Eleven

The next morning, Falerian was nowhere to be found. The others packed their belongings and prepared to leave.

Only one middle-aged Marshlander man came to see them off.

'That was a good thing you did for our Traegl last night, Earther,' he said, only a little stiffly. 'If you do find others hiding out there in the Land, will you come back some day and tell us about them? Just ask for a guide in Westhaven; or send a messenger and I'll come and meet you. I'm sorry you can't all stay here, but it really isn't safe.'

Kerrig was unused to kindness, or being apologised to, and he was quite gruff with his reply. All the same he did manage to say he might return some day, if he had anything to tell them. And perhaps by then they would have managed to read Zirpa's weaving, and have a story for him in return.

◆◆◆

A rested and refreshed Traegl led them back through the Marshes until they reached firm ground. Since they knew that going north wasn't an option, Traegl had led them south and east, curving a path a safe distance from the town of Westhaven. Even so, Kerrig could feel the weight of the buildings as they passed it. All those people, crowded on top of each other. He shuddered; it was unnatural.

They found Falerian waiting for them, just south of the town. She waved when she saw them, for all the world as if they'd arranged to meet at this exact place and time.

'Hello!' she said, bouncing with enthusiasm on her invisible cloud. 'I did some more thinking last night, and I've definitely remembered about that island. Someone told me all about it, ages ago, only, I didn't remember until last night. You're going to love it! Follow me, everyone!'

And so, in the days that followed, they travelled on as before; except that the Air Walker drifted ahead of them, leading the way south.

That had been a point of contention in itself.

'All the stories I've heard say that, if there *is* a "Protected Island of the Elements", it's in the east,' said Traegl.

'Yes, well, *stories*,' said Falerian, dismissively, 'Stories like that kind of thing, don't they? East, sunrise, new dawn. Symbolic as anything, the East. But South? Frozen, dark, cold, sunless... no halfway decent storyteller would put an important symbol of hope and unity in the south. But then this isn't a story, is it? This is real life. And real life is really bad at symbolism.'

Volnar grinned.

'Yeah, all that "Long ago when the world was new" stuff is mostly just for kids. Stories are nice an' all, but they ain't *real*. Now, if you want a true story, I can tell you about the Great Rat Stampede. That one really happened, and I should know 'cos I was there. It were a few years ago, when I was only a kid myself; and it all started when we was on a raid in the market.'

◆

'I was dead nervous, because it was my first time leading the younger kids on a table-crawl. The leaders was all getting too big, see, and I was the oldest kid what could still fit under the trestles.'

'Is this a story about stealing, Volnar?' Kerrig said with a frown. 'Because I'm sure that's not a good sort of story to tell in front of impressionable ears.'

'Nah, we wasn't stealing,' said Volnar, blithely. 'We was tidying up. All sorts of stuff falls off the tables, and gets smooshed up on the floor if you ain't quick, and then all the nice people at the market gets muck on their nice shoes. Markets can be really messy places,' he said, confidentially.

'Especially if you jostle the table just so when you're passing underneath it, right?' said Ash, with a wry smile.

'Yeah, that's a good trick,' agreed the youngster. Then he caught himself and added, 'But not one that I would ever show Maddie how to do. Because that would be wrong.'

Volnar assumed a saintly expression, although the effect was rather spoiled by his peeking out of the corner of his eyes to gauge the reactions of the adults. He gave up in the face of Ash's grin, and went on with the story.

'So there's me under this one table, looking out through the hanging tablecloths to see the others is all in position. And we starts going up and down our rows, picking up stuff off the floor. And it's all going OK until Lousy tries for something a bit out of reach, and goes tumbling out of his hiding place with his arms full of bits of fruit.

'Well the guards is all over him in a minute, and I knew I gotta do something. But I can't go out and grab him, because there's still three younger kids needing me to get them home safe. And then I see the rat.

'A right biggun, sitting in front of me with her paws full of something green, eating away like she's got all the time in the world. And there's this loose thread hanging down in front of me, just begging to be pulled. So I grabbed the big rat, and tied the thread to her, and let her go. And then there's another rat, so I grab another thread, and tie that one off as well. And the whole tablecloth starts coming undone, and I hear the merchant shout, and more threads come loose, so I look around for more rats, and then I see Lousy getting dragged past me on the way to the guard house, so I snags some threads on one of the swords, and they pull the whole table over. And the merchants are shouting at the guards, and people are dropping stuff - and I see the little ones picking it all up, good as gold, so I grab Lousy and we go. And the kiddies are smart enough to come when they see me signal 'em, so they're alright. And Rasser has seen my trick, and tied up a couple of rats of her own, so things are proper messy now.'

Volnar's expression turned nostalgic, and his eyes glazed over as if he could see his friends still.

'We cleaned up enough that day to keep everyone fed for a week,' he said, smiling fondly. 'Which was just as well, because the market was covered in guards for days after we'd pulled our little stunt. We moved around a bit after that, because the merchants started pinning down their tablecloths with spikes and stones, and it got a bit more dangerous to go under the trestles. Still, good times. Good times.'

◆◆◆

They walked on until noon, then stopped to eat. Traegl led Kerrig to a small spring where they could refill their water bottles. The Marshlander proved her skill by perfectly funnelling the water into the skins after Kerrig had pulled out all traces of dirt.

After they had rested, the group got back into formation for the march. This close to the Western Marshes the paths were taking a long time to dry out from the rain, so Kerrig was still in front and the Marshlander bringing up the rear. Even with their combined skill, it was slow going.

That evening, Volnar lamented their lack of progress.

'It's going to take forever to get anywhere at this rate. We're safe now, right? So why are we still covering our tracks?'

Ash and Traegl exchanged glances.

'Bandits are still a risk,' said Ash.

Traegl nodded. 'True, but in that case we're better off conserving our energy and moving faster. The patrols from the Mines won't be able to find us now, we've been masking our trail too well.'

'Unless they have an Avlem with some kind of Tracking Talent.'

'In that case we're finished, tracks or no tracks. And, again, speed will be a better defence than stealth.'

'The sooner we can get to Fal's Island the better. Assuming it exists.'

'Could an Avlem with a Talent for Tracking find us there, do you think?'

The ex-soldiers broke off their private conversation and looked at Nesh. Kerrig had kept walking with the others throughout the whole exchange, and he wondered if the Sidrax and the Marshlander had even been aware of them while they talked. The two were clearly great friends, though the Earther's mind had difficulty accepting that any child of the People could be so comfortable around an Outsider. Perhaps Traegl had been separated from her family while she was still young, and she'd been brought up amongst the Outsiders as one of their own. After all, Kerrig hoped to do something of the sort with little Madrigal. But then, where had she received training in her Element? And how come she was so comfortable with her relatives now, if they were only recently reunited? He remember the mob that had joyfully welcomed the Marshlander home. Could that happy, extensive family really have such a tragic story to tell?

He decided not to ask. If his guess was right, then Traegl wouldn't want to relive her past for a comparative stranger. And if he was wrong then it meant... no. His instincts recoiled from the idea. The strangeness that was Ash and Traegl's friendship would have to be chalked up as yet another mystery. Kerrig was making quite the collection.

Meanwhile, the worrying twosome were questioning an amused Nesh and getting her to tell them all about Avlem Talents. The discussion got rather heated, so Kerrig took Maddie to one side and enlisted her help with preparing dinner. He would have liked to get Volnar out of there too, but the boy seemed to be enjoying the chaotic argument.

◆

The day passed without incident, except for the moment when Ash realised exactly where they were, and tried to tell a story about it.

'Hey, Trae,' said the Sidrax, sounding delighted. 'See that clump of rocks over there? Remember the last time you and I were out this way, on survival training, and Garbrat decided we should make camp near a "small stream" that was actually a...'

'Ash!' interrupted the Air Walker, loudly. 'Ashie, darling, I think I know this story, and it is *not* for young ears. Or old ones, really.' She turned to the curious faces of the others and added, 'Trust me on this, you do not want to hear the end of that sentence.'

Traegl was looking slightly green. 'Agreed,' she said, and reached over to cuff the Sidrax on the back of his head. 'That's for reminding me of it. Ugh!' She shuddered and grimaced. 'Well, I'm not going to be eating anything this evening, that's for sure.'

'I was only trying to join in with the story-telling thing,' said Ash, looking rather hurt and bullied.

'Save it for this evening,' his Marshlander friend advised him. 'And until then, work on thinking up a story that won't make Mr. Kerrig drop you down a three-stride hole for corrupting young minds.'

The Sidrax warrior bit his lip and looked nervously at the older man. Kerrig looked back, trying to keep his expression completely neutral while he struggled not to smile. Misguided though they undoubtedly were to have joined the service of the Outsiders, he was starting to rather like the two young women. And that was astonishing in itself, when he considered that one of them was an Air Walker.

He counted the days, and realised that it was barely a week since he had been living in the Mines, content to acknowledge only other Earthers. At this rate, his old companions would hardly know him by the time he got back home.

Kerrig spent the rest of that day's walk trying to decide if this was a bad thing.

◆

When it was time to put the children to bed, Ash said that he had remembered a suitable story.

'It's a legend, an old Sidrax one,' he said. 'The sort of thing Maddie's parents would tell her. Maybe they already did, and she'll recognise it. Anyway,'

Ash assured Kerrig, 'It's completely appropriate. I promise.'

Ash sat down beside the fire and took a deep breath. Then he started his story. It was haltingly told, and short, but Kerrig was touched to recognise the younger man's attempt to copy the proper story-telling style.

'Long ago when the world was new, and all things were alike,' he began, then broke off to comment, 'Hey, that actually fits the story pretty well!'

Traegl gave him a Look, and Ash blushed.

'So, yeah, everything was the same back then, until Wisdom asked each creation what shape it wanted to be. And all the people and the animals each chose their shapes, until at last it was the turn of the first Sidrax to choose a shape. And they said, the first Sidrax, that they wanted to be the same shape as Wisdom itself.

'And Wisdom laughed at how cheeky that was, and instead granted the Sidrax the power to take any shape they could understand, in return for having no standard shape of their own.

'"And you will spend your lives learning about every creature in creation, and you will live and die in only those shapes that you have truly come to understand," said Wisdom. "And when you understand Wisdom, you will know my shape at last."

'And that's how come the Sidrax can change shape like we do, and why we are always learning. And maybe, one day, we will find out the shape of Wisdom.'

The next day, Maddie surprised Kerrig by choosing to walk in her child form. At first she stayed at the Earther's side, but by mid-morning she had drifted over to walk nearer to Ash.

'I like your story yesterday,' she said. 'Not as much as my Stony-Man's stories, but I do like it.'

The older Sidrax gave her a small smile. 'Thanks, Mads,' he said. 'Yeah, I think I'll need to practice a lot before I can tell stories like Mr. Kerrig. I'm glad you liked it.'

They walked on in silence for a bit, then Maddie spoke again.

'So, if I want to make a shape, I have to know all about it first?' she said.

'That's right,' Ash told her. 'Not in words, maybe, but you have to know how every bit of you is meant to look, and feel, before you can make the shape safely.'

'But I can be a donkey, and no-one teached me how.'

'Yes, they did,' Ash said. 'Your parents showed you when you were a tiny baby. I think maybe you were born in your donkey shape, so it must have been a shape that your mother liked. And she showed you how to be a donkey, and how to be this shape, too, when you were still so young that you didn't need words.'

The little Sidrax was quiet for a long time, and seemed to be thinking this over carefully.

'So, if I make a new shape now, I need to learn it with words?' she said.

'That's right. Words, or pictures. Like when I showed you how to make your skin like a lizard before. You had to touch it, and see it, and understand before you could copy it.'

Madrigal nodded, seriously. 'So, that's why you can't make a donkey shape,' she said at last. 'Because you don't understand donkeys.'

'Exactly.' Ash beamed at the girl, and patted her on the shoulder. 'You're a smart kid, Mads. Real smart.'

Maddie reached out and patted Ash on the arm.

'You're smart too,' she assured him. 'And don't worry, I can teach you how to be a donkey.'

Ash laughed, and Kerrig fought to keep his own face straight.

'It's a deal, Mads,' he said. 'And I'll teach you how to be a bird. There's a lot to learn, but it's worth it to fly.'

'BOOOORING!' The Air Walker was hovering about them, grinning upside down at the two men and the little girl. 'Why do all that brain-work when I can take you flying right now?'

The Air Walker reached down to the Sidrax child, and Kerrig felt the air swirl around her. Instinctively, he put his hand on the little girl's shoulders, and saw that Ash had done the same.

Falerian laughed at them. 'You two are such a pair of old fusspots,' she said. 'Don't worry, fellas, I'm not going to drop the kid. Let her have some fun.'

Reluctantly, Kerrig relaxed his hold on the little girl, and the Air Walker pulled her up to float in the air beside her. She took the child's hands and spun her in a circle, then let go and used the air itself to send Maddie dancing over the heads of the others.

Maddie laughed delightedly, but Kerrig saw Ash inching closer to catch the girl if she fell. The Earther saw the wisdom of this, given how easily distracted the Air Walker seemed to be. As he was watching, the flow of air was suddenly cut off, and Maddie dropped like a stone.

Kerrig thrust his power into the ground, breaking up the earth below the falling girl until it was as soft and yielding as he could make it. The older Sidrax moved to stand underneath her, preparing to take the brunt of the impact, but it never came. At the last moment, the Air Walker took back control and lifted the child back up into the sky. The little Sidrax shrieked and giggled as she was swooped and swirled overhead, and the watching adults heaved synchronised sighs of relief.

At last, Falerian set Maddie back down on solid ground.

'Be a bird if you like, kid,' she told the girl, 'But remember there are other ways to go flying, if you know who to ask.'

'I ask you,' Maddie said, without hesitation.

'That's right,' the Air Walker told her. 'And, if I'm feeling in the mood, I can fly you anywhere you want. In fact,' she added, 'I might be taking you all flying soon. Look.'

Everyone looked where the Air Walker was pointing. By the light of the noonday sun, with their stunted shadows pointing them southward, they saw a massive river. And there, in the middle of the river, was an island.

Chapter Twelve

They reached the north bank of the river in the late afternoon. Traegl and Kerrig were discussing the best way to cross, when Falerian interrupted them.

'I'll get everyone across,' she said. 'But first, I have to signal the lookout. There's a complicated, multi-Element system of protection around this island, and it needs to be deactivated from the other side. Wait here, and I'll send the signal.'

Sure enough, the Air Walker went to the bank and made a series of complicated arm movements. Kerrig couldn't see anything coming back from the island, nor could he sense any change in the ground, but a minute later Falerian was waving them over.

'I'll take you over two at a time,' she said.

Kerrig and Maddie went first, floating smoothly over from shore to shore. The waters of the river churned white as they passed, and it looked cold. Kerrig felt more than a bit ill when he looked down and saw nothing under his feet, so he focused all his attention on Maddie until they touched down safely on the island.

Ash and Volnar were sent over next, seeming more curious about the trip than concerned. Finally, only Nesh, Traegl and Falerian remained. Kerrig watched as the three women stood close together, Nesh grasping the sleeves of the others for support, or reassurance. Kerrig thought that he was perhaps not the only one to find the short flight unnerving.

Nesh and Traegl touched down, but Falerian remained hovering. This wasn't unusual - Kerrig didn't think he'd seen her touch the ground once. But when she raised herself back up and away, Kerrig began to worry.

By the time he called out to her, she was over the water. She grinned and waved, then cupped a hand to her ear and pointed at the rushing water.

At last the Earther heard her voice, carried on a thin breeze.

'Enjoy the Island, grandpa! Tell them Fal sent you!'

The party exchanged worried glances as the Air Walker flew away and out of sight.

'Where's the Flying-Lady?' said Maddie.

Volnar shrugged. 'Gone flying off,' he said. 'Adults don't stick around, 'cept when you don't want 'em to. Come on, let's explore.'

Maddie scrambled after Volnar on four nimble hooves. Kerrig lunged for her but missed, and he didn't want to use his Earther abilities to trip her up. She might get hurt.

The adults sighed as one and started to chase after the children.

So much for peace and security on the mythical Island, thought Kerrig.

They rounded a copse of trees and came face-to-face with a very serious-looking farmer, who was holding Volnar by his ear. Maddie, in her donkey form, was head-butting the man, but he wasn't moving. Confronted with three adults running toward him, the farmer stomped his foot and trapped all of them in earth up to their knees. Kerrig blinked, then started to smile.

'You're an Earther,' he said, delightedly. 'Out here - I was starting to think I'd never see another.'

'You won't see another sunrise if you trample my seedlings,' swore the farmer. 'Now who are you, and how did you get here?'

After a moment where everyone seemed to be waiting on one of the others to start, Nesh spoke up. Strangely, even trapped halfway through an awkward stride, the Avlem managed to project an air of grace and poise. She gazed sternly past the farmer as if he were of no importance at all, and related a heavily-abridged account of their travels to date. She left out their jailbreak, portraying the group as simply on the run from oppression. She couldn't explain away the army uniforms, but the farmer didn't seem interested. In fact, he didn't seem interested in any part of their story, beyond the initial introduction of each new character. It was only when she got to the part about Falerian bringing them to the island that he showed interest.

'An Air Walker, you say? And what were the likes of you doing in company with one of the Flying Filth?' Especially that one, who claims to be an Earther.'

Kerrig gently felt for the other Earther's power, and discovered that the farmer had stopped controlling the soil once it was in position around their legs. With a careful push of his own power, Kerrig released his friends from their bindings. Kerrig moved to take Volnar from the farmer, but the boy didn't seem particularly happy about the rescue. Ash laid a hand on Maddie's neck, tugging gently on her mane until she backed away from the angry farmer.

'I *am* an Earther,' Kerrig said, his delight fading to disappointment. 'And I will vouch for Falerian, who has not trespassed on your farm or your island. She proved herself on the road, so we don't hold her tribe against her. And now,' he said, 'It's been a long day and we're tired. If you would show us where we can make camp for the night, I think everything else can wait for the morning.'

The farmer surveyed them, then appeared to make up his mind.

'There's room in the house for you and the boy,' he said at last. 'Your animal, the Outsiders, and their lackey can make do in the barn. So long as the animal is tied up, and the Outsiders don't steal anything.'

Traegl protested at being called a lackey, but not the sleeping arrangements. As she said later, a barn was hardly the worst place she'd ever spent the night. She was also fuming over Falerian's sudden departure, and Kerrig found himself agreeing with her at least in part. Why had she just disappeared like that? Almost as if she were afraid of staying too long. Was there so much anti-Air Walker sentiment on this island that she felt unwelcome? If so, that suggested a large Earther population; which thought had Kerrig so excited he couldn't sleep.

He walked out to the barn rather than disturb Volnar, and found Nesh sitting outside gazing up at the sky, where the moons were in complementary phases. Neither was full, but by the light of the brightest Kerrig could make out an unfamiliar, alert cast to the Avlem's expression. She turned to look at him as he approached, and her eyes seemed unusually clear and focused.

Kerrig sat down too, letting the passive power of the earth soak into him. It was good to be out here, on the Island of the People, in his Element and at peace.

After a while he turned to Nesh and said, 'Can't sleep either?'

She sighed. 'Traegl's out like a candle, and Ash and Madrigal are curled up in their favourite animal forms, but I couldn't get comfortable. I don't know why straw should be so difficult to sleep on; I must be too well used to beds of earth and stone.'

Kerrig smiled. 'You should be indoors, then. It's a real Earther building, with the walls made of compacted soil and the floor raked soft. Very different from the caves of home, but completely Earther. It's... it reminds me of the stories my uncles used to tell me, about how things used to be. You have to see it - such a great example of Earther traditions.'

Nesh gave a crooked smile. 'I'm sure our host would be flattered by your enthusiasm, Kerrig,' she said. 'And I'm equally sure that he wouldn't want an "Outsider" to set foot in his home.'

She was still smiling, but there was a distinct bitterness to her tone. Kerrig frowned.

'No need to be like that about it,' he said. 'I mean, yes, you are an Outsider, but it's alright. You're not like other Avlem.'

The Avlem made a sound that might have been a laugh or a sob. 'The eternal exception, that's me,' she said. 'Always the outsider. You'd think I'd be used to it after more than 25 years, but it still manages to catch me by surprise. It's almost enough to make me wish I were anything but Avlem.'

Kerrig nodded sympathetically. 'Yeah, it must be uncomfortable for you. Still, it's not your fault, you know. Being Avlem. And maybe you'd be happier if you went back home. To your family, I mean,' he said. 'Not back to Avlenia. Well, unless you wanted to, of course.'

Nesh gave him an old-fashioned look. 'Where my family and their friends would be thrilled to welcome a convict back into their houses,' she said, deadpan. 'You've only got to think about how much the Avlem guards in the prison mines liked me to guess how happy my kith and kin will be to see me again.'

Kerrig was taken aback by the venom in her tone. He didn't know what to make of it.

'Well, go and find some Avlem who don't know you,' he suggested. 'There are plenty of new towns springing up all over the place.'

Nesh sighed. 'Maybe I will,' she said. 'Now that the children are safe and settled, there's no need for me to stay.'

Kerrig nodded, and smiled. 'Now we can all be with our own people,' he said, happily. 'I don't know why Falerian didn't stay, but she's done us a good turn and no mistake.' He gave a small but heartfelt laugh and said, 'Who'd have thought that I'd ever say that about an Air Walker?'

The days flowed into weeks as Kerrig adapted to his new life. He lost track of the others quickly, except for Maddie who had refused to leave his side. She hadn't revealed herself to be anything other than a donkey around the other Earthers, and so had been granted a permanent home in the barn in return for working on the farm.

He quickly learned that the Earthers and Marshlanders raised and processed crops, while the Fire Breathers kept animals - mostly goats. A couple of Marshlanders kept ducks, and various members of all three tribes worked at turning the plants and animals into useful things. There was a central area where trade happened, and people met socially, but apart from that the tribes stayed in their own homes.

Kerrig was surprised to discover that his fellow-Earthers didn't share his ability to easily work stone. He supposed it came from his being brought up underground, and being more familiar with rock than with soil, but it made him stand out and his didn't like it. Unfortunately for him, the other Earthers did like it, and he found himself called on to fix the balance on a pair of millstones, and repair three different stone walls before he'd been on the island a week.

One good thing about these jobs was that they let him travel around the island, or 'Camp Freedom' as the inhabitants called it. He discovered that there had once been an Avlem-Sidrax training camp on the island, until a small band of the People managed to take control of it. There were still a few army buildings left, on ground unsuitable for farming, mostly because it was too rocky.

'Although,' said his host, a man by the name of Balmar, 'Now that you're here, perhaps some of that ground can be used after all.'

And so Kerrig made his way towards the eastern end of Camp Freedom to inspect the state of the fields there. They were certainly bare and stony, with only occasional tufts of coarse grass breaking through between the rocks. He wondered what he was supposed to do here - it would take him months to break down all this stone into dust, and even then it still wouldn't be good growing soil. He continued on towards the buildings anyway; may as well check that the whole place really was unusable before going back.

But when he entered the largest of the surviving buildings, Kerrig discovered Volnar and Nesh sitting inside, busily working on something.

'Hullo,' he said, surprised. 'I thought you'd left,' he said to the Avlem.

'We're going,' said Volnar. 'Just as soon as we finished building the raft.'

'Raft?' asked Kerrig, as he looked around. He could see now that they had taken some of the blankets from Zirpa's place and cut them into strips, about a hand-breadth wide, which they were braiding together. The result was a medium-weight rope, and they already had quite a few coils of the stuff at their feet.

'Ash got us some logs,' the Avlem said, without looking up from her work. 'He said he persuaded one of the Fire Breathers to lend him an axe, but he sounded awfully embarrassed about it, so I didn't push for details. Anyway, he came back after a couple of days and showed us a pile of fallen trees not far from here, so we're going there to make them into a raft as soon as we've got the rope we need to lash them together.'

The Earther was impressed. 'It sounds like you have it all planned out,' he said. 'How did you work out how to make a raft? I wouldn't know where to start.'

'Trae helped,' said Volnar. 'Here, you can take over plaiting for a bit - I'm going outside to cut up some more blankets.' The Fire Breather thrust his work into the Earther's hands, picked up a knife, and headed out into the sunshine. Kerrig sat and looked at the mess of fabric in his hands, but he only fumbled for a moment before he worked out what to do. His movements weren't as swift or as neat as Volnar's, but it was coming out OK.

'Why is Traegl involved?' Kerrig asked, once he was able to spare part of his attention for something other than counting the pattern of the weave. 'I would've thought she'd be busy building a life for herself here. This place isn't particularly isolationist, or overly-traditional. It should suit her down to the ground.'

'I don't think anywhere is going to suit Traegl just yet,' Nesh said. 'She's still young, and not ready to settle down to a steady life. At least, that's how I understand it. She asked me to come and find her when the raft's ready to go, and said she'll come along. Her affinity with water should get us safely down the river.'

'Why not just cross to the shore? It would be safer than travelling by water. Easier, too. A few Earthers and Marshlanders working together could make a temporary bridge, without your having to do any rafting.'

Nesh shook her head. 'Thanks,' she said, 'But Volnar and I want to travel down the river; it's faster. He wants to get back to the Citadel, and I'll need to go north and east to find a new town where they'll be likely to accept someone like me.'

Kerrig frowned. 'It's dangerous for young Volnar to go back to that place,' he said. 'He'll be arrested again, and we won't be there to look after him.'

'I know,' Nesh said, 'And I'm hoping to persuade him during the journey to settle in a new town with me. But he's absolutely determined at the moment, and if I don't go with him, he *will* go by himself.'

The two adults shared a look of despair at the folly of youth, which bypassed all their many differences. They worked on in silence after that, and Kerrig let himself enjoy the peace and quiet. When Volnar came in with an armful of blanket strips, he didn't break the spell; he just sat down on the floor and began working on a new length of rope.

It wasn't until the shifting shadows made it hard to see that Kerrig noticed the time passing. He took his work to the door to get the best of the light and the lengthening shadows reminded him that it was a long walk back to Maddie and his lodgings. He excused himself from the working party, and wished them luck with their raft.

If he hurried, he'd be back before the first moon rose. Maddie was expecting him, and they hadn't quite managed to find the right time to explain to their host that she was more than just a donkey.

◆

What with his regular duties on Balmar's farm, and the many extra jobs that people had for him, Kerrig was only able to fit in a visit to Volnar and Nesh about once or twice a week. He had discovered that the other Earthers - and, in fact, most of the People he met - took a dim view of his continuing to associate with 'Outsiders and traitors', but he was able to use the excuse of working on the stony ground to justify his trips there.

On his most recent visit he had come up with the idea of bringing pieces of stone back to install as a drainage layer under the heavier clay fields - which gave him an excuse to take Maddie along to pull a cart. Once they were out of sight of others, Kerrig took over pulling the empty cart, and Maddie switched to her two-legged form.

After she had hugged him for a full minute, Maddie told him that Ash had been visiting her most nights, to get her to keep up with her training. She proudly showed off her ability to change just her ears, then her hands, and finally her skin. Kerrig still found that last one a little disturbing, but Maddie's happy smile was infectious, even when coming from a face that was oddly scaly.

Kerrig told Maddie about Volnar and Nesh building a raft, and how they had worked on it for a long time to make sure that it was safe. Kerrig and Traegl had built a pond for them where they could test their raft for various situations. It was a good pond, and Kerrig thought he might keep it after the others had left. And, if the land proved completely unusable for farming, this might be a good place to set up home for himself. A little stone-working business, and enough raw material to create any sort of house he pleased... yes, it was a good plan. Once the others left.

◆

As he approached, Kerrig wondered if they had already gone. On his last visit he had seen the raft pass every test, and Maddie mentioned that Ash had said he might have to go away for a while soon. When he caught sight of the completed raft propped up against the side of the largest building, the big Earther felt strangely happy. Life would certainly be easier when the others were gone: no more balancing two conflicting sets of friendships. He would be able to settle down to life as an Earther amongst Earthers, maybe even get married and preserve the traditions of the People for another generation. It was going to be good, and yet Kerrig still felt glad that he hadn't missed his chance to say goodbye.

Kerrig and Maddie left the empty cart outside and pushed open the unlocked door. He wasn't sure what he was expecting - it could have been anything from a scene of frantic preparations to a celebratory mood of eating and relaxing before heading out - but he certainly hadn't expected to walk in on a mixture of anger, confusion, and desperation.

'It's a dome, I tell you,' said Volnar. 'Ash, are you sure you tried every angle?'

'For the last time, yes! As soon as I get too far from the island, it hits me like a runaway cart. Even if you could all somehow fly, it wouldn't change anything.'

'Neither will shouting,' said Nesh. 'Any luck discovering the source of the safeguards?' she asked Traegl.

'No,' she said, sounding frustrated. 'The ones who were willing to talk to me have never heard of any such safeguards, and the rest are still spitting at me when I get too near. And they wonder why I want to get out,' she muttered, darkly.

The Marshlander had pulled all the insignia from her uniform, but it was still distinctly not of the People. Kerrig decided that this would be a good time to make his presence known, so he led Maddie into the room.

'Mads! Good to see you, kid!' Ash swept the child up in a big hug, and was soon joined by Nesh and Volnar. Traegl was less demonstrative, but still smiled and waved at the girl.

'What's all the fuss about in here?' Kerrig said, when the hug disengaged.

Nesh's smile fell away as her expression hardened.

'We can't leave the island,' she told him. 'It turns out that "Camp Freedom" is even more of a prison than the Mines. We're trapped here.'

Chapter Thirteen

Kerrig felt his blood run cold. 'What do you mean, trapped?' he said.

'Exactly what it sounds like,' the Avlem told him. 'Have you been down to the river since we arrived?'

Kerrig had to think about that for a moment. 'Not right down to the water,' he said, after a minute or so, 'But I did some work on the Drishmel farm last month, repairing their western wall. That runs pretty close to the edge of this island.'

'How did you like it? Any ideas of going for a dip once you'd finished your work?'

'Oh, no,' Kerrig said. 'It was far too cold for anything like that!'

Ash frowned. 'Kerrig,' he said, 'It's not even autumn yet. Last month was really warm - maybe too warm. How come you were cold?'

'I-' Kerrig hesitated. It had been hot, especially for a man used to the cool darkness underground. When he'd been building stepping stones across a duck pond, he'd stood in the cool water and found it a welcome relief. But the thought of going down the river just a few days later had made him shiver and hurry home.

'I... don't know,' he said at last.

'None of us do,' said Volnar, 'It's creepy. We've all tried different ways of getting to the river, but as soon as you get too far from the middle of the island, something turns you back. Feeling cold, scared, even suddenly tired. And the harder you push, the worse it gets.'

'It's in the sky as well; I couldn't fly out,' said Ash. 'But - and this is interesting - other birds didn't seem to have any trouble. And there were fish too, coming in and out of the little stream that feeds from the Camp into the river. But when I tried to follow the other birds, I suddenly felt so afraid that I almost fell out of the sky. I don't even know what I was afraid of, just that it was terrible.' He shuddered, and Maddie gave him a hug.

Kerrig's expression hardened. 'I'll put the word around,' he said. 'Another sanctuary turned into a prison is simply unacceptable. We need to break this, and the others will help.'

Nesh raised an eyebrow. 'Why would they do that? Most of the Elementals here don't like us, why would they help?'

Kerrig gave a small, bitter smile. 'Because they don't like you. You're trying to leave, and they want you gone. And I suspect there will be more than a few who are as angry about this trap as I am.'

He turned to Volnar. 'You start on the Fire Breathers, and I'll talk to the Earthers. And Traegl can tell the Marshlanders. Maddie, let's go back now. Never mind about the cart, I'll take it back empty. This is more important.'

'Um, can I stay here?' Maddie asked shyly. 'I don't like shouting.'

Kerrig's brisk, emergency-minded mood faltered. 'There's not going to be any... No, you're right; there probably will be shouting. At least to start with. You can stay here if you want. But if you find a way off the island, don't leave without me.'

'You're coming with us?' Traegl said, echoing the surprise on everyone's faces.

'I won't be trapped again,' he said. Then, with a wry look at Nesh, 'I've tried freedom and found I rather like it. If this trap can be broken, then I'll stay and make sure this place remains as free as its name. But if it can only be escaped, then I'll escape - and I'll take as many People with me as I can.'

◆

Persuading the other Earthers of the need to act was harder than Kerrig had thought it would be. He hoped that Volnar and Traegl were having better luck, because he felt as though he was getting nowhere.

First, Balmar had wanted to know why he was back so early, and what he'd done with the donkey. Then he wanted to know how Kerrig was going to fix the drainage in the lower field without the rocks that he hadn't brought back, and incidentally, why hadn't he brought any back? And where was the donkey?

Kerrig tried to explain again about the trap, and how important it was to find some way around it, but the farmer hadn't finished making his point about the drainage.

'It's all very well coming in shouting about fancy traps and what have you, but without that drainage, I can't start on the winter wheat. And where will that leave us, hmm? All that grain that your donkey's going to munch on over the winter. The field won't drain itself, you know.'

'Maddie won't be here over the winter if we find a way off this island. Go ahead and plant your winter wheat. Even without extra drainage, you'll have the same harvest as every year.'

'The same harvest as every year is no good if we've got extra mouths to feed, is it? We barely have enough as it is. You and your Outsider friends can't live here and not expect to have to pull your weight.'

Kerrig gave up. 'You're right,' he said. 'So wouldn't it be better for everyone if my "Outsider friends" and I were able to leave? All I want to know is if you have ever tried to leave Camp Freedom yourself, or know anyone who has.'

'Leave? Why would anyone of the People want to leave Camp Freedom? It's perfect.'

◆

It was more than two weeks before Kerrig was able to meet up with the others again. Ash had brought Maddie home that first evening, but not stayed to see Kerrig. According to Maddie's rather confused account, he had simply flown overhead, watching her as she walked home. The little Sidrax was happily sleepy for the next couple of days, and told Kerrig that she really wanted to show him what she was learning, but Ash said not to, yet.

The reports, when they came, were not encouraging. No-one wanted to leave, or even talk about leaving, because Camp Freedom was perfect. Kerrig himself felt reluctant, and hoped that the trap could be broken after all. This place was so... *right*.

But at the next meeting of the raft committee, there was a distinct shortage of good news.

'No luck, I'm afraid,' reported Traegl. 'No-one knows anyone who's ever been down to the river - and I've been talking to Marshlanders! You'd think if anyone would want to get down to a massive body of water, it would be one of us.'

'Have you tried going to the river yourself?' asked Nesh.

'Yes, I tried,' Traegl replied. 'The day after you told me about the problem. Same thing - a sudden, overwhelming urge to go back to the farm. I was absolutely convinced that a rat was going to get into the duck house, and I had to make sure all the nests were secure. It was so weird. I don't even like the stupid ducks.'

Maddie giggled at this. Volnar laughed loudly, then looked embarrassed.

'What about before that?' said Nesh. 'Did you try going down the river at any time? Like you said, what could be more natural for a Marshlander than to go to the water?'

'No, it never occurred to me,' said Traegl. 'I think everyone's afraid of the river, even me, but I don't know why.'

'Afraid?' said Kerrig. 'What makes you say that? I didn't get any sense of fear from the Earthers, just indifference.'

'Same here,' said Volnar. 'Most of the Fire Breathers agree that all that water is cold and gross, but it's not scary.'

'Maybe it's just Drishmel's family,' said Traegl. 'A couple of weeks ago, their little boy ran off after his pet rabbit, and made it past the storm wall before his mother caught up with him. Madam Leuran grabbed him with a water line, but she was shaking like a leaf.'

'The storm wall?' said Kerrig. 'I was working on that recently. Couldn't bring myself to go past it, though. And you say the boy just ran out there - without hesitating? So someone *has* been down to the river!'

'No, he didn't get as far as the river. Like I said, Leuran grabbed him before he got there. But yeah, he passed the storm wall without blinking.'

'How old is the child?' Kerrig asked.

'A bit younger than Volnar, I think,' said Traegl. 'But older than Maddie.'

'So it's not about age,' Kerrig said. 'Is there anything different about the boy? Anything that might explain how he can pass through the barrier?'

Traegl thought for a moment, then shook her head. 'He's just a normal child, as far as I know.'

'What happened to the rabbit?'

Everyone looked at Ash with various expressions of incredulity.

'I'm serious,' he said. 'Where did the rabbit go? Did it get down to the water's edge, or did it turn back?'

'Oh, you think there might be something about the rabbit that let it through? And maybe the boy too, because he'd been playing with the rabbit that day?' said Traegl.

'I don't know,' said Ash. 'I know that I can't get through just by being a different shape, so it's not that. But a rabbit - a natural born one, not a Sidrax in the shape of a rabbit, doesn't behave like a person. Maybe it doesn't feel things in the same way. Whatever it is that makes us feel anxious or afraid, the rabbit isn't affected.'

'Perhaps it doesn't understand,' said Maddie. 'It hasn't got the words.'

Now it was Maddie's turn to have everyone stare at her.

'Drishmel's boy,' said Kerrig, slowly. 'Does he have any sort of trouble with his ears?'

'Well, I don't *think* so,' said Traegl, slowly. 'But you do have to get him to pay attention before he understands you. He says it's just noises unless he is looking at you when you talk.'

The others looked at each other and frowned. *Could it be that simple?* thought Kerrig.

'So,' he said, 'We need to block our ears? That's all?'

'Not quite,' Ash said. 'The winds blow strongly, and they get stronger when you try to push on through. There must be someone watching, to make the air respond like that. Probably the same people sending the whispers.'

Traegl frowned. 'I didn't hear any whispers,' she said. 'I just got this awful sick feeling, like everything was about to end.'

Nesh smiled, a little sadly. 'You don't have to hear something clearly to understand it. The quieter the whisper, the more likely you are to think it's your own thoughts speaking to you.'

The Marshlander shuddered. 'That's creepy,' she said. 'Who would do something like that?'

Kerrig felt his face twist into an ugly sneer, and he gave a bitter laugh.

'Air Walkers,' he said. 'Who else? Looks like I was right about the Flying Filth all along.'

Nesh looked disapproving. 'Kerrig, you don't know that for sure. Maybe there's an Avlem somewhere with a Talent for Air Control. Or someone using long-distance Voice Projection.'

'It's Air Walkers,' Kerrig insisted, against his own rising doubts. 'The last thing our Airhead guide did before she left was to send me a message on the wind, "Tell them Falerian sent you". It sounded like she was standing right next to me, instead of being twenty strides away over rushing water. She must have known about the barrier and held it back for us as we went in. She even told us about it.'

Kerrig threw up his hands in despair, although whether at Falerian's lies or his own naïveté even he didn't know. His fingers brushed through a layer of water, and he saw that the Marshlander had created a thin dome of water that went from the floor to a point well over their heads.

'If they can talk to us, they can listen,' said Traegl. 'This should interfere with that a bit.'

Kerrig became aware of the stopping of a thought, not his own after all, that had been making him wonder if he was being unfair to Air Walkers. He saw his own shock reflected on the faces of the others.

'Falerian's always been a jerk,' Traegl said at last. 'I should have known that this island was another of her stupid jokes.'

'It's a bit worse than a joke, Trae,' said Ash. 'And Falerian does tell the truth sometimes.'

'So long as there's something in it for her,' agreed Traegl, grudgingly. 'She's not even a reliable liar. Completely untrustworthy, that one.'

'She's an Air Walker, what did you expect?' said Kerrig. 'Let's get our exit organised. We've got a lot of people to talk to.'

◆

They quickly realised that 'talking' was not going to be easy, even if people had been willing to listen. Traegl had played off her water-dome as a joke on her friends, but water-domes popping up all over the camp would be sure to arouse suspicion. Not to mention the creeping doubts that would come in once they were unprotected.

Kerrig went home alone again that night. His ears were blocked with perfectly shaped pieces of stone so that all he could hear was his own heartbeat and breathing. Even his footsteps sounded muffled, and Kerrig focused on his Earth sense for some measure of normality.

As well as making earplugs for everyone, Kerrig had picked out some pieces of slate to act as writing materials. These would be their voices and ears from now on, apart from Maddie, who couldn't

read or write. She was going to stay with Ash until
they left.

•◆•

With his newly-fitted earplugs in place, Kerrig
took the scenic route home along the northern
shore, a part of the island he'd not yet explored.

Before he got to Balmar's farm, he saw a
large barn right by the water's edge. Curious, Kerrig
opened the door and saw stacks of grain, bags of
wool, crates of eggs, and sacks of vegetables. Enough
to feed the whole island twice over.

•◆•

Kerrig entered his host's house with a
cheerful "good evening", but his face didn't match his
voice. He held up his slate, which read: *I have to tell
you something important.*

Balmar started to read this out loud, but
Kerrig shushed him with a gesture. On the back of
the slate, he wrote: *AIR WALKERS ARE LISTENING!*

This got the farmer's attention, and he
appeared to whisper his reply. Kerrig pointed to his
own blocked ears, and handed his host a slate pencil.
Balmar took the pencil and the slate and wrote: *I
thought you liked Air Walkers? Why are your ears
blocked?* Then, as Kerrig reached for the slate to
reply, added: *Have you fixed the drainage yet?*

Kerrig ignored this last question, and wrote
out instead a summary of the situation. It took both
sides of the slate, and Balmar took his time reading
it. Kerrig watched his face, but the farmer didn't
seem to be reading aloud.

When he finished reading, Balmar started to
talk, then stopped himself, wiped the slate clear, and
wrote *Are you sure?*

Test it yourself, Kerrig replied. Is there a
place on the island you never go to?

138

Balmar admitted that he'd never been further north than his own fields, even though the woods there seemed pleasant enough. Kerrig suggested they walk that way together.

So, ears still blocked and slate in hand, Kerrig led his host north into the woods. As soon as they passed the first tree Balmar began to slow down. Then he stopped, took Kerrig's arm and tried to return to the farm. He was talking fast, and appeared increasingly upset with every minute.

Kerrig reached out and put his hands over Balmar's ears. The other man struggled for a moment, then relaxed. His eyes were wide, and Kerrig nodded. He took his hands away and at once the farmer blocked his own ears.

Kerrig led his host to the barn and opened the door. There was a moment when Balmar didn't seem to understand what he was seeing, then he sank to the floor, his jaw slack and his arms limp. Kerrig expected him to bolt now that he could hear again but nothing happened. Curious, Kerrig removed one of his own earplugs and felt no compulsion to leave.

'How? How did they do this?' Balmar was saying over and over in whispered horror. 'Some of those sacks are mine. I remember making them. Why did I never wonder where they'd gone? Have the Airheads been controlling our minds?'

Kerrig laid a comforting hand on the farmer's shoulder. 'They can't read minds,' he said. 'But they do listen to words, and they can whisper suggestions so quietly that we mistake them for our own thoughts. If the thefts are small enough, they could be making you believe you'd miscounted, or even put the losses down to rats or foxes.'

'But if they are always whispering in our heads,' asked Balmar, 'then why can't I hear anything now?'

Kerrig smiled a grim, triumphant smile. 'Because they're not perfect. They can't be listening to all of us all of the time. This barn has "go away" in the air all around it. The biggest risk now is that we run into someone coming to collect this bounty.'

'I hope we do meet the sludge-sucking Airheads coming to take all this,' said Balmar. 'The flighty, sneaking thieves!'

Kerrig hushed him, and quickly replaced his earplugs.

If we want to leave this place, we can't let them know we know, he scrawled on the slate.

Balmar started to answer, but Kerrig pointed to his ears and made a shushing gesture. Balmar snatched the slate and wrote: *I want them to pay!*

Kerrig smiled again as he wrote: They will. Who will the Outsiders blame when all their prisoners escape right under their noses?

The farmer smiled.

◆

Kerrig and his host quickly spread the word about the Air Walkers and the stolen harvest. For once Kerrig was glad of Balmar's proud and stubborn reputation, as it meant that few of his neighbours needed more than his word. There were some outspoken ones, but either quarrels between farmers were common enough for the Air Walkers to ignore or else there really weren't enough of them to monitor the whole island.

After a few days of this, Kerrig went to the old barracks for a hasty evening meeting under another of Traegl's water domes.

'I've been using these a lot lately, especially after dark. I guess the guards don't listen so hard when everyone's supposed to be asleep.'

'That's assuming there's more than one or two on at night,' Ash added. 'You know how thin the army's been stretched lately, Trae. There won't be more than a single squad assigned to this whole operation, and one of them will be a Sidrax officer. Even with a dozen Air Walkers working shifts they won't be listening to everything. You've done boring guard duty, Trae. You know what it's like.'

Traegl grinned. 'Look alert when the captain comes by, and count the seconds until your relief arrives? Sure. So long as this is just another boring day, no-one's going to be paying that much attention.'

Kerrig relaxed a little at this news, and urged Traegl and Volnar on in their efforts to persuade the Marshlanders and Fire Breathers to escape with them.

Traegl was willing enough, though her neighbours seemed unwilling to listen to a 'traitor'. Volnar, though, saw little point in continuing to talk to the Fire Breathers.

'They know about the Air Walkers, and they know I'm leaving - if they want to come along, fine. And if they want to stay here, then let 'em. What do I care?'

Kerrig took a moment to think about his answer. The boy had been living in the Outsiders' stronghold, of course he didn't understand the ties that bound you to others of your Element. After a couple of deep breaths, Kerrig said,

'If they really understand the situation, and really want to stay, then no-one will stop them. But we can't just leave people behind - we have to give them the chance to make a decision.'

To the Kerrig's relief, something of this did seem to get through to Volnar. The Fire Breather boy still grumbled about it, but agreed that he ought to have another go at warning the Fire Breathers.

Once Volnar had left, and after making sure that Maddie was out of earshot, Kerrig asked,

'What will the army do when they discover that we've worked out how to beat their trap? When I went back to the Mines they had a full scramble going on, with extra soldiers and crossbows for the guards. Life inside probably got a lot worse for the other prisoners there, not to mention the Earthers.'

Nesh looked almost guilty but then seemed to shake it off. It was Traegl who answered, assuring Kerrig that even if they could spare the manpower the army couldn't respond without admitting that 'Camp Freedom' was really a prison.

'Will they care about that sort of thing?' Kerrig asked. Nesh gave a bitter laugh.

'About the only thing the Citadel cares about more than money is its shiny reputation,' she said. 'You can trust me on that.'

Traegl made interested noises, and even Kerrig considered that there might be a story there, but Nesh refused to be drawn further. Eventually, Traegl gave up and returned to discussing the escape.

'The only real risk is from the Air Walkers somehow catching on to what we're doing and actively working against us, but if they haven't noticed yet, I think we're safe.'

'There's still a risk,' Kerrig said. 'And it doesn't take into account what even a single squad of angry Air Walkers could do to the People who stay behind. Or to those who are leaving, if they catch us at it.'

'Us?' said Nesh. 'You're definitely coming along, then?'

Kerrig nodded. 'We can't break this trap without finding and confronting the Air Walkers and that's a job for trained fighters, not ordinary People. We're better off trying to slip away quietly, and hope we can get some distance away before anyone notices that we've gone.'

He sighed. 'The best thing would be for everyone to come along, but even with Balmar's backing there are Earthers who won't willingly leave. Some of the Marshlanders too, I should think. That's something that they have in common with us Earthers; we get attached to places. Leaving is always a last resort.'

'You don't say,' Nesh replied, dryly. 'Well short of kidnapping all of them, we'll have to just go with as many as are willing to come. There's a double new moon coming up; we'll leave then and do everything as quietly as possible.'

And they did. In the end less than half the Earthers and Marshlanders decided to leave, while only a handful of Fire Breathers chose to stay. They waited for the darkest part of the night, and gathered near the north-eastern corner of the camp. Everyone was given written or whispered instructions, then had their ears filled up with soft clay. Once they were ready, all lights were extinguished.

The raft had been dismantled, and the logs were now carried down to the water's edge by the departing campers. The first Earther and Marshlander stepped forwards and pushed at the river. The Marshlander blocked the flow from upstream, forcing the water to pile up against his hands; the Earther firmed up the uneven riverbed. Both were operating using their sense for their Element, Kerrig could tell. He was waiting in line as the fifth Earther, paired with the Drishmels. Their son was supposed to be with the other children but Kerrig could feel that he'd tagged along with his parents. Little, impatient feet. Kerrig tried to memorise their impression on the ground, so as to know them again in the noise of many.

The logs had been laid by the Earthers, lengthwise along the safe path. Nesh and the Fire Breathers - those not able to sense the Earth or Water - had practised walking with one foot touching the side of a log at all times. Everyone walked in a chain: with one hand on the shoulder of the person in front. From his station nearest the island, Kerrig paid attention to the footsteps of those passing him. Most of the Fire Breathers had brought their goats along, tethered and muzzled for the trip, the larger ones pulling carts. Sharp little hooves dug into the ground, seemingly untroubled by the darkness or the rough going. It seemed to take forever to get everyone across. It was dark and cold, and so nerve-wracking that Kerrig thought his earplugs must have slipped, letting the Air Walkers' whispers get into his head and cause his stomach to twist and thrash like a dying fish.

At last the crowd thinned, and Kerrig felt a spray of water behind him. Someone tapped him on the shoulder and urged him to take his turn walking the log-path. The last of the Earthers crossed the river, with the final Marshlanders bringing up the rear. They walked on towards the place 500 strides downstream that had been agreed as a rendezvous. Now only the Earthers could feel the path, although the Marshlanders could at least stay out of the river. The others stayed close, feeling their way forward through the moonless night.

Maddie's donkey shape was sure-footed, even while pulling a supply cart; and Ash was in his mongoose form, riding on her back. The young man had offered to guide people in his wolf form, but Kerrig suggested that having a wolf at their side in the night was not most people's idea of reassuring. Nesh was walking with great confidence, which didn't surprise Kerrig. Not only did the Avlem woman do everything with great confidence, she had also lived for many years in the Mines where total blackout was just a burnt-out torch away.

They reached the crowd of milling feet, and Kerrig tentatively loosened one of his earplugs. He heard nothing and felt no different. They'd made it.

He sank to the ground in relief and felt others doing the same. Kerrig let himself drift off to sleep with a victory chant ringing in his brain.

We did it! We're free! sang his heart. He was almost asleep before his mind snapped back with, *That's nice. Now what?*

We're past the worst danger, thought Kerrig, but where are we going to go now? Back across the river, into the Air Walkers' mountains? Of course not. North, to wander around on the Fire Plains for the rest of our lives? The Fire Breathers might go that way - and Nesh too, maybe - but Marshlanders won't agree. They'll want to go west, back toward the Marshes, which just isn't feasible. For one thing the Air Walkers guarding the island are almost certainly to our west, and for another there are at least two Avlem towns lining the edge of the Marshlands. Getting past those without being seen would be almost impossible.

Not as impossible as going East, of course. That way lay the Citadel, and the hub of the Sidrax-Avlem government.

Kerrig drifted into a troubled sleep and searched the Land in his dreams all night long.

Chapter Fourteen

The next morning was chaotic. Kerrig half-expected the noise to carry all the way back to the Airhead guards. The grazing goats were milked and breakfast prepared, which seemed to take all day. At last the fires were doused and people started to drift eastward along the river road, mostly to get some space for their own conversations. By the time the carts were loaded there was a long procession ambling along beside the river.

Everyone seemed completely relaxed, apart from Traegl, Ash, and Nesh. Even Volnar looked happy to be moving in the right direction at last.

Kerrig moved towards the young Fire Breather, and saw Traegl moving in from the other direction. They joined up with Volnar and walked together in peaceful silence. After a while, Volnar commented that this was about as perfect as he could imagine: No work and no worries, just strolling in the sunshine.

'Strolling in the sun is all well and good,' Traegl observed, 'But there's the little matter of our being homeless. Where are we strolling *to*?'

'I'm going to the City- the Citadel,' said Volnar. 'Don't know why you lot are all coming along though. I thought I'us the only one as wanted to go there.'

Kerrig shuddered. 'You certainly are. I think we'd all be safer heading north across the Plains.'

'You go where you like,' Volnar told them. 'I'm going to the Citadel, and this road's my best way.'

'The Citadel isn't safe for any of us,' Kerrig said. 'We need to decide on a place to settle, not just amble along like this unprotected and unprepared for trouble.'

'What is it with you and trouble?' said Balmar, who had wandered up from behind. 'You always seem determined to expect the worst. All that fear-mongering back at the camp - why, I'll bet it wasn't nearly so bad as you claimed.'

'But you *saw* the...' Kerrig started, but the floodgates had been breached and a dozen tired, footsore farmers congregated to vent their frustrations at Kerrig and his friends.

'Going around stirring up discontent - ought to be ashamed of yourselves!'

'We were all perfectly happy until you lot came along.'

'And dragging children into the business - that's just despicable. Why, my kiddies liked living in Camp Freedom just fine.'

'And little Volnar, too. He could've had a happy, normal life with us if you hadn't decided to use him to convert the Fire Breathers to your crazy schemes!'

'Hey,' said Volnar, 'No-one uses me for anything! And I never wanted to stay on your rotten island.'

The young Fire Breather stormed off until he had caught up with another group further along the road. Kerrig considered the adults around him and wondered if he could get them to change their minds (again) about the wisdom of leaving their prison-camp. Probably, but he realised that he actually didn't care. They could bicker and blame to their hearts' content, because he, Kerrig, needed to make sure that Volnar didn't get too far ahead. They really needed to start going north soon, even if only Nesh, Maddie, Ash, Traegl and Volnar came with him. Getting too close to the Citadel and the Outsiders' civilisation was not an option.

By late afternoon the farmers' complaints had died down to some low-grade mumbling, and the discussion had turned to where they should spend the night. When the road opened out onto a grassy meadow the question seemed settled. One by one the families and individuals claimed their spots and made themselves comfortable. Several small cooking fires sprang up, and a couple of Marshlanders set to fishing.

For the first time since he learned the truth about Camp Freedom, Kerrig truly relaxed. He sat beside a fire, eating hot fish fresh from the river, and surrounded by free People. As he watched the western sky fading from orange to black, Kerrig took a moment to enjoy the peace.

It didn't last. Kerrig was approached by Ash and Nesh. They were apparently as concerned as he was about getting too far east, because they had decided to head north within the next day and wanted to know if Kerrig would join them.

'Maddie shouldn't stop her training now, but she won't want to leave you,' Ash said. 'And Trae's still undecided.'

'I know it's too dangerous to keep to the road,' Traegl explained, 'But part of me just doesn't want to leave the river.'

Kerrig was about to answer when one of the Fire Breathers interrupted.

'Who's Maddie?' he asked Kerrig, without looking at the two Outsiders. 'And why are you even talking about going anywhere with them?'

A life in the mines had taught Kerrig that there was no such thing as a private conversation, but even so this farmer's rudeness was enough to give him pause. And so it was Ash who got in first:

'Maddie is the little donkey who's been hauling your baggage around since we escaped that trap of an island. Good little worker, isn't she? And she's a nice kid, too. And we had to tell her to hide herself; to not let anyone know she's Sidrax like me because jerks like you would bully her for it.' Ash was breathing hard, and looked angry. Kerrig was taken aback; he couldn't remember ever seeing the younger man truly angry before.

The Fire Breather didn't seem impressed.

'You can do what you like,' he said. 'We don't need Outsiders and traitors getting in our way.'

'You lazy idiots need looking after,' Ash shot back. 'This isn't your cosy little farm, goat-herd. Do you even know anything about wilderness survival?'

'We know everything we need to know, Shifter. This is the Land, and we're the People of the Land. What's more, these are the Fire Plains and I'm a Fire Breather. This is my ancestral home, I don't need any Outsider telling me how to live here.'

'You stubborn idiot...!' Ash began, but the Fire Breather simply smirked and walked away.

◆

The last of the sunlight disappeared, and the small fires began to dim as people settled down to sleep. Kerrig dozed, until he was woken by someone shaking his shoulder.

'Kerrig, wake up.' It was Nesh. The Earther forced his eyes open, and could just make her out in the dim glow of the banked fire.

'What is it?' he said, trying to keep the irritation from his voice. The Avlem woman could be annoying, but she didn't seem the type to disturb him without good reason.

'You're needed on watch,' she said. 'None of the farmers will take a turn, so it's up to us. I've got the next group over; can you watch this lot?'

'Yes, of course,' Kerrig said, still half-asleep. 'We should have had a watch set last night, as well. I suppose we fell into bad habits after being off the road for so long.'

'We did have a watch last night,' Nesh told him. 'Ash and Trae took half the night each. But they can't watch everyone while the group's spread out like this.'

Before Kerrig could select a suitable response to that revelation, Nesh had walked back to her own fire. The Earther sat blinking in the darkness, and gave his full attention to his Earther senses.

The little feet at the edge of his range didn't register at first. Animals of the night were going about their own business, and he supposed that was perfectly normal. It was only when the small, sharp hooves of the goats began to grow restless that Kerrig realised something was wrong. Then he heard the growling.

Carefully, Kerrig picked a branch up from the pile beside the fire and poked at the banked embers with it until the end caught light. Holding his torch high, Kerrig searched for the source of the sound. A glittering row of amber eyes glowed in the reflected light, barely ten strides away. Kerrig froze.

The mines held many dangers but Kerrig had never faced down any wild animal bigger than a snake, and even those were rare. The noise and the torches were usually enough to keep them away. Experimentally, Kerrig waved the lit branch at the growling eyes. They didn't come any closer, but neither did they back off.

Quickly and quietly the Earther roused the sleepers nearest him.

'Move back towards the river,' he told them. 'Don't argue, just move.'

Kerrig felt Nesh's approach, her confident steps in sharp contrast to the stumbling shuffle of the sleepy farmers.

'What is it?' she asked.

'Some kind of wild animals,' Kerrig told her. 'We need to move people without causing a panic. Wake your lot, then find Ash and Traegl. I don't want to leave this fire - I think it's keeping them away.'

'They must be after the goats,' she said. 'Build up the fire, I'll start moving people.'

Kerrig poked at the embers with what was left of his branch. The fire glowed brighter, but not by much. The Earther cursed under his breath - this was a job for a Fire Breather, but Volnar was in one of the other groups, and the farmers would probably just argue again.

So it was a relief to see one of the other fires flare up, not too far away. Then another, and another. At last, Volnar came into view, and Kerrig's own fire roared.

'Ash says make a trench between us and the creatures.' The boy sounded tired, but not scared. 'Traegl and the others is going to flood it. Then come and join everyone else on the river bank.'

Kerrig didn't waste time. He pushed his power into the ground and opened up a semi-circular ditch that touched the water at both ends. It wasn't perfect, and he saw one of the fires topple and go out as he disturbed the ground beneath it. But he could feel that all the feet of the creatures stood on one side of the ditch, and all the goats and people stood on the other side. There was a sudden feeling of cold and damp as water from the river was directed into the trench, and Kerrig felt the animals on the far side back away.

There was still plenty of growling, but none of the creatures approached. There was one nasty moment when the Earther registered some of the growling as coming from the wrong side of the water, in the gap left by the toppled fire, But when he grabbed another burning branch and waved it towards the source of the sound, he recognised the familiar solid black colour of Ash's form and relaxed. The Sidrax and the wild animals exchanged threats for a while, until the creatures finally slunk away.

Kerrig made a point of waiting for Ash, and walking with him to the huddle of farmers and children gathered beside the river.

'That was brave, standing up to the creatures like that,' he said, slightly louder than strictly necessary. 'You could have been hurt protecting us.'

The Sidrax grinned, his sharp teeth catching the firelight. 'Nah, I recognised the type,' he said. 'All bark and no bite. Most animal fights are about who can put on the biggest show, you know. And you had my back.'

◆

Kerrig had hardly settled down to his watch again when Traegl came to find him. She looked exhausted but determined.

'Kerrig, you have to take control of this rabble before someone really gets hurt.'

'Why me?' he asked. 'I'm heading north, and I thought the rest of them were staying on the road.'

'I expect this near-miss will have scared some sense into the worst of the troublemakers,' Traegl said dryly. 'If you step up now, I think the group will stay together.'

'Surely Nesh would be better at it - she's very organised, and she cares about people.'

'She's also Avlem,' said Traegl. 'It shouldn't matter, but it does. You're an Earther, and a traditionalist (well, mostly). People listen to you, when you give orders instead of suggestions.'

Kerrig shrugged. 'I'm not good with people,' he said.

The young Marshlander laughed. 'Neither were most of the officers I've known. But you are good at getting things done. You took charge to get us out of Camp Freedom, you just need to carry on being in charge.'

'That was different,' said Kerrig, defensively. 'I was directing an emergency. That's what I do - all my life I've kept people safe from dangers in the mines. Breaking out of that Airhead-fuelled trap was no different from clearing people away from a dangerous fault.'

'This emergency isn't over,' said Traegl, bluntly. 'If you don't get this lot sorted out they're going to self-destruct. Sort it out with yourself however you like, but the fact is that some of these farmers aren't fit to lead a goat to water, much less a group of people to safety. Nesh and Ash are Outsiders, and I'm not trusted because of my time in their army. Volnar and Maddie are too young - that leaves you.'

Traegl yawned and stood up. 'I'm going to get some sleep,' she said. 'Think about it - and have orders ready for us in the morning. Don't let them discuss it, just tell us where we're going.' She yawned again, and stumbled off towards the fire with a mumbled, 'G'night.'

''Night,' Kerrig echoed, absently. He sank his feet into the Earth and listened to his Earther senses. He felt Traegl arrive at her bedroll and fall into it. There were too many individuals around the fire for Kerrig to identify, but at least he would be aware of it if any of them moved around in the night. Further out there was only the movement of nocturnal animals.

I'll have to work with Maddie and Ash, he thought, *to distinguish natural animal movement from Sidrax imitation*. But the worms, moles, foxes and badgers were all moving normally, as far as he could tell. None showed any inclination to move towards the camp, so Kerrig let his mind wander while his Earther senses kept watch.

Could he take charge of all these Marshlanders, Earthers, and Fire Breathers? Would they listen to him? Where could he take them? Where could such a mixed crew settle and be welcome?

Nowhere, supplied his mind. *But who says you need to settle? The Shanzir never did.* Kerrig blinked in the darkness as the idea took hold. A new tribe, in the model of the Shanzir? Was it possible? He glanced to the north-west, to where Zirpa lay buried many days' journey away. 'Well, old lady,' he said, quietly. 'It looks as though you'll live on in a few more memories than either of us expected.'

◆

Taking charge was neither pleasant nor easy, but Kerrig found that it did help to think of it as a mining emergency. He had never raised his voice underground, and rarely had to resort to physical force. His ability with stone was enough of a threat to cow the belligerent, and his firm authority was enough to make most people obey him before they had time to process that he'd given them orders. It still took nearly two hours to get everyone moving in the morning, but on the first day it had been noon before the carts were packed up. It was an improvement, and that was all anyone could hope for.

Kerrig didn't bring up the 'new Shanzir' idea directly. First he sent Ash ahead to scout out their route from the air. He also trained some of the younger adults of the Earthers in using their Earther senses to get the lie of the land. They already knew how to feel the soil beneath their feet for rabbits and other burrowing types who might take their crops, but now Kerrig showed them how to feel the weight of a person, animal or building that lay above the ground. When Ash's reports said that they were approaching a small town, a couple of Kerrig's students were able to confirm the claim. That night, the gap between Ash, Nesh, and the former campers was slightly less pronounced. Maddie, although now revealed to all as Sidrax herself, refused to budge from Kerrig's side. There was some attempt on the part of the Campers' children to make friends, but the steady disapproval of their parents made most back off after a while.

They were heading almost due north now, to Volnar's annoyance. But the riverside road was getting larger, and they were more likely to meet soldiers coming the other way. Better to strike out across the plains, even if the terrain did shake up the carts. They spread out during the day, and camped in close formation by night. It was becoming a routine, and they were in no hurry. They needed time, after all, to get their goods ready to trade when they got to their first town.

The trade idea had been carefully introduced after a talk with Nesh and Ash. They started with the Fire Breathers, partly because they were the ones with the livestock, and partly because there were a couple of the older Fire Breather girls who would listen to anything that came from Ash. He was polite, but didn't seem to respond to any one of them in particular.

The goats were milked every morning and evening, and brushed every day. The long hair made good thread, and most of the ex-campers had brought their spindles along. The simple weighted rods were easy enough to pack - but the weaver had decided to stay behind when he was told that only his smallest loom would fit on the carts. The result was that they had lots of yarn, but no loom. Likewise, plenty of milk but no butter churn or cheese press. So it was easy enough to introduce the idea of going into a few towns and trading for things. And if anyone wanted to stay on in a town, having some goods to trade would be a start.

◆◆◆

Kerrig took Volnar aside one day, and asked him if that's what he wanted to do.

'I know you're used to the Citadel,' he said. 'If you wanted to find a place to live in a town, then I'll help you. Not to live alone,' he said, quickly, 'But if you can find a good apprenticeship, then I'll find a way to make it work.'

The Fire Breather boy looked confused. 'Are you throwing me out of the caravan?' he said. 'I pull my weight!'

'Of course not! But you seem so unhappy about being on the road, I thought that maybe you'd rather live in a town,' Kerrig said. 'If it's not that, then tell me - what do you want to do?'

'I want,' said Volnar, with the patient air of one who has said this too many times, 'To go back to the Citadel.'

'But that's impossible,' Kerrig told him, just as patiently. 'So why not settle in a town instead? It can't be that different, surely?'

'Because I need to know they're alright!' the boy snapped. 'Sangomel, and Lim, and the others. Olra was getting too big even when I was there, and that was last winter! I'm the next Oldest, and after me there's only Rasser, and she's too young. And I'm their best protector, only I got picked up shielding a couple of the new kids, and now I'm not there for them. And you lot keep dragging me around the Land and getting me stuck in places and now you want to stick me in a town for the rest of my life!'

Volnar was breathing hard when he finished, and glared at Kerrig as though trying to set the man's hair on fire with his eyes. Kerrig had a sudden urge to back away - who knew what an angry Fire Breather might do? But he forced himself to stay calm, and instead made a seat for the boy from the ground.

'Volnar, I'm sorry,' he said, and tried not to sound as frustrated as he felt. He was annoyed with the child for expecting him to be a mind-reader, but more annoyed with himself for not making time for this conversation earlier.

'Why didn't you say anything about this before?' he said, carefully. 'I thought you were just missing life in the Citadel. I didn't realise you had people waiting for you there.'

The boy from the Citadel streets mumbled something that Kerrig didn't catch. Eventually, after some coaxing and repetition, Kerrig discovered that Volnar had expected them to refuse to let him go back once they knew about his gang.

'Adults say it's wrong for us all to live together, and we have to get split up and sent to shelters and workshops and stuff,' said the Fire Breather, with an air of wary experience. 'And we have to hide the babies when the charity ladies come around, because they always want to take them. And, OK, one time we let them have this one baby, because we found it when the mother was dead, and it was too little to live without better food than we had, but that was one time. Normally, we don't get kids until they can at least crawl. And usually they're walking before they really get thrown out.'

Kerrig sank his fingers into the soil and forced himself to breathe. He was no stranger to a hard childhood, but he'd never imagined anything like this.

'How many?' he managed at last, when he could trust himself not to shout or weep. 'How many children did you look after?'

'It varies,' Volnar said. 'When we get big enough, we go out and get proper work. But it's got to be a real job, not just being put in a workshop because you're a kid and the adults don't know what to do with you. Quite a lot become soldiers, and that's a good life. And some of the soldiers in town let us get away, because they grew up cleaning the markets too.' He suddenly frowned. 'Not all of 'em, though. Some of 'em are really mean, like they want to forget they ever lived like us.

'There's usually about a dozen of us at once. Sometimes only six or seven, one time we had nearly twenty. But the charity ladies came through and took most of them off, so we're careful about numbers now. Too many, and we split up, some to the inner keep and some out into the fields.'

Kerrig felt as though each question was digging at an open wound, but he couldn't not ask. Volnar might never open up like this to him again, and the Earther found himself wanting - needing to know.

'You seem very organised,' he said, after searching for a suitable question in vain.

'For a bunch of kids? Yeah, we are. But it's the Oldest what keeps it organised, and that's supposed to be me soon. Maybe even now. If Olra gets a good job offer she'll have to take it, but she won't if I'm not there to take over as Oldest. And if she gets picked up like me, I don't know what'll happen to the others. I *need* to get home, Mr. Kerrig. I need to go now, and we're getting further away all the time.'

Kerrig nodded, and started thinking, furiously.

'Volnar, I can't let you go off on your own,' he said at last. 'Not because you're young, but because it's a long way, and the road is dangerous. Also, you're still an escaped prisoner. We've managed so far by being in a crowd, and keeping away from soldiers who might know to look for us, but you'd be a sitting target. No,' he said, before the boy could object, 'Your going back right now is not possible. But we might be able to find a way to make it safer.'

'Really?' Volnar looked cautiously pleased, as though expecting a trick.

'We're establishing ourselves as traders,' Kerrig said. 'And once we have built up a bit of a stock, it's only natural that we should take our trade to the Citadel. We'll go in, quite legally and openly, as the merchants we are. And you can find your friends under the trestles, where I trust you'll ask them not to clean up after us too thoroughly.'

'But that'll take months,' Volnar protested. 'And I wanted to be back there before winter. They need me.'

Kerrig sighed. 'I'll see what I can do,' he said. Then, because Volnar was looking mulish, 'I mean that. I won't let this go until we have a solution. Meanwhile, the more we have to sell in the next town, the faster we'll be ready for the Citadel.'

Volnar took the hint, and picked up the carding combs.

◆

The first trading day was approached with all the group-level stress of opening a new seam. Everything was in place, everyone knew their jobs, but there was still an outside chance that the whole thing would come crashing down and end with people fleeing for their lives. Kerrig had chosen to keep all the recognisable faces from the Mines safely outside the town, along with Ash and Traegl, since they were likely identified as deserters by now. He sent in the most level-headed of the ex-campers, along with Maddie in her donkey form.

'That child's got more common sense than most adults I know,' Kerrig told them, before they set out on their trading mission. 'If she's unhappy about something, trust her instincts. And if she wants to leave, then it's time to leave.'

To Maddie, privately, he added, 'I know you can be good when work is boring, so I know you won't push to come home early just because of that. But if there's something wrong, you know how to get back to me.'

Kerrig left them to get ready, and headed over to the other side of the camp, where Ash was wearing a track in the long grass with his pacing.

'I wish I could go along,' he said. 'Just to watch over Maddie. I don't like her going off with strangers.'

Kerrig nodded, glumly. It was a feeling he shared.

'Keep working on a town-safe form,' he advised the younger man. 'Even your mongoose isn't exactly a domesticated type.'

Balmar came over at that moment to tell Kerrig they were ready to go. He walked back with the other Earther to see the final checks for himself.

'How can you stand it?' Balmar asked Kerrig, once they'd gone a few paces away from Ash.

'Talking to a Shifter about his Shifting. It's not natural!'

'What, talking to a Sidrax?' said Kerrig, dangerously.

'Well... you have to admit,' said Balmar, seriously, 'All that turning into different animals - it just isn't *normal.*'

'You do know,' the Earther said, 'That the donkey you're loading up is Sidrax, don't you? I think you'd better stay with the camp after all. I wouldn't want you to be uncomfortable around Madrigal.'

Kerrig suddenly stopped, and beckoned someone over from the group around the fire.

'Can you help out in the town today?' he asked the young Marshlander who'd responded to his wave. 'Balmar's not feeling quite up to it.'

And Kerrig left the blustering Earther behind as he continued over to where Maddie was waiting.

Chapter Fifteen

True to his promise to Volnar, Kerrig talked to everyone in the caravan and the towns about the Citadel, and how to approach it. Unfortunately, everything he learned focused on how difficult it was to get permission to trade there. Even the campers without a criminal record still had no official history in any 'respectable' town, and regular merchants in the Citadel itself paid hefty taxes to be protected from itinerant competition.

The more he looked at it, the more he realised that he wasn't going to be able to get Volnar to his friends anytime soon. Not safely.

'Then I'll go unsafely,' Volnar said, when Kerrig told him the bad news. 'I have to go, one way or another.'

Volnar hadn't been idle during their trip, and Kerrig discovered that the boy had been working an angle of his own.

One of the Earthers to escape Camp Freedom with them was a potter called Mashpa. Back in the camp, she'd owned a brick kiln, a treadle-powered potter's wheel, and a small workshop. When they left the island, she'd packed up her basic tools and a small sack of fine clay, and left the rest behind. Her Fire Breather assistant, who had built the kiln for her, decided to stay on the island. Their disagreement on this point had been very vocal, and

Kerrig had feared the Air Walker guards would pick up on it. In the end, they had parted ways. Volnar was quick to offer his services as her new assistant and, although they didn't have a kiln, he was able to bake small things for her using his own carefully controlled fire.

He informed Kerrig of this with an air of great pride, and a little smugness.

'I keep tellin' you, I don't need adults fixing things for me. I can look after myself,' Volnar told him. 'So, thanks for trying - no, really - but now it's my turn.' And the boy did seem genuinely pleased that Kerrig had gone to such a lot of trouble. 'I know you didn't really want to go to the Citadel at all, but thanks for offering,' he said.

'I still don't like your going off on your own like that, just the two of you,' Kerrig said.

'I know.'

'I could forbid you to leave,' he said. After all, thought Kerrig, there have to be some advantages to being the leader, right?

Volnar just laughed. 'You could try,' he said. 'And now I'm off to see how much Mashpa and I can get in the way of supplies to take with us on our journey. I expect there will be haggling involved - good training for my new life working above the trestles, eh?'

Kerrig watched him go, and tried not to feel as though he'd failed the boy. He almost succeeded.

◆◆◆

It took the pair of them just over two days to reach the gates of the Citadel, where they gained entry without difficulty. Kerrig knew this because he sent Ash to fly after them, watching for trouble. When the Sidrax returned after three days and a night of hard flying, he reported to Kerrig that all was well, and then promptly curled up in his smallest form and slept on Maddie's back for a full day. All of which meant that he was wide awake to take his turn on watch that night.

It was not quite dawn when he woke Kerrig. The first thing the sleepy Earther noticed was that Ash looked as though he'd been asleep himself - his short hair was standing on end, and his eyes were wide as though he was holding them open on purpose.

'There's a storm coming,' said the Sidrax. 'We need to get under cover before it hits.'

Kerrig frowned. 'So, it's going to rain?' he said. 'That's not great, but we've been rained on before. Set the Marshlanders to keeping the supplies dry, and set up a couple of shelters for fires to keep everyone warm. No problem.'

Ash shook his head. 'You really have spent your whole life underground, haven't you?' he said. 'This isn't just a rain shower - it's a storm. Like... um... like a tunnel collapse in the sky, maybe? Everything gets shaken up - winds strong enough to pick up a grown man, and rain thick enough to drown in. It'll take every Marshlander we have to hold it back, and even then it might not be enough. We need to get underground, under stone. Soil will just wash away.'

Kerrig got to his feet and shed his blanket of earth. Now that he was out from the covers, he could feel something different in the air. It smelled like old fires, and crackled in his hair.

'Let's wake the others and get to work,' Kerrig said, but Ash stopped him.

'Don't let them know how bad it is yet,' he advised. 'People will panic, and then everything will take longer.'

Kerrig gave the younger man a Look.

'I know,' he said, flatly. 'I've been handling emergencies since before you were born, young man. I might not know about storms, but I do know about people. Let's wake Traegl and Nesh; they at least can be trusted to work without panicking.'

By the time the rest of the camp woke up, Kerrig and Traegl had created three large bunkers, carefully dried out inside, and roofed over with stones collected by Ash and Nesh.

When the first of the children woke up and showed interest, Nesh explained that it was going to be a rainy day, so they had made these big dens to keep everything dry. This was enough for the younger children, who could hardly wait to start fetching things to go in the dens. The older ones were less enthusiastic, but accepted their tasks without too much complaining.

It was the parents that gave Kerrig the most trouble. Many of them insisted on the children having breakfast before being allowed to play in the dens, and the delays caused by these arguments lasted until everyone could see the huge bank of thunderclouds looming in the sky. Once most of the adults had grasped the urgency things moved more quickly, but there were still a few who decided that berating Kerrig for his handling of the situation was more important than doing their part to prepare for it.

So when another pair of parents started shouting for their child to get inside, Kerrig paid no attention - at first. Adults calling to their children in tightly cheerful tones had become background noise by then. But when the shouts continued and the pretence of lightness fell, Kerrig did notice.

It was easy enough to find them, a Marshlander couple and their almost grown-up son, all calling for Shebbok, the youngest. Others started taking up the call as Kerrig approached.

'Where did you see him last?' Kerrig asked, and everyone had a different answer: in one or other of the dens, beside the cooking fire, with the overturned and tied-down carts (Kerrig noted in passing that it was gratifying to see the rope from the aborted raft being put to use after all). Reports put the boy everywhere and nowhere, and as the clouds rolled closer it was obvious that there would need to be a search party.

Nobody wanted to be left behind, but Nesh and Kerrig managed, through a combination of orders and persuasion, to limit the search to two groups of three. The rest of the adults were told to stay in the dens to watch over the children. Maddie was explicitly told not to go outside until the adults in their dens said it was safe, no matter how much she wanted to be with Ash and 'her Stony-Man'. The adults, in their turn, were warned that heads would roll if any child in their care got so much as damp.

The searchers spread out from the camp in opposite directions, each using their own abilities. Nesh had elected to join the search despite not having any Elemental sense. Kerrig was touched by her willingness to help, but doubted how much use she would be. In the end, he took Nesh along with him and Traegl. It seemed the fairest way to let her help without making other People uncomfortable.

Kerrig was therefore surprised to find that Nesh was leading the search, and taking them unerringly towards a faint pattern in his Earth sense that might have been a child's feet. Unfortunately, the rain pounding into the soil interfered with his ability to distinguish details - the falling rain obscured his Earth sense almost as much as it hampered his sight and hearing. Traegl was pushing at the rain, causing it to fall either side of them. Kerrig was grateful to her for keeping them dry, but she couldn't do anything about the biting wind. It was sapping at his strength, slowly and steadily, and the big man could only imagine the effect it was having on the lost child.

◆◆◆

When he felt feet approaching from the other direction, Kerrig thought that it was the other search party. Only when they got closer did he notice that one of the three was child-sized, and the two adults were strangers.

'You found him!' Nesh dashed out from Traegl's protection to embrace the child. 'Shebbok, are you well?'

The boy wriggled like a kitten, and Nesh dropped her arms.

'You're cold,' he told her, then added, 'I want my dad.'

Kerrig raised an eyebrow at the child's rudeness, but considering everything he decided it was a matter for the parents. And getting back to the dens really was the best idea at this point.

'Thank you for finding him,' the Earther said. 'We have shelters nearby, if you'd like to wait out the storm with us.'

'Let's get back,' said Traegl. 'I never thought I'd say this, but I can't wait to get back to a decent fire.' Traegl was using one hand to push the rain away from Kerrig, the boy having latched onto the other one. The two Marshlanders were seemingly torn between enjoying their Element and wanting to get warm.

Then the newcomers got nearer and the wind... stopped. It was still howling, and whipping the long grass, but around the six of them the air was as still as if a door had been closed on the storm.

Air. Air Walkers. More of them!

'Oh, that's better. Thank you,' said Traegl, and started to walk back the way they'd come as if she hadn't just been rescued by monsters.

'It's lucky for us that you were out here,' agreed Nesh, as they retraced their path. It didn't take long for them to get back. They dropped the child off with his parents, and then Traegl directed the strangers, the Air Walkers, to join them in another den. Kerrig followed, because he had just started to get warm, and refused to let the presence of these... people drive him away from a perfectly good fire.

Five minutes later he was regretting his decision. This den had no children in it, and so no reason for everyone not to talk as loud and as long as they pleased. And everyone was clamouring to know how the strangers had managed to find the lost child.

'There's a town not far off, and we've lived there for a while now,' the Air Walker woman replied, 'It's safe enough, but we always keep a listening watch during bad weather.'

'It's easy to get lost out here,' added the man. 'And people always expect the Fire Plains to be warmer than they are.'

The Earther watched the faces of his friends, waiting for the moment or realisation and revulsion. It didn't come.

'I'm surprised there are any Air Walkers in these parts,' he said, at last. 'Why aren't you up in those Peaks of yours? After you sold out the rest of the Land to the Outsiders in exchange for them, I would have thought you'd at least have the decency to stay there.'

There was silence for a long moment, then Nesh took hold of Kerrig's collar and pulled him away from the circle around the fire.

'If you'll excuse us for a moment,' she said to the others.

◆

The next minute, she had taken them both out into the rain. They stopped in the lee of a cart; but even there they needed to raise their voices to be heard.

'What was that about, Kerrig?' Nesh demanded. 'I thought you'd got over this "all Air Walkers are evil" nonsense!'

Kerrig yanked himself free of her grip and glared. 'Nonsense?' he roared, louder than necessary. 'It's a couple of Air Walkers! Do you not remember Falerian? That wretched "Camp Freedom"? They can't be trusted!'

'They helped us - Shebbok might have died without those Air Walkers! What is the matter with you that you can't be decent to people like that?'

'They. Are. Air Walkers,' Kerrig said again, as if explaining something to a particularly dim-witted child. 'Traitors, killers, and liars. I'm not saying they never do anything good, I'm saying we can't trust them to keep on doing good. The Flying Filth look after themselves first, and don't care what happens to anyone else.'

Nesh sighed and threw up her hands. 'I'm not asking you to be nice to a whole tribe, Kerrig; I'm asking you to keep a civil tongue in your head when talking to these particular Air Walkers - these *people* who have already proved their worth. I remember you vouched for Falerian readily enough, despite her ancestry. What's different about these two?'

'Absolutely nothing,' Kerrig replied, grimly. 'I'm sure they're exactly as trustworthy as Falerian turned out to be.'

Nesh scowled. 'Alright, bad example. But you were happy to accept one Air Walker as an individual; why can't you accept these individuals as well?'

'Because I've learned my lesson! There are no good Air Walkers, just ones who haven't been found out yet!'

Nesh slapped him, and the cold rain didn't quite take the sting out of his burning face.

'I suppose there are no good Avlem or Sidrax either,' she said.

'Oh, now you're just taking things personally,' Kerrig said, dismissively.

'And that all Marshlanders and Fire Breathers are the same, too,' Nesh continued, as if he hadn't spoken. 'So tell me, Kerrig, are you proof that all Earthers are self-pitying bigots?'

The rain pooling in his ears made Kerrig wonder for a moment if he'd misheard.

'How dare you?' he said at last, when he realised that he hadn't. 'Self-pitying - if you had any idea what the People have suffered, the lasting damage that the Outsiders have done to the Land...'

'Your people don't have a monopoly on suffering, Kerrig,' Nesh countered. 'I spent twenty-five years in prison for going up against those same "Outsiders".'

Kerrig bit down on the sarcastic responses that sprang to mind, ranging from the observation that he had been there twice as long, to a mock apology for the state of his ancestral home. He didn't particularly want to be slapped again so soon.

'I'm sure it was hard for you,' he said, as sincerely as he could manage, 'But the situations hardly compare. You can put that suffering behind you, now that you're free. You have a life, your children will be free - it's not like being of the People. You are Avlem, and you cannot begin to understand what it means to be us. The People lost everything when your lot arrived. *Everything*, Nesh. Don't pretend you can understand that.'

The wind had started to drop, but even so Kerrig had to strain to hear the Avlem's reply.

'I don't,' she said, almost gently. 'Even though I lost everything, my family didn't. The Avlem who chose to leave our homeland might have felt threatened by the Sidrax Empire, but they hadn't been conquered. This isn't about comparing experiences - no two races can do that. No two people for that matter. We're not competing to see who has suffered more; all I want is for you to acknowledge that suffering is not a purely Earther experience, nor even an Elemental one.'

She sighed, and continued, 'You're wrong about it all being behind me too. When I was sent to the Mines my family disowned me. I no longer have any name but "Nesh"; my family name and title are gone. If I were to have children, they would be nameless as well. Maybe things are different for Elementals, but among the Avlem your name is second only to your Talent in terms of identity. It hurt to have it taken away. It still hurts, sometimes.'

The rain still fell, but not as hard as before. Kerrig closed his eyes and tipped his face up to the sky until the heat faded from his face.

'I didn't know,' he said, after a long silence.

'You shouldn't have to know,' Nesh said, mildly. 'No-one makes it to our age without some grief, secret or otherwise. Kindness isn't earned, it's everyone's due. Now, can you be trusted to be decent to our guests, or do I have to leave you out here in the rain to finish cooling off?'

Kerrig did go back inside, and was stiffly polite to the Air Walkers while Traegl drew the water from his clothes and hair. The storm had passed, but the soft rain still fell until well after sunset, and so they made themselves comfortable in the shelter and dozed until daybreak.

In the morning, the Fire Breathers set up a large fire in the open between the three shelters, and everyone gathered around to make breakfast and hear the story of The Rescue. Shebbok's family repeatedly thanked the strangers, and no-one, it seemed, could talk of anything else. Kerrig bore it for as long as he could, then excused himself to see to the collapsing of the storm shelters. He found a few other Earthers there already, and commended them on their initiative.

'Good to know there are some here who don't expect me to do their thinking for them,' he said, as he joined a group who were carefully unmaking one of the storage bunkers. 'Well done, all of you.'

'Thanks,' said one of the women - Halg, he thought she was called. 'But I suspect we all just needed to get away from the others for a while. If you know what I mean.'

Kerrig raised an eyebrow, but didn't frown. 'You mean the Air-' he began, and she cut him off with a firm nod and noise of agreement.

'I can't say I care either way about Shifters or Avlem,' said another, 'But my mother said the Airheads weren't to be trusted.'

This earned a round of approving noises from the others, and started a collection of stories that lasted until they had cleared the outer rim of the camp entirely. Air Walkers who broke their word; foolish friends-of-friends who had fancied themselves in love with an Airhead and lived to regret it; Air Walkers who cheated honest workers, who spread diseases, or sent storms. Any bad thing that could be done, someone had a story about an Air Walker doing it.

'What were those two even doing out there anyway?' Halg said. 'Probably they got young Sheb lost in the first place, just to make themselves look good when they found him.'

'Maybe they even started the storm,' said someone else. 'Those winds last night weren't natural, I tell you.'

A small part of Kerrig's brain suspected that this was not true at all. The other Elements had a limited range of influence - no Marshlander could pull down a raincloud, nor Fire Breather control the sun. But even if these stories weren't exactly true, he wouldn't put it past Air Walkers to do those things if they could. And it felt good to be around people who understood - who wouldn't criticise him for speaking his mind.

They moved inwards, clearing the inner ring, and Kerrig enjoyed being an Earther among Earthers. This was how it ought to be, he thought. The People in their tribes, and my people at my side.

Then the Marshlanders came over and wanted to know why they hadn't been asked to help, and the Earthers replied that nobody was asked they just got on with it, and if the Marshlanders hadn't been too busy making up to their new Airhead friends maybe they would have noticed.

And the Marshlanders went to inspect the collapsed bunkers and said that they hadn't been dried out properly and would turn to quagmire unless they were correctly drained. And the Earthers accused the Marshlanders of going beyond their Element, and the Marshlanders told the Earthers that they were dry-bred idiots who thought they owned the Land because they could push dirt around.

Then one of the Fire Breathers made a crack about things getting heated and it all went rather downhill from there.

Chapter Sixteen

They were moving again by noon, but not in a single group. The party had fractured into huddles, each walking apart from the others according to how badly they'd fallen out.

Kerrig, in an attempt to keep things from getting worse, had chosen not to walk with the Earthers from before. Since he didn't want to walk with the Marshlanders and Fire Breathers that had created a protective ring around the Air Walkers, that left him to choose between the remaining Marshlanders, the Earthers who hadn't been involved in the fight (and who were looking rather smug about it) or the Outsiders.

He ended up walking with Ash, the two of them either side of Maddie, who was pulling one of the carts. The older Shifter laid a hand on the copper-coloured neck and absently patted her mane in a gesture that Kerrig recognised. For a moment he felt a stab of jealousy at the easy way 'his' Maddie trusted the other man. It reminded him that, no matter how he tried to ignore it, Madrigal was Sidrax. Of course she trusted another member of her race - little Maddie trusted everyone. She was too young to know about wars, violence and betrayal - she just saw people. The old Earther almost envied her.

Kerrig forced himself to make casual conversation with Ash, rather than let his thoughts dwell on their dark past. He fought the urge to see if Nesh was watching them. See, he wanted to say to her, I can be civil to non-Earthers.

The younger man was pleasant enough once you got past the fact that he would occasionally change the shape of his hands when he gestured. Kerrig found himself learning more than he ever thought there was to know about muscles and bones, and why most Sidrax couldn't speak in their animal forms ('Do you have any idea how many different parts have to come together before a mouth and throat can be used for speech?'). He also discovered that Ash was still some weeks away from gaining a donkey form of his own.

'Maddie is being very helpful,' he said, petting her soft ears gently, 'But there's a lot she can't tell me because she doesn't have the words. I can do the hooves, and even most of the head, but the muscles in the body are still unknown. If I tried it now, I'd have a weird mesh of donkey limbs with a wolfish body. No good for pulling carts, and almost certainly painful.'

Ash sighed. 'For the first time in my life,' he said, 'I'm wishing I had trained as a fighter rather than a scout. All my forms are small and fast. If I'd trained for the front line, I'd have mostly big forms, like an ox, or a bear. Clumsy, but at least I'd be good for carrying things.'

He broke off with a sudden snort of laughter. 'Sorry, I just pictured my old captain in her bear form, pulling a cart. And the children would want to ride on her back, in all that thick fur.'

Kerrig's heart clenched. It must have shown in his face, because Ash stopped laughing.

'What is it?' he said at last, concern and curiosity in his tone. 'You're not... Kerrig, don't tell me you feel bad about that business with the captain?'

The Earther stared at the younger man in disbelief. 'Feel bad?' he said. 'Of course I feel bad about it. I ki-' He broke off with a glance at Maddie, then resumed in a much quieter voice, 'I killed her! And I know it was in defence, and to protect others, and all of that, but I'm still a killer. I can't bear to think of it, much less laugh about it. I don't want to be alright with what I did.'

Maddie swung her head around and nuzzled Kerrig's arm until he gave in and patted her neck. The three of them walked on in silence until they got within sight of the town; both men resting one hand on Maddie's mane.

◆◆◆

It was nearly evening, and they were invited to make camp in the town square. The people seemed friendly, and willing to trade goods and stories alike. Shebbok and his family were prevailed upon to recount their thrilling adventure many times that night. During the tellings both Air Walkers were thanked by name, and the villagers' reactions to this caught Kerrig's attention.

Although pleased that the boy had been found alive and well, the Earther got the impression that no-one was entirely comfortable with hearing their Air Walker neighbours praised. He felt a twinge of satisfaction at the thought that the traitors were no more welcome amongst their Outsider friends than they would be amongst the People, but then he caught sight of Nesh, and winced. She would tell him off again if she caught him thinking that way.

Kerrig decided to avoid her until they were well clear of this place. Unfortunately, in trying to avoid the one Avlem he ended up in the thick of the locals, most of whom were Avlem themselves.

'And I suppose they'll be selling up now, as soon as they can get organised. Can you wait for them, or will they have to catch up with you?'

The unfamiliar voice belonged to an older Avlem woman, her mouth pursed in a knowing smile, while the lines around her eyes drew a permanent, disapproving frown. She was talking at Drishmel, who saw Kerrig and latched onto him with relief.

'I couldn't really say, Ma'am,' said the Marshlander, with the air of one cutting off a stream before it could become a torrent. 'When and where we go - and who goes with us - why, that's down to Mr. Kerrig here. He's in charge, you know.'

The frown-lined eyes lit up, and the woman pounced on the hapless Earther like a snake on a mouse. 'Mr. Krig! Just the person I wanted to see. "Always go to the top", that's what my father used to say. So, how long can you wait for Erben and Sanwe? They'll have to pack of course, and sell off anything they're not taking with them. And I'm prepared to make them a very good offer for their broadcloth loom.'

Kerrig glared at the babbling woman, but it had no effect. For a moment he considered just walking away, but there was a determined set to the woman's jaw that suggested she would follow him. There appeared to be only one way out of this conversation, so Kerrig faced his fate like an Earther.

'I haven't heard anything about your Air Walker friends joining us when we leave. If you want to buy their furniture, you'll have to take it up with them.'

The big man moved to leave, but the neighbour was persistent.

'Why of course they must go with you! The poor dears, it's no life for them living in an Avlem town like this. They need to be with their own sort.' The eyes seemed to be trying for sympathy, but their habitual frown-lines turned the look hard.

'I couldn't agree more,' said Kerrig. 'But since we have no Air Walkers in our party, they'd be no better off. Are you sure it isn't you who'd be more comfortable if they left town?'

He didn't want Air Walkers around anymore than she did, but Kerrig prided himself on never being a hypocrite. This woman's faux concern reminded him of all that he hated about the Avlem.

'Well I...! It's attitudes like that keeping your people from fully integrating with civilisation, you know. Oversensitive, imagining offence where none was meant. All I said was that Erben and Sanwe would surely be better off with their own kind, and you're all Elementals, aren't you? I don't know what sort of bad blood there was between your tribes five hundred years ago, but surely you can put it behind you.'

Five hundred years? thought Kerrig, furiously. *More like fifty.* But he didn't correct her. She wouldn't have understood, anyway.

To Kerrig's surprise, however, the Air Walker couple did ask to travel with them. He wanted to ask them why, but every time he tried to frame the question he was reminded of the awful pinch-eyed shrew. He refused to be anything like such a creature, which meant not prying in the Airheads' personal business.

His curiosity was satisfied at last by proxy, when Maddie sat down near the newcomers at the fire that evening. Kerrig hovered, close enough to keep a protective eye on the child, but still at a healthy distance from the Air Walkers.

'Do you miss home?' asked the little girl, without preamble. 'I do, and my Stony-Man is going to take me home one day. He promised. Are you going home again one day too?'

'Oh, sweetie, it's not... we've lived in a lot of places, Erben and I. We don't really have one place to call home, but we're happy anywhere so long as we're together.'

'So, you have lots of homes?'

'In a way, I suppose,' said Erben. 'But "home" doesn't have to be a place. Right now, for example, "home" is this caravan. It's quite exciting to be the first Air Walkers in the new Shanzir.'

'We're not calling ourselves that,' Kerrig said, sharply. 'The Shanzir are dead, and should be remembered, not replaced. All the other tribes have translated our names since Sidrean became the common language, so when the time comes, we'll choose a Sidrean word to describe ourselves.'

'What's this about us being a tribe?' said Balmar. 'I don't need another tribe; I'm an Earther, and that's good enough for me. It ought to be enough for any true Earther.'

Kerrig sighed, and silently cursed the trouble-making Air Walkers. This was exactly why he hadn't wanted to discuss the full idea just yet. Once a few trades more trading days had been completed, and people had a chance to get used to life on the road, then he might have brought it up. Ah, well...

'This is something everyone should hear,' he said, and raised his voice to call them. Once everyone was gathered around, Kerrig started to speak. He told them all of his idea to develop a new tribe, based on the Shanzir of old, and explained what he had learned from Zirpa. The Air Walkers chipped in with some extra lore of their own: According to them, the Shanzir would stay for weeks at a time in one place if there was enough in the way of goods, skills, or knowledge to trade.

'My grandparents told me that the Shanzir would sometimes spend the whole winter up in the Peaks, spread across two or three villages,' said the Air Walker woman. 'In my grandma's village it was such a regular thing there were even a couple of houses set aside for them.'

'That's nice,' said one of the Fire Breathers. 'But what about those of us who don't want to spend the rest of our lives trudging from town, begging for scraps?'

'Trading is not the same as begging!' said one of the other Fire Breathers. 'Or did you "beg" for that winter coat I sold to you last year?'

'You overcharged me for that coat.'

'Come over here and say that!'

'Alright, now break it up,' Kerrig said, pushing a wall of Earth between the two Fire Breathers. 'No-one's going to be forced to join anything - anyone who wants to live in a town can stay in one of the places we pass through.'

'An Avlem town? No thank you. Why can't we establish a town of our own? We've got the whole of the Fire Plains to choose from, we should be able to find somewhere with decent soil for crops.'

'You seriously expect Marshlanders to settle in this desert? How'd you like it if we forced you to live in a swamp?'

The voices got louder, and Kerrig noticed a couple of parents ushering their younger children away to a safe distance. He was tempted to just drop the loudest shouters down a pit, when Erben said,

'Well, there's always the Island.'

The mood stilled, balanced on a knife-edge. Then people started to laugh. A ripple that spread through the camp, a sense of camaraderie that only seemed to increase when the Air Walkers exchanged puzzled glances and wanted to know what was so funny about the Island.

'Why would we go back to the Island after everything we went through to get out of that place?' said someone at last, when the laughter died down.

The Air Walkers still looked confused.

'But why are you going towards the Island, in that case?'

Kerrig felt as though every eye in the camp was fixed on him. 'But... we're heading north and east,' he said. 'We left Camp Freedom behind us in the south-west. Of course we're not heading towards it again.'

The argumentative Fire Breather from before nodded, slowly. 'That's right,' he said. 'Check the sun. Wherever this Earther's leading us, it's not back to that cursed trap.'

Erben frowned. 'The Island isn't a trap. And it's in the East. I've been there.'

'In the east, you say?' Kerrig said, cutting off the jeers of the crowd. 'Then we might as well keep going as we are. This road runs north and east, so we'll arrive at the coast eventually. And in the meantime, we can continue to trade in the towns we pass through. Nothing needs to be decided yet.'

◆◆◆

They were two days out from the town when the sickness started. The year was on the turn; ever since the storm each night had seemed colder than the last. Kerrig longed for the security of the Mines - it could be cold there too of course, but there was no rain, and no tearing winds.

He'd asked the Air Walkers to do something about the winds. They asked him to level out the hills. He took their point, but not gracefully.

When he noticed the first children shivering, he told them to walk in the shelter of the cart, and wear an extra blanket each. The party started travelling later each morning, and stopped earlier each night, and everyone took time to make the camp as warm and dry as possible. Ash took to sleeping in his wolf form, and Kerrig found him early one morning carrying a couple of sleeping toddlers.

'They came over in the night,' explained Ash, a little embarrassed. 'Seems I'm warmer than a blanket - but I don't think the parents would like to find them with me.'

Kerrig took one of the children.

'Let's return them together, just in case,' he said. 'Though if the children make a habit of this, it's going to come out sooner or later.'

But the next morning brought something worse than a parent's ire. Kerrig was up before dawn again, and found a nearly frantic Ash, shifting back and forth between his man and wolf forms in a blur. Hand-paws shook tiny shoulders, and he was keening softly as he held his head close to the faces of two terribly still children.

'They won't wake!' Ash said. 'Help me!'

Kerrig pushed the young man aside and examined the children anxiously. He laid one hand on each little chest, feeling desperately for signs of life. When he felt two fluttering heartbeats, the big man breathed a sigh of relief. They were not dead, but they were both in the grip of a raging fever.

Within hours the camp had become a hospital. Nesh stepped up to direct everything, and for once Kerrig was not sorry to have a bossy Avlem around. Kerrig himself was busy with other Earthers creating quarantine areas for the sick children, and lots of smaller shelters for the healthy families. Unfortunately, the ground was proving difficult.

Ash came to find him, looking so pale and drawn that Kerrig thought of sending the Sidrax straight into the quarantine den - as soon as they had one. But Ash absolutely refused the Earther's suggestion that he take a rest.

'I need something to do!' he said, sounding desperate. 'Everyone's busy, and all Nesh will say is, "Go and help look after the children, Ash." I don't know how to look after children! I just let them use me as a pillow, and I didn't even notice that they were so sick they almost died! And they might still die if we can't get them warm and fed, and I can't stand it!'

The ex-soldier was almost snarling, his face an unsettling blend of different animals. But for all that, Kerrig was suddenly struck by how young and helpless he looked.

'We can always use some help with digging,' the Earther said. 'If you've got a shape that can do that.'

Ash blinked, pulled up short from his emotional outburst. 'I... mongooses are good underground,' he said. 'But I can't dig half so fast as an Earther. Won't I just get in the way?'

Kerrig sighed. 'We've hit a problem,' he admitted. 'There's a layer of wet clay about two arm-lengths down, and it's impossible to work with. There has to be an Earther and a Marshlander pushing it back into place every minute or the clay starts to slide and dislodges everything above it. We simply can't spare enough people to maintain that sort of control night and day, not as well as looking after the sick children. We need to find somewhere new to set up the shelters; but the wretched thing reads as damp soil to Earthers, and as groundwater to Marshlanders. We can't build through the clay, and we can't find the edge of it.'

Kerrig scrubbed a hand through his short hair. 'If you've got a shape that can explore underground, and tell us where we can dig safely, then you'd be helping a lot.'

Ash nodded, and looked thoughtful. 'What happens if you build on top of the clay - without digging into it?' he asked.

'So long as it's not disturbed, the clay seems stable enough. But we can't do that - the shelters would be too small to move around in.'

'If you can get them as deep as a man's hips, I think I can help with the rest. There's a building technique I learned about once - used in rocky deserts and places like that. I just wish I'd been paying more attention in class...'

The youngster broke off with a sigh. 'Look, I'll go and start digging around, see what I can find. And while I'm down there I'll try to remember about those desert shelters. Thanks, Kerrig!'

With a sense of purpose in his step, Ash moved to the edge of the camp. There, he shrank down into his mongoose form and began to dig. Kerrig watched until the jet-black tail was out of sight, then turned back to the working crews.

'We may have a solution to the clay problem,' he announced. 'We need shallow pits, no more than hip deep. Let's go!'

Chapter Seventeen

When Ash returned from exploring he was cold, tired, and covered in clay. Kerrig set the mongoose-shaped Sidrax down in front of the fire, and asked for his report.

After taking a moment, presumably to get his mouth into the right shape for talking, Ash said, 'The clay layer is deep and wide. We'd have to move a long way to get around it, and even then there are no guarantees we wouldn't find something worse. Sorry.'

The sight of Ash's whiskery little face with such a doleful expression might have been funny at another time.

'There's good news, though,' Ash added, with a cheerfulness that sounded only slightly forced. 'I remembered how to make those shallow shelters, and I think we can do it. All we need are some branches, or some large, flat stones.'

Kerrig raised an eyebrow and looked around at the treeless plains.

'We're a bit short of branches at the moment, Ash,' he said. 'But I might be able to flatten out some stones. How big do we need them?'

Ash tucked his head between his paws and started to pull dried clay from his fur. While thus hidden he said sheepishly, 'Um, about as tall as you. And the same across.'

A second eyebrow joined the first.

'Not a chance,' said Kerrig. 'Nothing we've found here is big enough to take that shape - it would be stretched thin enough to see through.' The Earther sighed, and dropped his head in his hands.

'We're going to have to move,' he said. 'Put the sickest of the children in the carts. Earthers ahead to smooth out the path, and Marshlanders keeping the children dry, which might at least stop them from getting worse. And those Air Walkers can help with that too, I suppose.'

Kerrig was thinking aloud now, and had almost forgotten about the younger man until Ash said,

'I think Sanwe and Erben will be too busy to do much more than they're already doing.'

Kerrig bit back a sarcastic comment, and substituted a noise that might have been something like 'Oh?'

Ash ducked his head. 'I could be wrong - I mean, what do I know about Elementals? - but it looks like the wind shield they've had up around the carts for the last few days has been taking a lot of work to maintain.'

A wind shield, fumed Kerrig silently. He wondered for a moment if they'd started after he asked for their help, but suspected they'd been helping quietly ever since finding the lost child in the storm.

A surge of anger spiked through him. Going around being nice at people, and then making sure he didn't find out. It was a trick - a plot to make him look bad because he knew better than to trust a pair of backstabbing Airheads. Getting everyone on their side like that, it was... well, it was exactly the sort of underhanded behaviour he would expect from the Flying Filth.

He thought of Zirpa, but dismissed the memory. She was clearly the exception, not the rule. One decent Air Walker didn't redeem the tribe, any more than Nesh could redeem the Avlem.

'So, Mr. Kerrig - the carts?'

Kerrig blinked, and realised that Ash was still there. Yes, deal with the situation first, and rage about untrustworthy Air Walkers later.

◆◆◆

When Kerrig went to update Nesh on the plan he found her looking more frazzled than he'd ever seen her. Before he could say a word, she held up a hand to stop him.

'Unless you're here to tell me the quarantine dens are ready, go away. Three more children have caught this sickness, and half the others are showing early signs of going the same way. I give it a few hours before we have our first adult victim, and then it's going to be chaos.'

She looked at him, and Kerrig chose the better part of valour.

'There's a small... delay. But it's going to be alright,' he said, hoping that he could make that be true. 'You need to rest,' he told her. 'Food, water, and a break. You didn't survive half your life in prison mines without learning that.'

Nesh looked as though she wanted to protest, then her common sense won out and she nodded.

'Let me know the minute the dens are ready,' she said. Then she stood up - and almost fell down again. Kerrig offered her his arm, and she balanced herself against him for a moment before letting go.

'Thanks,' she said, with a small smile. 'I must have been sitting still for too long.'

'Now that was a problem we never had back in the mines,' Kerrig replied, and felt proud of the smile his weak joke elicited.

After dropping Nesh off at the nearest cooking fire, Kerrig went looking for Ash.

'We can't move camp,' he said. 'Tell me everything you can remember about those wilderness shelters of yours; they're our only chance now.'

'But you said we didn't have enough wood or stone,' Ash said. 'And without something to make the upper walls, there's no way to-'

'Walls? We can make walls,' said Kerrig confidently. 'How big and what shape?'

'You can? But... no, never mind how. The shape goes like this.'

Ash turned his nails into claws and quickly drew a couple of rough diagrams. Kerrig watched, confused for a moment, then nodded.

'You mean, like this?' The Earther pulled at the ground until a hollow wedge formed under his hands. He pressed his fingers into the opening at the wide end, making a shallow pit inside and forming the outer into a thin wall.

'Yes. But how can the soil keep its shape like that without an Earther holding it in place?'

Kerrig grinned. 'Get digging, Ash. We need a small clay pit off to the side of the camp. Soil, water, a bit of clay and a lot of fire - we'll build the best shelters anyone's ever seen!'

Once the process was started, the dens went up quickly. Earthers created the basic shape, then the Marshlanders and Fire Breathers came in to dry out the walls and bake them firm. The Air Walkers followed the Fire Breathers, directing the heated air deep into the drying earth, and making air holes into the back walls of each den. Kerrig gritted his teeth and managed to thank the Air Walkers for their help. Their expressions of surprise were very satisfying.

That's right, I'm on to you, he thought. *So much for undermining my authority with your 'good deeds'.*

As soon as the largest shelter was finished, Nesh directed the sick children be moved into it. There were now a dozen little patients, either deeply into a fever-sleep, or else shivering with the early symptoms. By sunset every child in the group was ill - including Maddie. The little Sidrax had a corner to herself, with enough space for her donkey shape. Kerrig watched anxiously as she changed shape despite being unconscious.

'Is that safe?' he asked Ash. 'She's asleep - what if she makes a mistake with the shape?'

Ash knelt down beside the copper-coloured head and listened to her breathing. Then he laid a hand on her ribs, and counted under his breath.

'She's breathing well, and her heartbeat is normal,' he said. 'I wouldn't worry too much. This is her birth form, the one she knows best. If you see her change into any shape except donkey or girl, let me know. New, less familiar shapes can give a child trouble, but not a birth shape.' Ash stroked Maddie's mane once, and stood up.

'Donkeys are hardy little creatures,' he said. 'Maddie's probably going to make a speedy recovery. Especially with her favourite Earther looking after her.'

Ash's grin met Kerrig's expression and faltered. Then the older man smiled, and Ash laughed.

'I wish we could make a medicine out of your frown,' he said. 'It would scare off every disease from here to Sidria.'

Kerrig moved to check on some of the other children in the den. 'I wish it worked on Nesh,' he said, ruefully. 'She's certainly never been afraid of me. I don't think that woman's scared of anything.'

Maddie recovered after only a few days, but by the time she was up and about, Ash was sick. He curled up in mongoose form and disappeared into a nest of blankets. By that point, about half the adults were down with the fever, mostly the ones who had sat up for days with their sick children.

Kerrig tried to arrange a rota of care, and sat down with Nesh to work out who was well enough to be given which tasks. The big Earther wasn't usually one for detailed planning, and the names swam before his eyes as tried to write down the Avlem's suggestion. Then the room swam, and he blinked...

When he opened his eyes, he was lying down under a blanket of soil, looking up at anxious faces that were distorted beyond recognition. Kerrig blinked, and the room was empty. He blinked again and it was dawn. Blink. Bright afternoon sun poured through the low door of the hut.

When he was finally able to keep his eyes open, Kerrig sat up and looked around. He was in one of the huts they had built to be a quarantine, and there were more than half a dozen other men in here with him. He got unsteadily to his feet, feeling weak but otherwise healthy. He stumbled outside and nearly knocked into Ash, who was carrying two buckets of water.

'Mr. Kerrig! You're awake!' he said. 'And up. Are you sure you should be? What did Madam Leuran say?'

Before Kerrig could answer, the woman herself came hurrying over. 'Goodness, I was only gone for a moment. What are you doing out of bed, Kerrig?'

He opened his mouth to reply, but she cut him off with a gesture, and reached up a hand to feel his forehead.

'Temperature's down, then,' she said, apparently to herself. 'Any dizziness now, or double vision? No? Excellent. You can have a few hours out here in the fresh air, then I expect to see you sitting or lying down somewhere nice and damp - well, earthy, in your case. Can I trust you to take care of yourself?'

The matronly Marshlander bustled down into the hut without waiting for a reply, and Kerrig looked at Ash. The younger man gave a sheepish grin.

'I hope Nesh gets better soon,' he said. 'Madam Leuran is a good woman, but...'

'I know what you mean,' said Kerrig. 'How long has Nesh been ill?'

'Since before either of us, I think, but she wouldn't admit it. She passed out only a few hours after you did though, and has been mostly asleep for the past two days.'

'Two days?' said Kerrig, horrified. 'I've been asleep for two whole days?'

Ash nodded. 'You and half the adults in the camp. I only woke up yesterday, just in time to see Erben go down. Sanwe will probably be next - she won't leave his side. But the good news is that it does seem to only last for a few days; and you don't get it again once you're better. So all we have to do is wait for it to run its course.'

Ash set one of his buckets at the door of the hut Kerrig had been in, and carried the other to the next one along. The third hut had a higher door, and seemed slightly larger overall. The two men walked over to it, and Kerrig could hear children's voices coming from inside. It was not a happy sound.

A teenaged Marshlander was blocking the door, and arguing with a girl not much younger than herself.

'Everyone is supposed to take a rest after lunch, Madam Leuran says. That includes you!'

'*And* you,' the girl retorted. 'And don't shout, you'll wake the children.'

'How can I get any rest, or not shout, if you won't do as you're told?' the older girl said, in a voice like a pending avalanche. 'Go and lie down right now, before I take you outside and drown you.'

'You can't do that,' said the girl. Then, less confidently, 'You can't.'

Kerrig stepped forward until he loomed impressively over both youngsters.

'Now then, young lady, you mustn't drown a child just for being naughty,' he said. 'Much more effective to wrap them from neck to knees, so as they're still alive to learn from it.'

The younger girl squeaked and threw herself onto one of the makeshift beds.

'I'm resting! I'm resting!'

The Marshlander flashed a tired smile at Kerrig.

'Thanks, she's been impossible all day. Her mum didn't get sick until late last night, and I suppose she's just worried, but... it's getting a bit much for me, that's all.'

Kerrig sat on the grass and beckoned for the Marshlander to join him. The girl hesitated, then sat down and introduced herself as Boddan.

'I didn't get badly sick,' she said. 'Dessai did - my little brother - but he's better now. We live with our uncle, and he was OK until yesterday but now it's just me and I'm exhausted! I can barely keep up with Dess, never mind all of the kids in the camp. And they all feel better so they want to run around and make noise but they're supposed to rest and what if they get sick again or they disturb the adults so they don't get better or run out into the Plains and get lost or hurt and it'll all be my fault!'

Boddan burst into tears and buried her face in her arms. Kerrig awkwardly patted her on the back, and muttered some nonsense words in what he hoped was a soothing tone of voice. To his dismay this only caused the girl to sob harder and throw her arms around him. The Earther looked to Ash for help but the Sidrax seemed torn between pity for the girl and laughter at Kerrig's situation.

At last Ash relented. He sat down on the other side of Boddan and patted her shoulder. The Marshlander let go of Kerrig and turned a tear-blotched face to the Sidrax.

'I'm s-sorry,' she said, her breath hitching, 'I shouldn't have cr-cried on you like that.' Absently, she drew her tears from Kerrig's shirt, leaving tiny spots of salt behind to mark their passing.

'I'm sorry too,' said Ash. 'I've been out of bed for a day already, but I was too busy running around after the adult patients to come and check on the children. Please forgive me?'

Boddan blinked at the Sidrax, surprise banishing the remaining tears.

'You don't have to be sorry - I'm not your responsibility,' she told him.

'Those children in there are not your responsibility, either.'

'That's... different,' Boddan said, suddenly less sure of herself.

Kerrig smiled at this, but didn't argue. Instead, he said, 'Well, we're here now. Let's make it a shared responsibility.

◆

By the time the children woke from their afternoon nap, the Earther, Sidrax, and Marshlander had worked out a plan. They would take the children out on the Plains in the mornings and let them run about while collecting eggs and edible plants. Then, in the afternoon, they would come back to the large shelter and either rest or study. This part was Ash's suggestion.

'We'll set up a school of sorts,' he said, and seemed surprised at the blank looks he got from most of the Elementals.

'What's a school?' Kerrig asked.

So Ash explained about Sidrean schools, where people gathered in groups to learn from an expert. Even very basic skills like reading, writing, and cooking, were taught by experts. Kerrig thought it sounded a bit like the way he'd been taught by the Elders of his tribe; but that arrangement was only because he'd lost his parents. Sending children who had both parents alive and well to be taught by other people... well it must work, he supposed. And it would do while these children were waiting for the adults to recover.

The children themselves were less enthusiastic about the idea, wanting to play and learn on their own schedule, and no-one else's. But Kerrig and Ash between them were able to coax, cajole, or coerce the children into behaving themselves; and most found that they enjoyed it well enough in the end.

One child who needed no persuading was Maddie. The little Sidrax was already used to the idea of studying with Ash, and was delighted to get time with her 'Stony-Man' on top of that. Her innocence and enthusiasm seemed to encourage some of the shyer children, and by the third day Maddie had a small circle of friends.

This became a problem once the parents of those friends recovered enough to notice.

It was after lunch, and the younger children were sitting in the shelter practicing their writing by using sticks to draw in loose earth. Parents had been dropping by every so often to check on their children, but most seemed happy to let Kerrig get on with it. One Fire Breather couple, however, had taken one look, marched in, and grabbed hold of their two children before hurrying back outside. The schoolroom echoed in their wake with shocked and vocal objections, most of the children saying what Kerrig would only let himself think.

Telling the rest of the children to stay put, the Earther followed the family out into the open.

'What was that about?' asked the Earther, when he caught up with them.

The parents exchanged glances, then sent their children off 'to play' while they had 'a word with Mr. Kerrig'.

'Why was that... animal in there with our children?' demanded the father.

'What?'

'You know what I mean. That Shifter. It's useful enough as a beast of burden I suppose, but it has no place being inside, especially around children.'

'Yes,' agreed the mother. 'What if it trampled someone?'

'Madrigal has the right to learn, just like any child. She uses her girl-form when inside; she's no danger to anyone. And even in her donkey form she's perfectly docile. She's not going to trample her friends,' Kerrig assured them.

'You don't know that for sure. And why can't she learn from that other Shifter? She doesn't need to be in there with real children.'

The Earther forced himself to keep his temper.

'Ash is out on the Plains with the older children, teaching them to identify edible plants,' he told them. 'And it's "Sidrax", you know. Not "Shifter".'

'What?! You left children alone with that Shif-'

The Fire Breather's rant was suddenly cut short. His mouth kept on moving, but no sound came out. From behind him came the two Air Walkers with faces like thunder. Sanwe planted herself in front of the angry Fire Breather couple, while Erben came to talk to Kerrig.

'Excuse my wife, she's just giving a couple of idiots a piece of her mind. We thought it best if other people didn't hear the exact conversation. I expect there will be some language unsuitable for children.'

The Earther raised an eyebrow at this, but all he said was,

'Why?'

'I don't know - I keep on telling Sanwe that swearing is the mark of a weak argument, but when she gets her temper up... well, I'm just glad you can't hear her.'

'No, I mean, why is she defending Maddie and Ash? Are there really such strong ties between Air Walkers and Sidrax?'

Erben sighed. 'We didn't do it because they're Sidrax, we did it because they're our friends. And because we know how it feels to be judged for having the wrong ancestry.'

Kerrig felt his face burn until he couldn't look at Erben. Instead, he watched the faces in the sound-proof ring. All three were red with anger, but Kerrig thought he saw hints of shame in the expressions of the Fire Breathers.

He turned to go back into the schoolroom, then forced himself to turn and look at the Air Walker.

'Thank you, Erben. Both of you.'

Chapter Eighteen

Time passed. Everyone was finally over the illness; even Nesh, although her stubborn refusal to rest meant that she took longer to recover than anyone else. The children were settling into a routine and the adults were building up stock to trade. It was peaceful, but it couldn't last.

That night Kerrig gathered everyone at the dinner fire and made an announcement (and tried to ignore how bizarre that felt, even now). He thanked people for their efforts during the sickness, and told everyone to pack up tonight because they were moving off tomorrow.

The Earther braced himself for the inevitable complaints, and was not disappointed.

A good third of the Fire Breathers wanted to stay put and build a town of their own. Most of the rest of the farmers wanted to carry on with their trade route, but a handful mentioned trying for the Island.

'Oh, not that old story again!' said Traegl, with uncharacteristic venom. 'Another legendary Island where the People can pretend the world doesn't exist? It's probably just another trap - if there even *is* an island.'

'Trae? What's got into you?' said Ash. 'You're never normally so... angry.'

Traegl scowled at them. 'What? I'm not allowed to be angry about things? About being stuck, trapped, by my own people? About those Air Walker soldiers making me afraid of my own Element, and sending words into my brain until I couldn't trust myself? I'm not supposed to be angry about any of that?'

Everyone was looking at the young Marshlander now, but no-one spoke. Some of the other Marshlander farmers looked sympathetic, but mostly people seemed confused. Ash certainly did.

'I... wow, Trae, I had no idea...' he said, after a long, painfully awkward silence. 'Why didn't you say anything before? It's been months since we left that place.'

'You didn't seem to care,' she said, quieter now but still bitter. 'We got out of that trap, and you went on as if nothing had changed. Like it didn't matter that our own people set up something like... like that foul place.'

Ash reached out to Traegl, but she leaned away. He sighed.

'I'm sorry, Trae, I never realised how it would bother you, Elementals trapping other Elementals like that. I suppose I got so used to seeing you as a fellow soldier, I forgot that you're also of the People.'

The Marshlander stared at him like he'd grown a second head. 'That's not even... I'm talking about the army, idiot! Not 'The People' - *my* people. I didn't only join up for the good pay and the training, you know. I joined because I believed that the army was about making the Land a better place for everyone. Hunting bandits, catching criminals, protecting the weak - it was like being a professional hero. Even crazies like the captain, and bullies like Fal, didn't change that. There are going to be crazies and bullies wherever you go, that's just life. But that place... that island, the army was - *is* - running it. I trusted them, and they betrayed me. And you didn't even notice.'

Ash sent a helpless look to Kerrig, who could only shrug in return, equally lost.

'But, Trae,' Ash said, 'You *left* the army. We both did. Why did you desert in the first place, if it meant so much to you?'

She blushed. Kerrig noticed, with the part of his mind that was desperate to be anywhere but here, that he could see the exact moment when her face switched from being red with anger to being red from embarrassment. By all rules of manners, he should have turned away by now; turned away and taken others with him. This was a private conversation, even if it had started out at full volume. But despite everything, he couldn't make himself leave.

Traegl didn't answer for a long time, then suddenly she laughed. It was a halting, almost silent chuckle, and seemed to be drawn out from her against her will.

'I left because I'm an idiot,' she said. 'I knew I was ending my career, even while I still believed in it. Yes, I'd had it up to here with the mad captain, and yes, I wanted to help the children, but the real reason I went with you is...'

The young Marshlander finally looked away from Ash, and seemed to notice her audience for the first time. She looked horrified, and so embarrassed that Kerrig half-expected her hair to catch fire.

'...is nobody's business but my own!' she said, loudly, before sprinting away from the campfire.

Ash looked completely thunderstruck, standing rooted to the spot and blinking at the darkness that had swallowed the Marshlander. After a full minute, he stammered something about making sure she didn't get lost in the dark, changed into his wolf shape, and raced off after her.

It was after dawn when they returned, both looking utterly lovestruck and trying to hide it. Kerrig bustled the camp into busy-ness to give the youngsters time to pull themselves together - or rather, apart. The sudden move from friendship to romance took him by surprise, but that in itself wasn't too surprising. Kerrig had long ago made his peace with the fact that he was not interested in pairing off, beyond a desire to have children of his own. Romance was not something he noticed, but he understood it mattering to other people.

What did surprise the Earther was discovering that he was genuinely happy for the young couple. No misgivings about mixed marriages, or concerns over the fate of their children. It was a little disturbing to realise that the shake-up of his views and opinions had still not come to an end. Where would it stop?

Kerrig was distracted from these concerns when Ash sought him out, through the bustle of packing up. The young Sidrax had the air of a man on a mission, and waved aside Kerrig's congratulations as small-talk.

'No, listen, I've got something important to tell you,' said the younger man, impatiently. 'Um, I mean, Trae's important - obviously - but... anyway the point is, we got lost last night, so this morning I went flying, to get our bearings, and I saw it. The Island.'

'What?'

'I saw the Island, or at least, an island. And there's a town on the coast, too. Oh, and a stream, between here and the town. You know, if the Fire Breathers really do want to settle down and stop travelling.'

Kerrig blinked. 'Well, that's very... I didn't realise we were so close to the coast,' he said.

'Actually, we're not. I just have good eyesight as a hawk. Very good. I reckon it's half-day's walking just to get to the stream, and at least another day past that before we reach the town. No need to rush any decisions. Just, you know, information. Or whatever.'

'Good to know,' said Kerrig, briskly. 'Thanks, Ash.'

◆

Kerrig gave a direct order that morning, and told everyone to be ready to leave within an hour. Most of the farmers obeyed, albeit reluctantly, so that Kerrig was left to deal directly with a mere handful of dissenting Fire Breathers. To these, he explained that there was no water nearby, making this a bad place to establish a town, 'Unless you can persuade a few Marshlanders to stay and act as your personal water carriers.'

He then passed on Ash's message of a stream ahead, and left them to the discussion of their plans. He wondered which of them would end up as leader, and if he or she would find the job as unpleasant as Kerrig did.

It was almost noon before they were all on the road again, and this late start meant that it was early evening before they reached Ash's stream. The pro-settlement Fire Breathers were delighted, and began discussing where they would place their new homes, and whether they would use hunting or farming as their main source of food. Everyone else was busy setting up camp.

The place was made comfortable, but the meal that night was a poor affair. Thanks to Ash's lessons, the older children were able to forage for edible plants; and there was still some cheese and dried meat left over from trading in Sanwe and Erben's old town. Even so, supplies were running low.

'Get your stock in order,' Kerrig told them. 'We need to trade tomorrow if we want to eat tomorrow night.'

Chapter Nineteen

The next morning, the caravan headed east, minus a dozen Fire Breathers. Kerrig wondered if being fiercely independent was a Fire Breather trait, or if he was just really bad at getting people to stay with the group. His thoughts turned to Volnar and Mashpa, and he wished he had some way of knowing that they were safe.

Maddie must have picked up on his mood, because she turned her head to nudge at his arm, and didn't let up until Kerrig was walking with one hand on her neck. He petted her soft mane, and talked quietly to the little Sidrax as the caravan moved steadily towards the coast.

Kerrig had to admit to being curious. Growing up in the Sanctuary-turned-Mines, he'd never seen the sea, nor any body of water larger than a river. Even the river around the badly-named Camp Freedom had been larger than anything he'd ever seen before. As they walked, he reached out with his Earther sense, and tried to feel the rocks or the shoreline. Although he couldn't pick out anything different yet, he did notice that the Marshlanders were picking up the pace as the day went on.

'Can you smell that?' said one, coming up on Kerrig and Maddie. 'Salt in the air. We're almost at the coast!'

'You know the sea, then?' Kerrig asked, as the farmer drew level with them.

'Oh yes, my family had a trading boat running from the Citadel to the southern bank of the river for years. Salt air was my favourite when I was a kiddie. It still is!'

Kerrig watched the Marshlander hurrying ahead, and noticed that he and Maddie were dropping back in the line. He urged the little Sidrax forward, and she seemed happy to oblige. Her ears were forward and her head was up; the Marshlanders' enthusiasm was apparently infectious.

'Have you ever seen the sea, Maddie?' he asked. The little donkey shook her head, making her ears flap.

'Me neither,' he confided. 'Let's go see it together.'

◆

The town, when they got to it, was both grander and cruder than any others they had seen on the Fire Plains. The buildings were generally smaller, but there were many of them, and they had the look of being put up in a hurry and expanded later.

The largest, grandest building took up one whole side of the market square, and had the words 'Newharbour Town Hall' written over the door. Kerrig stopped to one side of this edifice and unhitched Maddie from the cart. At once, she switched to her child-form and stared around with big eyes, all the while clutching hold of Kerrig's hand.

Behind them, the Earther could hear Nesh giving directions for turning the carts into a display, and posting watchers around to guard against light-fingered visitors. It wasn't until she started sending people into the market to find things that the trouble started.

'I know what my family needs, thank-you-very-much, and I know what we don't,' boomed the familiar tones of Balmar. 'And one thing we don't need is some *Avlem* dictating to us. Any of us. Right, friends?'

The murmurs were low, but Kerrig could feel the tension as passers-by became an audience. Feet shuffled, groups subtly splitting and reforming along fault lines of opinion and allegiance. The big man sighed, and told Maddie to go stand with Ash. This could get ugly, fast.

'Balmar, a word?' he said, stepping between Nesh and the angry Earther. '*Now.*'

Kerrig led the way to a spot just behind one of the carts; near enough to be open, but just far enough to be hard to overhear from the market proper.

'If you have a problem with how I run things,' he said, 'I wish you'd take it up with me instead of fighting with each other. And that goes for everyone,' he added, looking around at the rest. 'It's also not wise to be openly rude about the Avlem if we want them to trade with us.'

Feet shuffled again, and everyone seemed very interested in studying the ground.

'*Does* anyone have a problem?' he said, pressing home a rare advantage. 'This is your chance. It's a large town and, now that we're a smaller group, I thought it would be safe to bring everyone in on this trading run. But if you're uncomfortable around so many strangers, then I'll take you to set up camp outside the town. Anyone?'

The crowd rumbled with low chatter, and hissed with whispers. Balmar was the first to speak up, although several others were around him, nodding their support.

'You've gone soft, Kerrig,' he said. 'But I get it. You're under a lot of pressure, and that's making it hard to think straight. The sooner we're on the Island, among our own kind, the better off we'll be.'

'Hang on, that's not...' Kerrig started to say, but he was cut off by the happy shriek of a passing local girl.

'Whaaaaaaat?! You're going to the Island!!?! I'm *soooooo* jealous! I keep asking my parents to move there, but they're all, like, "Integration is the future" and "You'll understand when you're older". And "Tidy your room". They say that one a lot. I wish I was going to the Island! Oh, I know! I can go with you!'

'Wait, what?' Kerrig began, before getting cut off again.

'Yeah, that's a great idea! I'll go tell my parents! Don't leave without me!' The girl bounded away, leaving a stunned crowd in her wake.

'So... I'll get my list from Nesh, shall I?' said Balmar.

◆◆◆

The excitable girl turned out to be an Air Walker of about sixteen. Kerrig hoped that her parents would forbid the move, or that the others in the group would object; but everyone seemed to have developed a sudden and disturbing level of faith in his leadership, and Kerrig couldn't justify rejecting the girl simply for being an annoying Air Walker.

'Are you sure about this?' he asked the girl's parents. 'Sending your daughter off with strangers? We won't be offended if you'd rather keep her here, I mean, I'd completely understand...'

But the parents were no help.

'She'll be fine,' said the mother, blithely. 'It will do her good to see the traditional life first-hand, instead of sitting at home and dreaming about how great it supposedly was. A dose of reality will do her good, and she can send us a message on the Air whenever she wants to come home.'

Kerrig grimaced at the reminder of that particular Air Walker ability, but he nodded acceptance anyway.

'The caravan is open to anyone who wants to join, and is prepared to do their share of the work,' he said. 'And, of course, she can leave whenever she wants. Although, I don't know when we'll be coming this way again.'

'That's quite alright, we understand,' said the girl's father. 'Our Pak's a determined little thing. She'll be fine.'

◆

'Pak' wasn't the only local who wanted to join the group, although she was by far the youngest and most enthusiastic. What interested Kerrig more were the ones who wanted to leave the caravan and stay in the town - and the ones who didn't.

Ash, he knew, would follow Maddie; and Maddie would follow Kerrig himself. But the Earther expected Nesh to make her new home in the town, not on the Island. But when their trading was done, and Kerrig told everyone who was going to the Island to gather at the town gates, there was Nesh.

'What are you doing here?' Kerrig said. 'This is the last Avlem town. We're well away from anyone who could know about your... whatever happened to you. I don't even know if the caravan is going to exist after we reach the Island, or if anyone is going to want to keep travelling when they can settle down with their own kind. This is your last chance to be with your people.'

'I know all that,' Nesh replied, as calm as always. 'You still don't understand - I can't introduce myself to another Avlem without revealing my past. It's in my name - or the lack of it. With Elementals,

I can be just "Nesh", and that's enough. Among Avlem, it will never be enough.'

Kerrig frowned. 'So use your old name,' he said. 'You remember it, don't you? No-one here knows that it was taken away, or removed, or whatever. You don't have to stay as just "Nesh" if you don't want to.'

The Avlem shook her head. '*I* would know,' she said. 'My old name is *gone*. Look, everyone knows about the Earther's Great Sanctuary getting turned into prison mines, right? And when you tell people where you're from, they know about your life there. So, why don't you call yourself "Kerrig of the Crystal Caverns", or even just "Kerrig"? Every time we meet new people, you give your name as "Kerrig, Earther of the Great Sanctuary". Why?'

'That's my name,' said the Earther, confused. 'I can't just decide to change my... OK, I understand. But I'm not ashamed of my life in the mines, you know,' he added.

'I'm not exactly ashamed, either,' Nesh said. 'But it changes how people look at you. And a person can get tired of those looks.'

The big Earther shrugged. He'd never bothered too much about noticing how other people looked at him, or at anyone else. Maybe it was an Avlem thing. But right now he had other things to worry about. Like how to get all the people and goods under his care safely across the broad stretch of open sea that separated the Island from the mainland.

Kerrig had sent Ash scouting yesterday, looking for the best place to cross. The sharp-eyed Sidrax had found a stretch of beach opposite the nearest point of the Island, but strong winds had prevented him from getting a better look at the Island itself.

'Natural winds?' asked the Earther, anxiously. 'Or an Air Walker defence?'

'I don't know,' admitted Ash. 'I've never flown over open sea before, it might be natural. But even if it is an Air Walker thing, we've got Air Walkers too, right? We can match anything they throw at us.'

Today, Kerrig tried to put those concerns out of his mind as he directed the caravan towards the beach. It took them only an hour to reach it, and Kerrig encouraged people to rest and eat while he organised the crossing.

Walking between the small groups gathered around the campfire, Kerrig sought out Traegl and Erben, and asked them for ideas about how and where to cross. Nesh joined them after a moment, followed by some disgruntled-looking Fire Breathers.

'What's the big secret?' demanded a Fire Breather. 'You're figuring out the crossing, aren't you? Without consulting a Fire Breather, I notice.'

Kerrig frowned in honest puzzlement. 'We're going over water,' he said. 'How can a Fire Breather help?'

She smirked at him. 'By reminding you that some of us were traders along the river before getting trapped in that miserable camp. And pointing out that the sea is cold. Fire Breathers don't just do flames, you know - we control the heat, too. However you plan to get over the sea, you'll want us Fire Breathers involved, keeping everyone warm.'

'I had no idea,' Kerrig said. 'Then... thanks, I suppose. I just wanted to work out a plan without having to deal with a dozen different ideas all arguing their point. But you're right - I should have asked a Fire Breather to join us.'

'And you should have invited this lady, too,' the Fire Breather said, pressing her advantage. 'Her Talent is perfect for a situation like this.'

'It is?' Kerrig said, looking at Nesh. 'What is your Talent, anyway? I don't think I've ever seen you use it.'

The Avlem woman blushed. 'I don't like using it, or at least I didn't used to. I'm a Finder - if I know what I'm looking for, I somehow just know the best place to start looking. It's not perfect, and it's got me into trouble sometimes, but here - yes, I can Find the safest and quickest path, and avoid things like hidden rocks and dangerous currents. But the more I know about what you're looking for, the more accurately I can Find a solution.'

'Oh. Uh, good to know. Well, let's get to work. Ideas?'

◆

The crossing itself was uneventful. Earthers and Fire Breathers baked layers of soil, sand and seaweed into a solid platform, Marshlanders controlled the flow of water around the raft, and Air Walkers pushed aside the worst of the strong sea winds. Ash flew overhead, protected by the Air Walkers, and watched for dangers from above, while Nesh sat at the front and pointed out the safest course. Maddie and the other children sat in the middle with one of the carts, surrounded by Fire Breathers. Everyone moved together, and shared mutual congratulations when they landed safely on the other shore. It was a great moment, made even greater by the welcome that was waiting for them.

Eight people stood on the shore, two from each tribe of the People. They joined their strength to that of the People on the raft, and greeted their own warmly. The travellers were pulled into their groups, until only Nesh, Ash and Maddie were left, standing with the cart on a mat of soil, sand, and seaweed.

Chapter Twenty

It took Kerrig a week to get his new home laid out to his satisfaction, between his work for the other Earthers of the Island, and his visits to Maddie. He'd been given a stretch of hillside to shape to his needs, and had constructed a comfortable space for himself. All the Earther chiefs had asked in return was that Kerrig did his share of the communal workload. Farms, houses, and workrooms were all maintained by the community, and once again Kerrig found his ability with stone set him apart from his fellow-Earthers.

Fellow-Earthers who had not been quite as welcoming as Kerrig had hoped. He hadn't expected to be hailed as a long-lost son, but he had hoped for a bit of warmth; or at least recognition for his months-long journey across the land. So far, only the chiefs had asked about the Great Sanctuary - and then only to establish Kerrig's claim to have been born there. No-one seemed to care about the occupied mainland at all, except to be glad that they were away from it.

The other Elemental camps were no better, as Kerrig discovered when he went to visit his friends. Traegl wanted to know when the caravan was going to leave, and nearly pitched a fit when Kerrig said he wasn't sure if there was going to be a full-time caravan anymore.

'Unless there's a lot of interest from the others, we're looking at the occasional trading visit to the coastal towns, nothing more,' Kerrig told her.

Traegl's face fell, but she didn't argue.

'I don't suppose I'll stay here much longer anyway,' she said. 'Even if we don't go back on the road, I'll go and join Ash as soon as he's settled.'

Kerrig sent Traegl what he hoped was a concerned frown, rather than a disapproving one.

'Are you not happy here?'

The younger Marshlander gave him a crooked smile.

'If I wanted to weave grass huts, I'd have stayed in the Western Marshes,' she said. 'This sort of super-traditional life has never been for me. Sorry.'

'Don't be sorry, unless you regret it. We're none of us living the lives we're strictly "supposed" to, after all.' Kerrig shrugged, and added. 'Even without the Outsiders, I would likely never have come here. I'd have lived in the Sanctuary - or whatever it was called before the invasion - and spent my life crafting it into a thing of beauty. Something like the Crystal Caverns, maybe.'

Traegl nodded, but didn't seem very interested. Kerrig, lost in thought, didn't notice when he stopped speaking aloud. His mind turned to the Crystal Caverns, and all that had happened there. As bad as it was, he found that he could at least appreciate the beauty of the Caverns again, without being crushed by the sadness. So much had been lost, but the beauty remained.

Just as he was gearing up for a long, philosophical ramble, Traegl broke in to ask what he had planned for the day. Kerrig returned to the present with a mental jolt, and cast about for an answer. He remembered that he'd been on his way to visit the other members of the caravan, and said as much. The young Marshlander invited herself along and they set off for the Air Walkers' settlement, high in the hills.

As they approached, the wild gorse of the hills suddenly gave way to a perfectly manicured lawn, stretching unbroken in both directions around the curve of the hillside, and for several strides in front of them.

'Odd,' Kerrig said, as they walked towards the green stripe. 'I never pegged Air Walkers as fond of gardening.'

'Me neither,' Traegl said. 'The way my parents go on, you'd think only Marshlanders could be trusted to know a root from a stem.'

'What about Earthers?' Kerrig asked, lightly.

Traegl grinned. 'You guys can grow moss, and root vegetables. And make very nice rock gardens.'

Kerrig hoped the young Marshlander was joking, but before he could defend himself they were both lifted off their feet by a blast of air that dropped them outside the ring of green lawn.

'No walking on the grass!' bellowed an angry voice. For one, rather dazed moment, Kerrig wondered how the warden had come to be here. The Earther felt his arms move into the brace position on instinct, even as he struggled back to his feet.

When he stood up at last, he saw a tall, red-faced character who could not have looked less like the Avlem warden. But for all that, the two shared a voice that could make the sky shake around your ears.

The angry Air Walker floated over to them, glaring at the footprints they had left in the soft earth.

'Just look - look! - what you've done to this lawn. Years of work, crushed underfoot! State your business, or be off with you.'

'We've come to see our friends,' said Traegl. 'You know, the new arrivals? They travelled with us, and we've come to visit them. And if you don't want people walking on your lovely, well-watered, carefully planted grass, then you should really make a path or something.'

Kerrig knew then that Traegl had definitely been joking with him before, because this was her serious voice. The Air Walker didn't seem to notice, though. Instead, he turned to address Kerrig.

'You should teach your daughter better manners,' he said. 'Although by the looks of it, no-one ever taught you any, either. You're Earthers, aren't you? Or Marshlanders - I can never really tell the difference.'

'I'm an Earther, Traegl's a Marshlander,' Kerrig told him, bluntly. 'She's not my daughter, she's my friend. Just like Erben, whom we've come to visit. If you like, I can remove our footprints from your lawn. But, honestly, they're fading already. Grass is hardy stuff, you know.' The Earther and Marshlander exchanged glances. 'Or maybe you don't. Grass is a plant, after all.'

The Air Walker's face turned redder than ever, and he drew in a breath ready to shout again, when he was suddenly jerked backwards himself. Kerrig saw Erben and Sanwe coming down the hill, walking hand in hand. Erben waved to Kerrig and Traegl, and Sanwe's free hand was just coming down from tugging the angry Air Walker.

'Don't mind the self-appointed welcoming committee,' Sanwe said, her voice carrying on the air while she and Erben were still a good way off. 'He's got a thing about non-Air Walkers.'

The Air Walker couple strolled passed their new neighbour, and walked - very deliberately - over the grass to join their friends. 'Unfortunately, he's not the only one,' Erben told them. 'Let's find somewhere more peaceful to have our conversation.'

Sanwe beamed. 'Erben, that was almost a barb! I'm so proud of you!' To the others, she explained that the Air Walker chiefs here had set themselves up as masters of peace and tranquillity, because Air is meant to be 'above everything'. Sanwe said that watching them squabble over who can be the most tranquil was actually pretty funny, but that the joke got old fast.

They set off down the hill, towards the Fire Breathers' area, and Traegl asked after the other Air Walkers who'd come from Newharbour.

'There were only two others, in the end,' said Erben. 'That rather excitable kid - I think her name's Prakka, but she talks so fast it's hard to be sure - so, there's maybe-Prakka, and her great-uncle, who didn't give a name. The great-uncle was already full of Air Walker superiority, so he fits right in with the chiefs, but the girl was hoping for something a bit more mystical, I think. She keeps trying to reach 'perfect tranquillity', as if something special is going to happen when she does. I guess all San and I can do is be there for her when the bubble bursts.'

As he said this, the girl herself floated into view. She was sitting, eyes closed and legs crossed, drifting on the breeze. Sanwe and Erben both reached up at the same time, and caught her just before she drifted head-first into a tree.

Probably-Prakka opened her eyes to see four anxious faces peering down at her, and explained that she was trying to 'become at one with the wind', because it was the only way to 'truly understand' her Element. And Kerrig said there was a difference between understanding a mountain, and letting one crush you to death; and did she think Fire Breathers had to set light to themselves before they could 'understand' their Element? Or Marshlanders needed to drown? And what would she have done if Sanwe and Erben hadn't been around to pull her silly head out of a tree?

And Prakka pouted and said that if she'd truly become one with the wind she would have flowed through the leaves and branches like the very air. And now she was cross and bothered, and further from perfect tranquillity than ever, so she might as well come with them on their walk, because she was clearly not going to make any progress toward peace and tranquillity today.

Her mood improved when they reached the Fire Breathers' camp. While Kerrig didn't have any particular friends amongst the Fire Breathers since Volnar had left, the Earther still recognised those who had travelled with them. He and Erben went to seek them out, while Sanwe and Traegl went to keep an eye on Prakka, who had wandered over to a group of youngsters standing around a fire pit.

◆◆◆

'This "tranquillity" business is new, then?' asked Kerrig. 'I mean, it's not something you used to do up in the mountains?'

'No, it's something they came up with on this Island, as far as I know. I think it's based on some idea from the Sidrax Empire, actually. Pretty funny, that.'

'You Air Walkers just can't get enough of Sidria, eh? I mean, first joining up with them to betray and conquer the rest of us, and now adopting their philosophy. No wonder so many of you moved into Outsider towns. You must feel right at home with them.' Kerrig didn't even try to hide the bitterness in his tone.

Erben was silent for a long moment, his face burning darkly. Kerrig thought he was ashamed, but when he spoke, his voice was brimming with tightly controlled anger.

'So that's the way you lowlanders tell it, is it? Well, let me tell you what my grandfather told me. And afterwards, we can decide between us just who betrayed whom.'

The quiet Air Walker took a deep breath, then began.

'Tell me, Kerrig; would you say that Air Walkers were good fighters?'

'That depends on what you mean by "good",' Kerrig retorted. 'But, yes, you're certainly... effective.'

'We weren't always so "...effective",' Erben said, precisely mimicking Kerrig's phrasing. 'We didn't have to be. According to my grandfather's stories, we lived a peaceful life. We didn't fight, or even hunt. We fished in the lakes, kept goats, and traded with the Shanzir for all our other needs. It was an Air Walker who discovered that we can live on the energy given off by our Element. Not comfortably, but so long as we have water, our Element will stand in place of food, at least for a while. Life could be hard at times, but it was never harsh. We were a peaceful people, safe in our high mountains - until the Sidrax came.

'They swarmed us, destroying our homes and killing anyone who resisted them. We sent messages on the Air for our cousin Elements to come to our aid, but none of the People responded. Meanwhile, the Sidrax took the form of terrible monsters, like nothing the Land had ever known. Have you ever seen a bear? I've seen pictures, drawings by explorers that I can't quite believe. Creatures as big as a rhinoceros, but with claws and teeth, and able to stand on two legs like a person.'

A vision of the Sidrax captain flashed into Kerrig's mind, and he grimaced. 'I know what you mean,' he said, with feeling.

'According to my grandfather, the Air Walkers were given a choice: Join or die. Some refused, and were killed. Did you never wonder why, out of all the Peaks, only a few are inhabited? Clear Ice, White Ice, and Greening were pretty much the only villages that surrendered unconditionally, and the remnants of the other Peaks were just about able to make a new home in Lowridge. Once the youngest and strongest were conscripted into the army, many smaller villages died out within a generation. And, with the Shanzir gone, we could no longer trade for essentials. There are villages in the Peaks, even today, that only survive because of the goods their children send home with their army wages.

'And so the Air Walkers were rolled up into the Sidrax army, like many a conquered people before us - and like many of the People after us, too. Your friend Traegl joined up of her own free will, so I hear; and yet we're the traitors for failing to hold off the might of the Sidrax Empire single-handed.'

Erben stopped, and breathed steadily for a long moment. Kerrig didn't dare say a word.

'You know, I try to help Sanwe control her temper. My parents always said that it does no good to get angry, and I agree with them. But there are times when, if I let myself dwell on things, I understand why my wife rages at the world.'

Kerrig was trying to decide if, and how, to apologise, when a shout from Sanwe caught his attention.

'You children need to learn to be careful,' the older woman said, while Traegl spread water over

Prakka's shoulder. There was a scorch mark surrounding a small hole in the girl's dress, and the skin below seemed rather too red. Prakka kept telling the Marshlander that she was fine, and could just blow cold air over her shoulder until it felt better, but Traegl wouldn't move.

Kerrig sent his best frown at the youngsters around the fire pit, and quietly demanded to know what the shale just happened.

Everyone seemed rather confused about exactly what had happened, but they all agreed that Prakka had said adding air to fire made the fire better, and there had been an argument about the relative value of each Element, and then Prakka had pulled the air from the fire, until it was almost out, before letting it back into the flame, thereby 'proving' the superiority of air. And the Fire Breathers had made the fire roar, and dared Prakka to try and put this one out with her 'fancy airy tricks', and then Sanwe and Traegl tried to calm things down, and then there had been a lot of flying sparks and chips of firewood, and suddenly Prakka had a burned shoulder but it really wasn't anyone's fault and anyway she was okay, and everyone was really, really sorry and could we just forget about this now, please?

Erben suggested that if they wanted to have fun mixing Elements, they should go somewhere that wasn't surrounded by people and tents and other things that could get burned, soaked, crushed, and/or blown away. One of the Fire Breathers said she knew the perfect place, and led the way to a piece of scrubland that became a beach.

'We've got everything here,' she said, confidently. 'Air, Water, Earth, and plenty of fuel for our Fire. Let's go!'

Kerrig quickly scooped out a fire pit, and surrounded it with a ditch. Traegl filled the ditch with water, while the Fire Breathers scrambled to fetch dead branches and dry seaweed to burn. Prakka, Sanwe and Erben stood with Traegl, and Prakka experimented with pushing air into the water, and lifting up bits of water on discs of air. When the time came to light the fire, Kerrig ordered everyone to stand back.

'At the first sign of trouble, Traegl will drown the flames, and I'll collapse the pit,' he said. 'The Air Walkers and Fire Breathers will keep the hot air and sparks from burning anyone. Are we clear?'

One of the Fire Breathers threw a mock-salute and barked out, 'Yessir, Sir!' The other youngsters giggled, and did impressions of Kerrig for each other's amusement. Kerrig asked if this was 'signs of trouble', and the group sobered up quickly. Once everyone was safely in place, the fun began.

The Fire Breathers pulled the flames into different shapes, and the Air Walkers focused blasts of air into the fuel to create flashes of brilliant white light inside the orange flames. Traegl got interested, and threw drops of water at the flames to create a rhythmic pattern of hisses and sputters. Everyone was having fun, and Kerrig enjoyed watching them. After a while, a few of the Fire Breathers started to get tired, and dropped out to sit with Kerrig and watch the display.

The sun began to set, so Kerrig and Traegl rounded up the children and led them back to their respective homes. Everyone was smiling in that happy-tired way, and Prakka was floating again (eyes open this time) and beaming with delight.

'That was fun!' she declared, to the world at large. 'Why can't we always be like that, just people hanging out together and being awesome? Why we gotta split up and be all weird with each other?'

'It's a mystery,' Traegl agreed. 'And our biggest weakness, if you ask me. Ash says the only reason the Sidrax invaders got their foot in the door was because we were too busy fighting and resenting each other to put up much of a resistance.' The Marshlander gave a half-smile, and shrugged. 'It's weird to think about, isn't it? If our ancestors hadn't been so clannish, Ash and I might never have met.' The smile became a grin, and she added, 'I must remember to thank my grandparents.'

Chapter Twenty-One

The next day, after he finished his share of community work, Kerrig set off visiting again; this time towards the out-of-the-way area where Ash, Maddie, and Nesh had been put. But just as he was leaving, Balmar came hurrying over to say that Kerrig had been summoned by the Chiefs.

So it was a disgruntled Kerrig who reported to the Earther Chiefs' Hall, and what they had to say did nothing to improve his mood.

Kerrig had, it seemed, been letting the side down badly ever since he had arrived with his motley crew. Not content with bringing Outsiders to the one piece of the Land that was still free of them, Kerrig had been crossing back and forth over tribal lines.

'You've been through an ordeal, young Kerrig,' said one white-haired worthy, 'And we've tried to be understanding. But if you persist in this un-Eartherly behaviour, we will be forced to question your commitment to your people.'

Kerrig raised a derisive eyebrow. 'Question away. What is that to me?'

Another of the masked chiefs made a noise of displeasure and disbelief. 'It'll be something to you if we decide you're not an Earther. Only Earthers are allowed to live in this village, as your Outsider friends know.'

Kerrig almost laughed. 'Not an Earther? Of course I'm an Earther. You've all seen me working in this village, using my Element. What else could I be?'

One of the chiefs shrugged, and said, 'A particularly clever Sidrax, perhaps? An Avlem with some kind of earth-moving talent? Or something else entirely - there's a large world outside the borders of the Land, and all sorts have come here since the invasion began. There's more to being an Earther than just our Element, as you ought to know. To be a true Earther is to live by our laws, and respect our boundaries. What true Earther would leave their home and travel around like a Fire Breather? And no-one truly of the People would willingly consort with Outsiders. Amend your behaviour, young man, if you wish to remain an Earther.'

The part of Kerrig that still longed for the security of childhood wanted to duck his head and apologise profusely. After his mother had died the Chiefs of the Great Sanctuary had been his parents, and he would never have dared to cross them even when they weren't wearing their official masks. But that part of Kerrig had shrunk over the course of the last year, and another part had grown to replace it. The part that loved Maddie, and learned from Zirpa; that supported Ash and Traegl, and disagreed with Balmar. The part that dreamed of rekindling the ideals of the Shanzir.

Kerrig raised his head and looked the assembled Chiefs right in their masked eyes.

'You're right,' he said. 'There's more to being an Earther than having an affinity for Earth. Just like there's more to being the People of the Land than just living here. And I *am* an Earther.' Kerrig took a deep breath, then went on, 'But I'm not just an Earther, I'm of the People. I love the Land, and all the people in it - not just other Earthers, or even other Earthers who think like me.

'Earthers, Marshlanders, Fire Breathers, even Air Walkers - we're all the People of the Land. And when we forget that, we become weak. Weak enough for Outsiders to come in and take the Land from under us.

'The Marshlanders blame us for not supporting them, and we blame the Air Walkers for fighting against us, but who helped the Air Walkers when the invaders hit the Peaks? Where were we when the Fire Breathers were being driven from the Plains? We were standing in our own corner, thinking of no-one but ourselves.

'And now we've been driven onto this Island and given a chance to start again. But instead, we're re-making the Land in miniature; sitting in our corners, sneering at each other. What's it going to take to make us the People of the Land again, rather than the backward collection of tribal "Elementals" that the Outsiders see?'

Kerrig stopped, breathing as if he'd been holding up a mountain. There was a long silence.

The masked chiefs shifted uncomfortably, and whispers flowed from mask to mask. At last, one of the masks coughed.

'That's quite the speech, young Kerrig,' said one. 'So, according to you, we've been going about things all wrong for a hundred years. And you're going to put it all to rights, I suppose?'

'Me? Great strata, I hope not. Being in charge of getting the caravan across the Land in one piece was enough for me. All I want is to be free to visit my friends, and for them to be free to come here, without anyone accusing us of betraying our Elements.'

The white-haired worthy 'hmm'd thoughtfully, and said. 'You believe that if the tribes had united, we would have defeated the Outsiders?'

Kerrig smiled. 'I believe that the People united could do almost anything.'

After being dismissed by the Earther Chiefs, Kerrig followed his original plan and went to visit Nesh, Ash, and Maddie. Traegl was there when he arrived, sitting apart with Maddie and Ash. It was a fetching and domestic tableau, which Nesh was watching fondly.

She greeted Kerrig without turning her head, and waved him over to sit next to her. The Earther made himself a seat between the family group on one side, and Nesh on the other. They sat in a companionable silence for a while, until Maddie noticed her 'Stony-Man' and came running over to hug him.

'Where have you been?' she said, into his tunic. 'It was days and days!'

Kerrig patted her hair, and said, 'I know, Little One. I'm sorry. Are you having fun here with Ash and Traegl? Learning about your shapes?'

Maddie chatted happily about what she was learning, and made her hands into different shapes to show off her progress. Kerrig still thought that looked weird, but he smiled anyway, and told her she had clearly been working very hard.

Kerrig and Maddie went to sit with Nesh, leaving Ash and Traegl to lean towards each other and talk in low voices.

'They're sweet together, aren't they?' said Nesh.

Kerrig nodded, then frowned. 'They've got a lot of problems ahead, though. People are going to have... *opinions.*'

Nesh raised her eyebrows at him. 'And what's your opinion?' she asked.

'I'm happy for them. Really. Even if it means I'm no longer considered an Earther.'

Kerrig bit his tongue, but it was too late. Of course, Nesh wanted to know what he meant by 'no longer being considered an Earther', and Kerrig ended up telling her everything. She listened in silence, her expression flickering between horror and pity.

'Kerrig, that's... I... I'm not going to try and tell you what to do,' she said. 'But your Chiefs calling you 'no longer an Earther', that sounds like, well, like what happened to me. And I don't want that to happen to you, if I can help it. So, if you have to stop coming here, or if we 'Outsiders' have to leave this island, then that's OK. I know how much it means to you, being with your own people.'

'Do you regret it?' Kerrig asked.

'What?'

'Whatever it was you did that got you banished, or disowned, or whatever. Would you still have done it, knowing the consequences?'

Nesh looked blank for a moment, then shook her head. 'I don't regret it,' she said. 'I could perhaps have been more careful, but my "crime"? I would do it again in a heartbeat. It was the right thing to do.'

'Then you understand my position,' Kerrig said. 'I've spent my life wishing for someone to set back time, put things back to how they used to be, but now... the Land I've seen this year can't go anyway but forward, and it's foolish to try and hide from that.' He shrugged and admitted that he could have been more careful himself, rather than calling the assembled Earther Chiefs weak to their faces.

'I was talking about myself really, but it probably sounded pretty bad,' the big Earther said. 'And I may have implied that I wasn't going to fix their problems for them, and they should get off their masked backsides and sort things out for themselves.' He dropped his head into his hands and groaned quietly.

'I'm going to get banished, I just know it. Me and my big mouth. This is why I stopped talking to the guards and prisoners back in the Mines - I'd say what I really thought, and get beaten up for it.'

Nesh looked surprised. 'You've never had a problem telling me what was on your mind,' she said.

Kerrig looked up and gave a small smile. 'You weren't scary enough,' he said. 'Just annoying.'

'And right,' Nesh added. 'Well, mostly.'

'Like I said: annoying.'

Nesh laughed and punched Kerrig lightly in the shoulder. 'Did you always have a sense of humour under that crusty shell?' she said, lightly. But Kerrig was rubbing his arm and frowning.

'How did you do that?' he asked. 'My arm's gone to sleep, and all you did was tap me in the shoulder.'

Nesh smirked. 'Just proving a point. I can be scary enough when I need to be - I just Find the best place to land a hit.'

'OK, you're scary,' Kerrig acknowledged. 'I'm glad none of the guards had that Talent, back when I was still mouthing off at them.'

'You're missing the point, Kerrig. Again.' Nesh gave him a wry smile. 'I could have done that, and worse, at any time. You've been downright idiotic sometimes, and I've been sorely tempted to try and smack some sense into your head more than once. But I didn't, because that's not who I am. So you can go on speaking your mind without fear. And, if the worst happens, you can always come and live with us. Traegl's already as good as moved in, and one more won't make any difference.'

Maddie, who had wandered off to make shapes, came running back at that.

'Yes, stay here!' she said, reverting to her child-shape so she could hug Kerrig properly. 'My Stony-Man, and Nesh-Lady, and Teacher-Ash, and me, all together. And the Marshy-Lady too, of course. She's nice.'

Kerrig laughed and hugged Maddie back. 'Alright, Little One, I'll stay for a while. But you know I'll always be your Stony-Man, no matter where I live.'

'I know.' sighed Maddie, happily.

◆

Kerrig visited them daily for two weeks, coming to the Earther village only to sleep and work. He was careful to be efficient and thorough in every task, not wanting to give the Chiefs any legitimate reason to disparage him. The fact that, a year ago, he would have considered 'fraternising with Outsiders' a perfectly legitimate reason to banish someone was something that Kerrig tried not to think about.

Maddie made a habit of coming to meet him in the afternoon, once his work was done for the day. The other Earthers were not very happy about this at first, but the little Sidrax proved very difficult to dislike. It helped that sly digs and insults went clear over her head, and she soon had half the village convinced that she really was a child. Her 'shapes' still made them unhappy, but Maddie liked to be in her child-shape when walking with Kerrig, so that she could tell him all about her day as they walked.

Kerrig was walking with Maddie one afternoon when a young girl from the village came running up behind them, calling for 'Mr. Kerrig' to stop.

The girl said that the Chiefs had sent for him, and she'd gone to his house but he wasn't there, and someone had seen him leave with Maddie and said which way they went, and she'd run to catch up with them, and Kerrig had to come now because it had taken her forever to find him and the Chiefs were waiting, and it was bad to keep the Chiefs waiting.

She said all this through gasping breaths, and Kerrig tried not to smile at her eagerness. He remembered being just as frantically eager-to-please at that age. So instead, he agreed that it was bad to keep people waiting, and he would be sure to apologise to the Chiefs when he saw them, and to tell them what a quick and clever messenger she had been.

Kerrig asked Maddie to go on without him, and to tell Nesh and Ash about being called to see the Chiefs. He said Nesh would understand, and that he would come and visit later. Maddie smiled and nodded, then changed into her donkey-shape and trotted home happily.

The two Earthers walked back to the village, and Kerrig reported to the Chiefs. They were seated in a rough semicircle, as before, wearing their ceremonial masks. Kerrig was surprised to see another figure in the room, seated at one end of the line, wearing a mask that he didn't recognise.

'Ah, Kerrig, at last. This is a Chief of the Marshlanders on the Island. I trust you have a good reason for your tardiness.'

'Apologies, honoured Chiefs,' Kerrig said. 'I was-'

'We trust that you have a good reason,' echoed another mask. 'We don't need to hear it.'

'There have been discussions,' said another. 'The Chiefs have met, and shared your idea about uniting the Elements. It has taken a while, but there are now more Chiefs in favour of your plan than against it.'

'My plan?' echoed Kerrig, awkwardly. 'What plan?'

'I told you: to unite the People, and destroy the Outsiders once and for all.'

Kerrig felt as though a tunnel had just collapsed on his head.

'What? I never said anything about destroying anyone! Why would you... How could you get that from what I said?'

The masks made a variety of surprised and annoyed noises. One said, 'You told us that you believed the People could have resisted the invaders if we'd stood together. So, now we're going to stand together; and finally throw those filthy Outsiders out of the Land once and for all!'

Kerrig dug his toes into the ground and tried very hard not to bring the Council Chamber down on the heads of the assembled Chiefs. He bowed instead, and addressed his next words to the ground between them.

'Honoured Chiefs, you are older than I am, so I know you must remember the wars of the invasion. It was a terrible time, with much pain and death. I was only a child, but I remember the scars it left on my tribe. I remember that it took my parents, along with many others. Why would you want another war, against the children and grandchildren of the ones who wronged us? The People can be united without having to go to war for it. Our travelling caravan proved that much.'

A new mask spoke up. 'Your travelling group only came together in the first place because you were united against an enemy, according to your own account. Nothing brings a group together like shared danger.'

'No-one's suggesting we rampage through the Land, burning Outsider villages to the ground,' said another, with withering scorn. 'We're just going to get rid of that ugly monstrosity they call the Citadel. Surely you don't support the Outsiders ruling over our Land? You want to see the People free to govern ourselves again?'

'Well, of course,' Kerrig said, automatically. Home rule was one of those dreams that all the People shared, no matter their age or Element.

'Then that's settled. As you said, when the People are united, we can do anything - even drive out the invaders. And since all the Chiefs have now agreed to this, we can move on to the next step.'

Kerrig looked at the assembled masks. 'All the Chiefs?' he asked. 'Are the Fire Breather and Air Walker Chiefs here as well?'

The Marshlander mask turned to the nearest Earther mask and exchanged a Look.

'Of course not,' said a mask somewhere near the middle. 'That's why the Marshlander Chief is here - to bring the Air Walkers' view. And we have spoken to the Fire Breathers, to get their opinion. And, in principle, the Chiefs are in favour of the Elements working more closely together. But that doesn't mean letting Air Walkers into our homes.

'Now that we're all agreed, we'll head to a piece of neutral ground to work out the details. Kerrig, you'll be there to represent your travelling caravan, and advise on the difficulties of working with multiple Elements. The best place would be the place where your Outsider friends have made a temporary camp. Naturally, we'll wait for them to leave. Will they be ready to go in a day or so, do you think?'

Kerrig frowned again. 'They've settled there, I don't think they're planning to leave. When we arrived, everyone said that no-one was using that piece of land.'

'It wasn't being used then, but now we need it. You understand that, don't you? In the interests of peace?'

The Earther sighed, and nodded his acceptance. 'I'll go and talk to them,' he promised.

•◆•

Kerrig emerged into the late afternoon sunshine to find Nesh waiting for him.

'Hello, Nesh,' he said. The weight of the uncomfortable meeting began to lift, and he smiled at her.

She wasn't smiling.

'Have you been waiting long?' Kerrig asked.

'Not at all,' replied the Avlem. 'I got here just in time to hear all about your idea for driving out the invaders, and how you were going to talk to us about giving up our new home, because your leaders need a place to discuss the best way to go to war with our leaders.'

Kerrig felt ill. 'Nesh, believe me, it's not like that,' he said.

She didn't look convinced. 'I suppose I should congratulate you on still being an Earther,' she said. 'Don't worry about talking to us, we'll be leaving this island just as soon as I can Find a way.'

She turned and walked away, then looked back over her shoulder. 'I'll tell Maddie you said goodbye. Traegl will probably come with us, so give her any messages you have for Ash or Maddie.'

'Nesh, wait - I'll come and talk to them myself.'

Kerrig started after her, but the Avlem held up her fists.

'Don't make me stop you, Earther,' she said. 'You people put us "Outsiders" aside because we're

233

not welcome in your homes. And now, you're not welcome in ours. Go back to your war, Kerrig of the Last Sanctuary. You never really left it.'

Chapter Twenty-Two

True to her word, Nesh, Ash, and Maddie were gone from their home when Kerrig went to look for them the next day. He'd hoped that a night's rest would have cooled the Avlem's temper enough to let him put his case, but the three 'Outsiders' seemed to have disappeared overnight.

Kerrig went to tell the Earther Chiefs, who commended him on his prompt action. Within days, he was summoned to the meeting in the newly-vacated house, sitting mostly below ground-level. Nesh and Ash had packed up everything they'd brought with them. Only the bare walls and furniture remained, left over from the first Earther settlers to come to the Island. Kerrig recognised the chairs, tables, and beds raised from the ground, and the shelves shaped from the walls.

Each party of Chiefs had brought a 'non-Chief' representative with them. Kerrig looked around for the Earther representative for a bit before realising that it was him. How was he supposed to represent the Earthers of the Island? He'd barely spoken to any of them, outside of what was necessary for working together. He eyed the other representatives, and got eyed back in turn. No-one seemed entirely sure what they were doing there, and opposing Elements were facing each other uneasily.

The first order of business was to reshape the meeting place to satisfy everyone's needs. The house was demolished and turned into an open-topped ring, with each Elemental party creating their preferred environment. This took up most of the morning, and resulted in some displays of competitive architecture between the Earther and Marshlander groups, much to the disdain of the Fire Breathers and Air Walkers.

At last, the talks began, and Kerrig tried to follow the discussion. It wasn't easy. At any one time, there seemed to be at least three separate points being argued at once. Nobody could agree on the best way to attack the Citadel (although they all wanted the place to be brought down). There was disagreement even between Chiefs of the same Element, and between Chiefs and the representatives with them. Kerrig eventually gave up, and went to sit at a distance from the squabbling.

He dropped his head into his hands and sighed. Over the years, Kerrig had imagined many ways in which the People might rise up against their oppressors. He'd never thought that he would be part of it himself, but he'd also never thought it would be so... petty. It ought to have been a day of glorious ambitions and rousing speeches, not a verbal brawl.

How are we supposed to govern the whole Land, if we can't even get a score of individuals to agree on things? Despite everything, Kerrig still wanted to believe that the Earthers, his people, were fundamentally noble and good. It was physically painful to feel that belief shatter, and for a long time Kerrig could only sit and stare at nothing.

When he sat up at last, Kerrig saw that Nesh was there, sitting on a fallen log barely three strides away. He offered her a tentative smile, and she nodded in return. Peaceful relations restored, perhaps? The Earther certainly hoped so.

'I thought you'd left,' Kerrig said, trying to sound casual. 'I'm glad you're still on the Island.'

'Really?' Nesh said, coolly. 'I didn't know you cared. We found a place to stay, for now. Until someone comes to move us along, at least.'

Kerrig's temper, already roughened by his fellow Elementals, suddenly flared up.

'Yes, I imagine it wasn't too nice to be kicked out of your home for someone else's convenience,' he said. 'Not that the People would know anything about that, of course. What a unique and distressing experience that must have been!'

Nesh rolled her eyes. 'Not this again,' she said. 'Don't you ever get tired of hearing yourself complain? And what are you doing out here, anyway? Shouldn't you be at the War Council meeting? Sitting on Maddie's old bed and working out how you're going to destroy her family?'

'Oh, for the love of... We're not going to destroy anyone's families,' Kerrig said. 'This is about the Citadel, the ruling elite. We're just taking back what's ours, and showing the governors that they can't push the People around any longer!'

'So, you only want to take down the Citadel?'

'Yes!'

'The Citadel where Volnar lives?'

'Yes! I mean, no - not Volnar's home, of course. This isn't about the ordinary citizens, it's about justice. You need to see the bigger picture!'

'The "bigger picture" gets ordinary citizens killed,' Nesh retorted. Both their voices had been rising with their tempers, but suddenly the Avlem became quiet.

'Don't go rushing into this thinking no-one's going to get hurt,' she said. 'If you fight, people will die - and not just the "bad" people, either. How many ordinary citizens' lives will you pay to get rid of us

"Outsiders", Kerrig? What's your precious Land worth, in blood?'

'I don't know,' Kerrig replied, matching her tone chill for chill. 'How much did your ancestors shed taking it the first time? If they give it back, there won't be any fighting. The People have never been the aggressors, not in this whole, sorry history.'

Nesh sighed and shook her head. 'I thought we'd got past this sort of "us and them" talk, Kerrig. What happened to living peacefully, and sharing the land?'

'You'd have to ask the Shanzir,' replied the Earther, bitterly. 'And don't talk about "getting past things" as though I were a child throwing a tantrum. Do you seriously expect the People to just forget what you've done to us? Shrug off genocide, and a century of oppression? You don't get past something like that.'

'I was talking about *you*, Kerrig,' she said. 'Not all Elementals, or even all Earthers. I thought that *you* had started to see past... to see beyond labels and bloodlines. Ash, Maddie, and even me - you were treating us as people when we were travelling together. What changed?'

'Nothing changed,' said Kerrig, unconvincingly. 'You're still alright, at least when you're not defending the indefensible. No-one's going to hurt you. You can even have your house back, once the meetings are finished. This isn't about you, it's about them. The armies, and governors. We're taking back our homeland, and you're treating it like a personal attack!'

'Of course it's personal!' Nesh said, her voice rising again. 'If it's not personal, then it's meaningless. You can't fight an abstract idea, Kerrig. When you declare war on the Citadel, people are going to get hurt. And that *will* be personal, no matter how high-minded you try to make it sound.'

◆

Kerrig stormed back to the meeting full of indignation and purpose. He'd hoped, after all this time, that Nesh would have overcome her Avlem-tainted view of history and come to accept the truth. Well, so be it. If she wouldn't listen to him, maybe the Chiefs would.

Kerrig marched to the edge of the meeting space and stared at the chaos. The arguments had split the assembly into smaller and smaller groups, each containing no more than three people, all arguing at once.

The big Earther stamped his foot, shaking the ground enough to get the attention of everyone, even the floating Air Walkers. The Earther Chiefs glared at him, but Kerrig was too angry to be intimidated.

'Stop this petty bickering at once,' he barked, fixing each attendee in turn with a look of withering disapproval. 'You shame the Land with your childishness! Is anyone here serious about standing against the Citadel, or is this just an excuse to fight amongst yourselves?'

'Mind your place, Earther,' said one of the Marshlander Chiefs. 'You are here as an adviser, nothing more.'

'No, sir,' Kerrig replied. 'Respectfully, I am here to make plans for freeing the Land from the rule of Outsiders. And, to judge by the state of the discussions so far, I am the only one here interested in doing so. Anyone who would like to join me is welcome. The rest of you can go back to your personal squabbles.'

Kerrig closed his eyes and took a careful breath. Losing your temper with authority never helped, he'd learned that well enough. But that was in the Mines, the desecrated sanctuary, a place this self-righteous idiot couldn't begin to understand. With a carefully moderated tone, Kerrig tried to explain anyway.

'For most of my life, until this year, no-one used my name. I was "Earther 27". Do you know what that means?'

One of the Earther chiefs shifted, uncomfortably.

'Yes, I know about the tribe that lo- that got trapped in the fallen sanctuary. You must have had a tough time of it, and I didn't mean to imply-'

'No,' Kerrig interrupted, 'Do you *understand* what that means, "Earther 27"? I was the Earther of sector 27; on my own, just me. I was responsible for that sector; I had to keep everyone alive, and safe, and I had to protect as much of my people's ancient architecture as I could, all by myself. And all the while, Outsiders ripped into the Border Cliffs; using brute force to do in months what should have taken decades. It should have taken whole families of Earthers generations to create hallways of beauty, deep underground. Instead it was hacked at by people who didn't know anything about Earth, or the Land, or our history, or our culture. They only knew that those cliffs contained valuable ores, so they tore them open.

'And all I could do was try to protect what was left until you free Earthers - and I had faith that you must exist - you free Earthers would come and rescue us. I knew you had to be out here, working as tirelessly as I was, but you weren't, were you? You were sitting around complaining about who got to be in charge, and who got the nicest home, and how much you disliked all the other Elements. And you know what? I did a lot of complaining too; about the Outsiders, the prisoners, the failings of other sectors, you name it. For years, I complained because I thought there was nothing else I *could* do. I was alone.

'You had homes, families, names - you had it all. I had sector 27. And it wasn't any of you who saved me from that in the end; it was an Avlem, a Fire Breather, and a Sidrax child.'

Everyone was staring at him, but Kerrig couldn't have stopped now for anything. A volcano had erupted in his heart, and decades of rage flowed from his lips.

'*Never,*' he said, 'Never tell me that I'm not an Earther, that I don't appreciate what that means. It means caring for this Land, all of it; whether it's a corner of an invaded and occupied mine, or an island.

'They called it "The Last Sanctuary", you know, before the Outsiders turned it into prison mines. But this Island really is a sanctuary. You could have done so much, but all you've done is dig yourselves in and wait for Time to fix things. Don't you know that Time only moves forwards? We're never going to get life as it was. But, if we work together, perhaps we can try for life as it should be.'

It took several days, and more than a little bickering, but eventually the Chiefs and their advisers put together a battle plan.

The meeting space was cleared away, and Kerrig looked for Nesh, Maddie and Ash to tell them that they could have their home back. But no matter how hard he searched, he couldn't find any sign of them. He felt a pang of regret at not seeing Maddie, but perhaps it was worth it to avoid another showdown with Nesh.

Chapter Twenty-Three

Making the plans had been hard enough, but carrying them out took months. Slowly, secretly, the Islanders ferried materials and people to a base camp on the mainland, carefully chosen to be both near the Citadel and hidden from all major roads. From there, it would be a half-day's march to the Citadel itself.

Kerrig had stayed on the Island at first, overseeing things and updating the plan with the Chiefs. By the time he got to the mainland base camp, it was well-established. The Chiefs who had gone ahead to set it up asked Kerrig to look it over, and he was impressed with what he found. The Earthers and Marshlanders had taken a wooded valley and turned it into a small fort, with defensive fire pits dotted all around. He walked the perimeter in the company of another Earther and a Marshlander, admiring the way they had used the trees to hide the camp from the road and the air alike.

'Are you sure no-one will come this way?' Kerrig asked. The other Earther invited him to reach through the soil and see if he could sense anyone nearby.

Kerrig tried it. 'Nothing but animals,' he said, impressed. 'As long as they are animals, and not Sidrax in disguise.'

'Oh, we don't need to worry about that,' said the Marshlander, confidently. 'The Air Walkers have this trick where they can sort of whisper at people to stay away. I don't know how it works, exactly, but-'

'Never mind,' Kerrig cut in, quickly. 'I've seen it before. Not a nice trick, but I suppose at least this time they're using it for the good of the People.'

'Still creepy though, right?' said the other Earther, and Kerrig couldn't help but agree.

They had only walked on a little further, when a large, black bird fell out of the sky and nearly landed on Kerrig's head. He caught the creature instinctively, and then recognised it.

'Ash?' he said. 'How did you get here?' Kerrig laid the bird on the ground, where it changed into a young man.

The Marshlander and other Earther leapt back in alarm and fumbled for their weapons. Kerrig put himself between his nervous companions and the unconscious Sidrax, and glared until the weapons were lowered.

'I know this man,' Kerrig said. 'He's no threat to us.' *Or anyone, in that state.*

Ash groaned, and Kerrig was at his side in a moment.

'What is it? Ash, stay with me. What did you need to say?'

'Why would he need to say anything? Except "ouch", maybe?' asked the Marshlander.

'He changed shape,' Kerrig said, without looking round. 'That takes effort, but this shape is one of the few that can use speech. He must have wanted to tell us something.' The Earther moulded the earth around the fallen Sidrax, then cut the shaped layer free of the ground. The other Earther saw his plan, and came forward to help.

'How come you know so much about Shifters?' she asked.

'Sidrax,' corrected Kerrig, absently. The two Earthers rose to their feet, carefully lifting the stretcher of earth. 'I spent the better part of a year with Ash and Maddie; you can't help learning a few things. I learned about other Elements too. Did you know that Fire Breathers control their Element by touching the heat of a flame, not the flame itself?'

The Earther knew he was babbling, but couldn't help himself. Anything to take his mind off how pale Ash had gone.

'Ugh, Fire Breathers,' said the Marshlander. 'I'm not surprised they couldn't shut up about their Element. Honestly, those guys are the worst. When are they going to realise that nobody likes them?'

The two Earthers exchanged glances, but the younger one shook her head.

'Don't ask,' she advised Kerrig. 'And, speaking of people nobody likes, where are we going to take this one? I can't imagine the Chiefs will be too happy about having some random Sidrax in the camp. I mean, we are kinda, mostly, y'know... at war with them?'

Kerrig blinked. 'But... this is Ash,' he said. 'The Chiefs know him - he lived on the Island for a while. He's not just some random Sidrax, he's a friend. And he's hurt.'

The Marshlander and younger Earther didn't look convinced. Fortunately, Ash chose that moment to come round.

'Trae,' he said, weakly. 'Take me to Trae, and Nesh. I have to tell them... not safe...'

◆◆◆

After some arguing on all sides, the youngsters went back to the camp, and Kerrig set off with Ash to find Traegl and Nesh. The Sidrax gave Kerrig a direction, then used the last of his energy to change to his mongoose form. The Earther carried Ash carefully in his hands, trying to shield him from any sudden movements.

He was unconscious again before long, and Kerrig worried about missing the right place, but he soon caught sight of Nesh, walking determinedly towards them.

Kerrig called out to her, and the Avlem changed course slightly to meet him. She frowned as they drew near, and didn't stop until she was almost nose-to-nose with Kerrig.

'You've got a nerve, coming here,' she said, then seemed to notice Ash for the first time.

'What have you done? No, I don't care. Give him here.'

Kerrig opened his hands in surrender, and Nesh gently picked Ash up. But the little creature flinched at her touch, and curled his tail around Kerrig's wrist. The Avlem took the hint, but she didn't look happy about it.

'This way, then,' said Nesh. 'But only because of Ash. And I don't want to hear anything about your war effort.'

Kerrig nodded and followed the Avlem silently. She led them through what looked like a solid hedge, twisting and turning sharply in strange places. They came out in a clearing, where Traegl was sitting and stroking the ears of a very familiar donkey.

Maddie's ears shot up at the sight of Kerrig, and she ran over to him, changing shape as she went. With only a slight stumble as she transitioned from four legs to two, the girl went to throw her arms around her 'Stony-Man'. But when she saw what he was holding, she hesitated.

'That's Ash,' she said. 'Why is he asleep? Is he hurt?'

Ash stirred in Kerrig's hands, and blinked his eyes open. The Earther laid the little body gently on the ground, then stood back to give the Sidrax room to change forms. Sure enough, a man-shaped Ash was soon lying there, looking up at four, concerned faces.

"M only hurt a little, kiddo,' he mumbled. Traegl knelt down beside her lover and kissed him gently. He smiled up at her, but winced as her hands brushed his bruises.

'You were right, Trae,' he said. 'It was stupid to go in alone. But it would have been worse for all of us to go. I only escaped because I have an undocumented lizard form. Thank young Maddie for that.'

Maddie smiled, although she looked confused, too.

'You had to escape? But why? You were only delivering a message.'

Ash grimaced. 'An unpopular one, by the reception. And the governors don't like being disturbed, it seems. Even getting to the main tower was difficult. I tried flying straight in, and got netted right out of the air.'

'Why were you carrying messages to the Citadel at all?' asked Kerrig. 'I know that you weren't trying to re-enlist just in time to fight against us. So what was it?'

'It was a sort of... semi-official letter,' said Ash. 'Requesting an audience with the governors. Nesh thought, I mean, we all thought - we all agreed, that if we could talk to them, then...'

The younger man wilted under Kerrig's level stare. His bruised face lent pathos to his sad eyes, and the Earther switched his attack to the mastermind of the scheme.

'So,' he said to Nesh, 'You thought you'd go and have a quiet word with the governors. Maybe give them a warning? Tell them the natives are getting ideas again, and they should act now to stop us?'

'Don't be ridiculous,' said Nesh. 'And I wasn't asking them to talk to me, I was asking them to talk to you. I mentioned that, as a fellow Avlem, I believed the grievances to be legitimate, and that being governors meant ruling for all the people of this land, not just the privileged few.'

'And you sent Ash to deliver your diplomatic message, brokering peace in a war that is not yours.' Kerrig gestured towards the injured Sidrax, where he lay. 'What did you expect?'

'Hey, I volunteered,' Ash said. 'Don't get stroppy with Nesh, she was only trying to help. I was the one who messed up.'

Traegl went in for a light slap, then changed her mind and ruffled his hair instead. 'Stop hogging all the guilt, idiot. You're good, but even I don't think you're perfect,' she said. 'Now, why don't you tell your story, love? Let's have your daring exploits in detail.'

Ash sat up carefully, and gave Traegl a wry grin.

'You know me far too well,' he told her. 'Well, like I said, I was flying in from the north wall. It should have been easy - drop the letter near someone in uniform, and let them deliver it. I dropped the letter alright, but before I could get away, I was netted right out of the air.'

'How was you netted?' asked Maddie. 'You was being a bird, not a fish.'

'They've got catapults,' Ash said. 'Like big crossbows, but they don't shoot arrows, they shoot rocks.'

Maddie flinched and brushed her hand over her leg.

'Arrows hurt,' she said. 'Do rocks hurt, too?'

'Yeah, probably,' Ash replied, with forced brightness. 'I wouldn't know, I dodged 'em all.' Then his face fell and he added, 'Too bad I didn't dodge the net they were tied to.

'I went down like a... well, like a rock. I was lucky with the landing - only got bruised, not broken. Then the guards found me, and I stopped being lucky.'

Ash shuddered, and leaned into Traegl's side. 'I knew some of them, Trae,' he said. 'Garbrat, Lembok - we trained together. I tried to tell them about the letter, but they found it and burned it in front of me, then...' He shook his head, and the unfinished sentence hung in the air like smoke.

'In the end, they threw me into a cell. It was dark, only lit by one small window, too small for my hawk form, and too high up to reach as a mongoose. I guess Lem, or one of them, must have known I trained in small forms. But they didn't know that I'd learned a new one since leaving the army - and it's all thanks to Maddie.'

He smiled at the little Sidrax. 'Remember when we practised being lizards?' he said. 'What I said about how to become smaller?'

Maddie thought for a moment, then replied, 'You said to practice. And I still can't get all the way little, like a real li'lzard. Li-zard,' she corrected herself, carefully.

'And I, being the show-off that I am,' continued Ash, 'practised making my lizard forms smaller and smaller. And some lizards, it turns out, can walk up walls.'

Kerrig was impressed, despite himself. 'You walked out of your cell?'

Ash looked smug, and changed into a tiny lizard right in front of them. He ran up Traegl's arm and kissed her on the cheek, making her squeak with surprise. He was fast, but not quite fast enough to avoid pay-back. Traegl picked him up by the tail and dropped him in a puddle.

'Show-off,' she said, not without affection. 'Stop messing about and finish your story. I take it you didn't simply run for the walls, like a sensible person?'

Lizard-Ash blinked up at them for a long moment before changing shape. 'You have no idea how huge you all are,' he said. 'I ran up the wall, through the window, and down for a bit, but I couldn't begin to tell where I was, or which direction led to safety. For all I knew, I was running right back towards the guards. And I was still sore from the... well, never mind. Anyway, the point is, I was lost. And I didn't dare change forms, because all my others were known. I'd be recognised and caught again, and kept in a box this time - assuming I was kept at all.

'I found a corner to hide in, and tried to make sense of what I could see, smell, and hear. Did you know lizards can see heat? And we need it, too - even hiding in shadows made me cold. So cold, I could hardly stay awake. And then night fell.'

Trae stroked his hair gently. 'I was worried,' she confessed. 'You should have been back within hours, and I knew you couldn't fly well at night. I kept the fire burning bright until dawn, in case you needed a beacon.'

Ash smiled at her. 'You're my beacon,' he said, with such sincerity that Kerrig looked away and pretended not to have heard.

'Hush, you,' said Traegl, grinning. 'You're embarrassing the grown-ups. So, where were you, while I was sitting up all night stewing beside the fire?'

'I was beside a fire of my own,' Ash said. 'Or rather, a fire belonging to someone we all know and miss. My little lizard body was freezing, and I made a dash for the nearest, hottest thing I could sense. I was back to being lucky, I guess, because I stumbled into a potter's workshop. And who should I find tending the kiln but young Volnar.'

After the expected exclamations, Ash resumed his story. 'Yes, he's doing well. Very well, in fact. His shop is in the inner ring, and it's stone-built. He and Mashpa are doing very nicely for themselves; they've got a real business going there. He told me all about it over dinner, and I caught him up on our adventures. And I told him he should get out of the Citadel before the attack - and get his friends out too, if he could. Sorry, Kerrig, but I had to warn him. He saved my life, and even smuggled me to the wall at first light. I had to say something.'

The Earther assured the younger man that it was quite alright. After all, they wanted to strike against the Citadel, not the People.

'Kerrig, I don't think you understand,' Ash said, earnestly. 'About half the people living in the Citadel are Elementals. And it's a busy, crowded place. There's no way to fight in there without hurting innocent bystanders.'

He took a deep breath, then said, 'When I left the Island with Maddie and Nesh, it was because we were all "Outsiders", not because I wanted to leave. And Trae, bless her loyal heart, came because of me. I didn't have any strong opinion either way on your argument with Nesh; I've been a soldier, and I know that there are times when violence is the only answer. But now that I've seen the Citadel... I'm sorry, Kerrig. You're my friend, but Nesh is right. Trying to take that place by force, is only going to get a lot of people killed, and the governors won't be in that count.'

◆◆◆

The four adults talked, and argued, all afternoon. Maddie wandered around, alternately practising her 'shapes', and sitting beside her 'Stony-Man'. The periodic presence of the child kept Kerrig from giving in to his temper, and as the sun was setting, the four came to an agreement.

'Talking to the governors is a good idea,' the Earther conceded. 'But I still say you had no right to speak for the People without asking.'

'Agreed,' Nesh said. 'I apologise. Shall we take this to the Chiefs, or do you think they would rather come here?'

'Why not meet halfway?' said Traegl. 'That way, we both get to keep our "secret locations" secret. Even though I think it's all a bit silly: Ash has already been near to yours, and you've seen ours.'

'Sometimes we need to be a bit silly,' Ash told her. 'But now, I think it's time to try being sensible, too.'

A familiar, unwelcome, voice broke in from overhead.

'Now then, where's the fun in being sensible?' said Falerian.

◆◆◆

The Air Walker grinned at them as she floated just out of reach. 'Calm down, chickees, it's alright. Yes, I heard everything (and what a story!) but trust me, if I wanted to spill your secrets to the Citadel, I'd already be halfway there. No, all I want is to join in with the fun.'

'Trust you?' snorted Traegl. 'Not likely. Not after the stunt you pulled with Camp so-called-Freedom. Go back to wherever you hide out when you aren't stabbing your friends in the back.'

'Friends? Are we really friends, Trae-Trae? Oh I'm so happy you think so. Best friends? Or is that privilege reserved for darling Ashie now?'

'So, what *did* happen at the river, if you weren't sending us into a trap?' said Kerrig.

'Well I didn't know it was a trap, did I? All they told me was that if I ever found Elementals who weren't happy about Outsiders, I should send them to Camp Freedom. It was supposed to be this little island paradise. I was ever so cross when I found out what it really was. I caught up with the army again, and the smelly, dirt-for-brains colonel wouldn't even see me! The nerve! Serves him right if I pull his silly Citadel down around his ears.'

'But you can't, can you?' said Nesh. 'So you want us to do it for you. Too bad, Miss Falerian. We're not your personal attack force.'

'But we could be allies,' said Kerrig, trying to play the voice of reason. 'After all, if she wants to fight the Citadel, then she's on our side. Anyway, we should let the Chiefs decide. As you pointed out, Nesh, you don't want any part of this. Come on, Falerian. The camp's this way.'

Kerrig walked away, and Falerian followed. And if she got rather ahead of him at times, he didn't care to notice.

◆

It took the better part of the next day to arrange the meeting, and another day after that to work through all the explanations and objections. Eventually, however, a new plan emerged, one that limited the violence to taking down the Citadel's walls - and even then only if the governors refused to talk to them.

Once the altered plan was explained to the People, there was a lot more enthusiasm for the fight. Messages were passed back to the Island, and some who had previously held back were now willing to take part in the campaign. Everyone practised disabling, non-lethal attacks, and all weapons were discarded in favour of pure Elemental strength. It seemed fitting for the People of the Land to fight thus, Elements against foreign skills and technology. Morale soared, and people spent more and more time with their training groups. Kerrig could feel his fellow Earthers all around, and learned to identify each one by stance and tread alone. It was almost like being a child in the Great Sanctuary again, albeit without the distinctive scent of rock dust that always hung in the air.

Training time passed swiftly, and soon it was the night before the battle. The moons blazed full and bright overhead, and Kerrig fell asleep watching them.

Chapter Twenty-Four

It was dawn, and Kerrig stood beside a fading fire. He watched the sun rise over the water, casting long shadows down the line of small camps, each huddled around their own fires. It was time - by nightfall, the People would have their justice.

The camps stirred, and the day began. As planned, the fighters formed up in their groups, and marched to the Citadel. Earthers and Marshlanders flanked the line, with the Fire Breathers and Air Walkers in the middle and slightly ahead. When they reached the Citadel, the Air Walkers' group worked together to boost the voices of all the chiefs, sending a challenge booming over the Citadel louder than any one Air Walker could have managed alone. The People demanded justice, and offered the Citadel the chance to surrender peacefully.

They waited until noon. When the Citadel failed to respond, the People charged. Earthers raised a wall of soil on the left, while Marshlanders held a wall of water on the right. Air Walkers sent gale force winds to knock down the wooden walls of the Citadel, and Fire Breathers projected heat to burn them. Kerrig was swept up in the feeling of power that came from the People, and he knew that they were unstoppable.

Then the rocks began to fall.

Small stones, the largest no bigger than a clenched fist. It should have been an easy matter to dodge them, or let them get soaked up by the earthen shield. But there were so many, and the charging crowd left no room for individuals to move quickly. Kerrig felt the ground shudder as a rock landed inches from his feet. Another passed between his ear and his shoulder, grazing his shirt. There were screams of pain and shock tearing at the line, and someone crashed into Kerrig from behind.

The Earther gathered up some of the fallen rocks and tried to use them to strengthen the shield, but the wall of soil was crumbling as the Earthers who had held it were struck down, or scattered. Kerrig heard the Air-boosted cries of the chiefs to retreat, and he joined the mass of bodies in running back to the camp. He glanced back, once, to see a field littered with rocks, and the still bodies of the fallen. Killed or injured, he couldn't tell.

◆◆◆

Back at the camp, the Chiefs and their chosen aides were in the middle of what might charitably be called a lively discussion. Or, more realistically, a blazing row.

'What the screeding shale happened out there?' snapped one of the Earther chiefs. 'I thought you Airheads said you could pull that wall apart!'

'We could have,' replied an Air Walker, coldly. 'Just like you Dirt Crawlers could've shaken the ground from under their feet, if not for the fact that *the Citadel has Elementals, too.* Lots of them. Anything we can do, they can counter.'

A Marshlander chief looked scandalised at the very idea. 'No true Marshlander would fight for the Outsiders against the People!' he declared.

Kerrig raised an eyebrow at him. 'I don't know about that,' he said, 'But I do know that no true Earther would fail to defend their home. Are Marshlanders really any different?'

'Whether they're against us on principle, or just protecting themselves, the problem remains,' said a Fire Breather. 'There's nothing we can do that they can't counter. There's not one of our Elements that can win this.'

Kerrig blinked. Thoughts poured into his head faster than he could process them: Volnar, the hospital huts, escaping from Camp Freedom...

'You're right,' he said. 'Not one of our Elements can win this. We can't be Earthers, Marshlanders, Air Walkers, and Fire Breathers, not if we want to take back our Land. We have to be Shanzir.'

'Yes, well, if we had a legendary Shanzir, wielder of all the Elements, we'd be laughing. But the Outsiders killed them all, so we might as well wish for the moons.'

Kerrig smiled. 'Let me tell you about the Shanzir,' he said. 'I met one of them, not so long ago. Her name was Zirpa...'

Kerrig stood guard under his shell of soil, protecting himself, and the three people with him. He didn't know any of them well, but could trust that they all knew what to do. The Fire Breather was maintaining three small but hot fires, while the Marshlander and Air Walker sprayed the flames with a fine mist of water. The smoke and steam rose around them, shaped into a thick cloud hiding the group from the Citadel.

All around, similar groups of four raised their own clouds, covering the open plain in white patches. As the gaps closed, Kerrig switched to his Earther sense to watch what happened next. Even though he knew the plan, it was hard to keep track of everything.

There were scattered thumps as rocks landed, but they were undirected and desperate shots, fired into the fog at random. One hit Kerrig's shield, clattering on the fire-baked earth. It would have shattered, but Kerrig held it together.

Three large groups of Earthers and Marshlanders were hidden in the mist, sinking their combined strength into the ground. Three lines of muddy water surged towards the wooden walls of the Citadel, hidden just under the surface of the ground. The swampy mess hit the foundations of the wall, and became more water than earth. Kerrig's sense of it grew faint, but he heard the panicked cries of soldiers as the wall toppled beneath their feet.

The ground shook as more shots landed, still seemingly fired with no clear target. When the rocks stopped falling, Kerrig knew that the walls under the catapults must have fallen. He nodded at the Air Walker, who turned and spoke three words into the fog.

'Group five, clear.'

Minutes later, an answer whispered in everyone's ears, barely loud enough to be heard. If he hadn't known the plan, Kerrig would have believed it was his own thoughts.

'*Charge.*'

◆

Kerrig and the Marshlander guided their companions safely between the lines of water-weakened ground, while the Air Walker cleared the mist ahead. The Fire Breather held a small flame in his hands, ready to light up the arrows for his bow.

The earth beneath his feet sank down, then firmed up as the Marshlander drew on the water there for ammunition. Kerrig helped by drawing the wet earth towards himself, emptying the hidden waterway until it collapsed into a damp trench. He'd been practising the new (or at least recently re-discovered) art of mud-slinging, and it seemed like a good time to try it out.

He threw the mess of earth and water into the face of the first soldier he met, dodging as the soldier tried to burn him. Kerrig buried the uniformed Fire Breather up to his neck in the trampled ground, and moved on to the next soldier.

But there wasn't *a* next soldier - there were lots. The Fire Breather must have run on ahead, because now the People were facing a wall of soldiers, standing on the ruins of the wall of wood.

It was a nightmare. The plan hadn't gone this far - once the walls were down, they had expected the Citadel to surrender. Kerrig was hardly able to move, or tell friend from foe unless someone tried to attack him directly. Meanwhile, he was trying to subdue the enemy without killing anyone. It was impossible - there was no room to move, or even see clearly.

The big Earther pulled a second skin of soil and rock over his body and tried to simply push his way through the melee, but it was too thick. Someone stumbled into him from behind, and he turned to see Traegl there. She had an arrow sticking out of her upper arm, but was still using her other hand to spray water into the eyes of the soldiers.

The two of them stood back-to-back, blinding and trapping all the soldiers around them, but the crowd never seemed to thin. Then something larger than Traegl hit Kerrig's right side, and he felt the crushing blow through his improvised armour. Pieces of protective earth and rock flaked away like old bark.

The second blow clipped his head, and knocked the big Earther to the ground. Kerrig looked up into the face of an impossibly huge animal. The creature raised a foot to crush him, but suddenly stumbled backwards. Kerrig saw just enough to recognise Ash, in bird form, going for the other Sidrax's face. Then the Earther's own instincts took over and buried him in the safety of the soil, where he could pass out in peace.

◆

He woke up in a tent, though still more than half encased in earth. He turned his head and saw other Earthers in a similar state, all of them lying in neat rows. Kerrig moved to get up, but the soil around his legs tightened, and a hand landed firmly on his shoulder.

'Not yet, young man,' said a deep voice from over his head. 'You were brought in here less beaten up than most, but I still want to check you over before I let you move.'

Kerrig allowed himself to be lifted and prodded until the healer was satisfied. When he was done, the healer pulled back Kerrig's covering of Earth himself, and the cool air made the hairs on Kerrig's arms stand up.

The healer made his rounds of the other sleepers, then beckoned Kerrig to come outside. The two Earthers walked together around the many healing tents dotted around the edge of the battlefield, each big enough to hold a dozen patients. As they walked, the healer filled Kerrig in on events.

'From the looks of your injuries, and where we found you, it was the mammoth attack that took you down. Great big creatures, as tall as two men, with thick hides and wicked tusks. They packed a punch, I can tell you. Gave you a nasty crack on the head, and fractured a fair few of your ribs. If the head strike had been a hair lower, you'd have lost the sight in that eye. A thumb lower, and you'd've lost the whole head. You were lucky, friend Earther, very lucky.'

Kerrig glanced around at the bodies not in tents. The ones beyond helping, who had met their 'death or glory' end facing others of the People.

'Luckier than those poor devils, anyway,' he said, not quite under his breath.

Kerrig asked for details of the battle, and the healer was able to describe most of it. The soldiers had pulled back to clear a path for the large Sidrax, and then had been mobbed by angry townspeople, demanding to know who was going to pay for the damage to their homes and businesses.

'You can't be serious,' Kerrig said. 'People stopped soldiers in the middle of a battle to complain about property damage?'

'Well, the fighting was still outside the walls at that point,' said the healer. 'And market traders are very particular about anything that damages their livelihood.'

'The wall was down, the whole place was in chaos. What were they thinking?'

The healer shrugged, and said that he cured broken bodies, not broken minds. And really, a mob was a creature of very little brain and lots of momentum. Once it had latched onto an idea, it was not going to let go.

'And so, the soldiers inside were being held back by angry merchants, and the soldiers outside were trying to dodge the falling elephant. That young Sidrax friend of yours was as bold as a mountain, for all he's an Outsider.'

'Was?' Kerrig echoed, sharply. 'You don't mean he's...?'

The healer looked confused for a moment, then shook his head.

'Dead, you mean? No, not at all. Though his lady friend is in a bad way. I'm heading that way next, if you'd like to visit.'

Kerrig thought of Traegl, fighting on with one arm while Ash scouted overhead for dangers. It occurred to him that the young Sidrax had probably acted to save Traegl, and that Kerrig's own rescue was by way of a lucky bonus.

'And what happened after Ash took down the other Sidrax?' asked Kerrig, hastily cutting off that train of thought.

The healer replied that it was mostly over by then. The biggest fighters were down, as were the biggest weapons, and the townspeople were blocking up everything.

'It helped that we'd fought so defensively,' he said. 'The townies liked that. We killed no-one, did you know that? Some soldiers died, but they were almost all victims of the falling mammoth-shaped Sidrax. Some of those trapped in the earth were trampled, and others fell from sky traps when the Air Walkers holding them were hurt or killed.'

The healer ducked into another tent, and beckoned Kerrig to follow. Kerrig immediately noticed the two nearest occupied beds, one a netted hammock and the other a shallow pool. Traegl lay there, her hair floating around her face, and her body submerged in herb-clouded water.

Ash lay on the floor beside Traegl's bed, his hand clutching at hers where it floated, barely below the surface. Nesh was standing further back, with a girl-shaped Maddie in her arms. Two young Marshlanders were sitting by the water, with both hands submerged and very serious expressions. The healer took up a position beside Traegl's head, and began his examination. He was quick, calm, and professional, just as he had been with Kerrig. But when he was finished, he didn't smile.

'She's no worse,' he said at last. 'But she's no better, either. Keep the water moving, you two, and I'll find someone to take over before nightfall.'

The Marshlander healers nodded, and

The healer moved over to the hammock and Kerrig realised that it was Erben lying there. He wondered why Sanwe was not with him - unless she had... No, there was no point in assuming the worst.

The healer seemed pleased with Erben's condition, and soon left the tent. Kerrig quietly made a seat for himself near the door, joining his friends in their vigil.

After a while, Nesh came to join him. Kerrig extended the seat, and she sat down. Maddie was asleep in Nesh's arms, and Kerrig moved to take her until halted by the pain from his ribs.

'She'll be glad to see you,' said Nesh. 'I knew my part in this fight was over once I'd Found the best places to hit the walls, but it still made me feel useless, being left to mind the children while you went off to risk your lives.'

Kerrig raised an eyebrow at her. 'I thought you didn't want to be involved at all,' he said. 'In fact, I thought you'd come out here to say "I told you so", and remind me that all this pain and suffering is because I pushed for a fight.'

He kept his voice low so as not to disturb the sleeping Maddie, but he couldn't keep the bitterness out of his tone.

Nesh put a hand on his arm, but didn't say anything. There was a long moment, broken when Sanwe came into the tent. She was wearing a sling, but seemed otherwise unhurt.

'Is he awake?' she asked, before the tent flap could fall behind her.

Erben stirred in his hammock and tried to sit up. His wife was at his side in a moment, floating herself up to perch at his side. Kerrig looked away. It felt like an intrusion, watching their happiness. He glanced at Ash, and flinched from the expression of envy and hope he saw there.

Kerrig and Nesh quietly slipped outside, the Avlem still carrying Maddie. They saw the healer return with two assistants in tow. After a few moments, Erben and Sanwe joined them outside.

'The healer told us all we need now is fresh air,' said Sanwe, cheerfully. Kerrig noticed that her sling hung strangely loose at the front, and the Air Walker caught his look.

'Yes, there's a space where my hand used to be,' she said, not losing her smile. 'It's going to take a while to adjust to using Air to pick things up, but when I think of what I could have lost...'

Sanwe threw her good arm around her husband and hugged him fiercely.

'No contest,' she said.

Erben chuckled, then broke off when he saw Volnar picking his way through the tents towards them.

'Volnar! How are you? Keeping out of trouble, eh?' Erben laughed hugely at his own joke, and Maddie stirred in Nesh's arms.

'Hey there, Little One,' Kerrig said, and smiled down at her. 'I think it's about time we got you to a proper bed.'

'The Marshy-Lady was asleep in a pond,' Maddie told him. 'Why is she in a pond? Is she being a fish?'

Erben laughed again, and Maddie wriggled until Nesh set her down. Kerrig caught one of her hands in his to keep her from rushing back inside to see Traegl.

'No, Little One, Traegl isn't a fish. She doesn't make shapes like you or Ash. She's a Marshlander, and sleeping in water makes her feel better - the way earth makes me better.'

'Oh, good. Then she'll be awake soon, and then I get to wear flowers!'

The adults exchanged puzzled glances. 'Er, flowers?'

'Yes. When Ash and the Marshy-Lady gets married, I gets to be a donkey and carry all flowers, and wear them on my hair, and in my tail, and all everywhere! They said so.' Maddie forgot all she'd learned about speaking properly in her excitement at the prospect of dressing up.

'Oh, how lovely - our first wedding in the caravan!' said Sanwe. 'Except that we're not really doing the "caravan" part right now. But you know what I mean.'

'My darling, I never know what you mean,' said Erben, 'But I love you anyway.'

Sanwe swatted him with her sling, then winced in pain. Erben laughed again, and said it served her right for abusing her spouse.

'Never get married, son,' he said, fixing Volnar with a serious look. The boy snorted, which set Erben off again.

It was a loud laugh, full-throated and hearty, but it was not loud enough to drown out the cry of pain from within the tent. Kerrig was nearest, and pulled back the tent flap just in time to meet the healer coming out. Behind him, Kerrig could see one of the assistants gently lowering Traegl's head under the surface of the water.

'I'm sorry,' said the healer. 'I couldn't save her.'

From behind the tent, a jet-black hawk launched itself into the clouds and screamed at the sky.

Chapter Twenty-Five

'It's not your fault,' Nesh said, looking out across the churned-up field. 'All this. I know you didn't really want to fight; you just wanted justice. I can understand that. Honestly, I hoped my people were more civilised than this.'

'They are,' Kerrig said, softly. 'But it's an Avlem and Sidrean civilisation, and that doesn't fit onto the Land or its People.' The Earther followed her gaze over the humps that marked the hasty graves. 'We don't have cities and academies, but we have our ways. Or we did, when the Shanzir still roamed.'

'The old ways are still there, we've just added some new routes,' Nesh said. 'But I agree, it's no use trying to make this land into a second Avlenia, or Sidria. The Land is its own place, and needs its own rules.'

'And its own rulers,' Kerrig added. 'Though Time only knows how that's going to work out. The chiefs still argue over the smallest things.'

'That we do,' said a new voice, or rather, an old one. The oldest of the Earther chiefs had emerged from his tent and come up behind them. Kerrig felt his face flush, but the older man only laughed.

'Being a chief is about respect,' he said. 'Not just getting respect from the tribe, but respecting them, too. And the other chiefs, and even other tribes. I'm still struggling with that one, but you seem pretty good at it. Don't forget that, when you meet the governors.'

'Yessir,' said Kerrig, automatically. Then, 'Wait, what do you mean meet the governors? Why am I going to meet the governors?'

'The Citadel sent a message. They will see exactly four representatives to discuss terms. Trying to pick one chief from each tribe is an exercise in futility, but it seems that most of them respect you. Even the Air Walker chiefs thought you could be trusted to carry their demands without "accidentally" forgetting about them. So, Kerrig, you, and three others, are going to see the governors. Do you have any recommendations for who those three should be?'

Kerrig hesitated, overwhelmed. After a moment, he said, 'I think Sanwe should come with me. She's more outspoken than her husband, and we'll need to be clear about what we ask for. Ash should come too. It's only fair, after nearly getting himself killed trying to deliver this message the first time.'

'An Air Walker and a Sidrax?' said the Earther chief. 'Kerrig, I don't think you've thought this through. You can only take three companions, and whether you pick a Fire Breather or a Marshlander for your third, the other tribe is going to feel slighted.'

Kerrig smiled. 'I know,' he said. 'That's why I've chosen Nesh to be the fourth. We have to start trusting each other, if we ever want to be the People in Unity again.'

'I thought I was an Outsider,' said Nesh. 'You said this fight was none of my business. Why do you want me with you now?'

The Earther struggled to meet her eyes, but eventually he said, 'I was wrong. This is about justice for the People of the Land, and that has to mean all people, not just the Peopl- the Elementals.

'You don't have to come, of course, but, well, you know the Land as well as anyone, and better than most. And you know about Avlem manners, too, so we can avoid any accidental rudeness. We don't want any... misunderstandings.'

Nesh gave Kerrig a small smile. 'A misunderstanding? That's an interesting way to describe the last century. But you're right, if I'm there, we shan't have any *accidental* rudeness.'

◆

The council chamber was impressive, if rather crowded. The three governors and four representatives sat in a circle, on exquisitely carved chairs. There was an awkward moment when Sanwe expressed interest in watching an Avlem carpenter at work, but she recovered smoothly by adding that it would be fascinating to see such a skilled crafter create things that no-one else could.

Awkwardness averted, the negotiations began in earnest. They were... disappointing.

Kerrig had expected lively debate, where he would struggle to stay calm while sensitive topics were discussed. After an hour he realised that 'negotiations' was code for endless droning; and only the ache in his ribs kept him awake while tedious minutiae were dissected.

He took a look at his fellow representatives while he pretended to listen to proposals for road maintenance on the Fire Plains. The three governors were business-like, but languid. They gave the impression that they could, and frequently did, keep this up all day. Nesh was watching them shrewdly, as if they were a rock she wanted to cleave. She didn't speak often, but when she did it was sharp and effective, like splitting slate. Sanwe seemed almost as bored as Kerrig felt, and she was using tiny currents of air to braid and unbraid her hair, much as Kerrig himself was drumming out silent rhythms with his toes. The wooden floor was far too thick and polished to respond, but the motion made him feel better. A bit.

Ash was the only one in the room who was showing any enthusiasm for the discussions. Kerrig doubted that the younger man was really so enthralled by the upkeep of roads, and made a mental note to prepare for the fallout when Ash's attempts at distracting himself failed.

There came a break for lunch, and the seven dispersed into their own comfort zones. Kerrig went outside, found a patch of grass, and lay flat on it, soaking up the feel of good, clean earth. He closed his eyes against the sun and let himself drift off into a light doze, until a shadow fell across his face. The Earther opened his eyes and sat up. Ash was standing next to him.

Kerrig wasn't very good at reading people's faces, but just one look at Ash suggested that now wasn't a good time for, well, anything. Wordlessly, the older man sat up and gestured for Ash to join him.

The two men sat in silence for a long time, looking out across the courtyard. The shadows moved. Eventually, Ash said,

'Do you think it would be alright for Volnar to take over for me in there? I don't think I can stand another minute of minutes and agendas.'

Kerrig took a moment to consider his reply.

'Volnar's a bit young for that, don't you think?' he said, carefully. 'And the Marshlanders won't like it if the Fire Breathers are given a voice and they aren't.'

Ash sighed. 'I'm sorry, I can't... I thought I could handle it, but, I...'

Kerrig carefully didn't look at Ash. When he heard a stifled sob, he reached out and pulled the youngster into a one-armed hug, letting Ash hide his face against Kerrig's shoulder.

'You're doing fine, Ash,' he said. 'Just fine. I don't think I can take anymore minuting either. What say we go in and light a fire under things?'

The Sidrax gave a watery chuckle. 'So you do want to bring Volnar in, then?' he said.

'Well, either that or you can turn into a wolf at them.'

◆

After that, things began to move more quickly. Sanwe and Nesh must have reached similar conclusions about the lengths of their respective tethers, because they started pushing for speed and practicality at every turn. And one such turn was the matter of Camp Freedom.

Nesh, Ash, and Kerrig were vocal in their condemnation of the place, and Sanwe said that she was horrified by what she'd heard of it. Air Walkers using their abilities to control others was dubious enough when it was used to drive people away from something, but to use it as a prison was going beyond 'dubious' and into downright immoral.

The three governors expressed surprise at the levels of outrage coming from the representatives.

'But Camp Freedom is an Elemental-led project,' said one governor. 'A humane way to discourage rebellion, and give the traditionalists somewhere to live. Why, the Air Walker who proposed the scheme was quite brilliant - and very enthusiastic.'

'Really now?' said Sanwe, dry as a desert wind.

'Oh yes,' said one of the other governors. 'And she was from a village somewhere up in Peaks, so she knew what she was talking about. What was her name? Val'rn? Something very traditional, I remember that much.'

There was a rustling of papers as the governors' clerks sorted through the stacks to find the correct documents. Kerrig, Nesh, and Ash exchanged glances. It couldn't be, could it?

'Here we are,' said the first governor, happily. 'Proposal for a reserve on the island in the Great River, by Falerian of the Clear Ice Peaks. I don't see how any of you can object to that, it was suggested by one of your own.'

'Exactly,' snapped Sanwe, '*One* of us. Not all, not most, not even some. One. Was she an appointed representative? A village chief? Even a family head? No. One crazy Air Walker with a plan, and you think that's an example of "Elemental-led"? Perhaps Nesh would like to come up with an idea off the top of her head right now, and we'll call that the official Avlem position on things, shall we?'

'Falerian's not crazy,' said Ash, in the silence that followed Sanwe's outburst. 'She's selfish, and vicious, and easily bored, but she's not crazy. Of course Camp "Freedom" was her idea. And she took us straight there. Curse the little fiend.'

'Come to think of it,' said Nesh, 'Has anyone seen her since the fighting stopped? I couldn't Find her in any of the healers' tents, and she wasn't among the fallen, either. Oh... sorry, Ash.'

'She probably cleared off once the fun was over' said Ash, with a forced, faltering lightness in his voice. 'She must have known we'd find out about her clever little idea once we started talking instead of fighting. Ha, "Nobody likes you, Falerian". That's what Trae always used to tell her. You were right, my love. More right than you knew.'

'The lousy traitor,' said Kerrig. 'I should have known she couldn't be trusted.'

'Because she's an Air Walker?' asked Sanwe.

'Because she's *Falerian*,' corrected the Earther. 'It turns out that some Air Walkers can be trusted, and some can't.

'Just like anyone, eh?'

Kerrig gave Sanwe a wry smile and inclined his head to her.

'Just like anyone,' he said.

One of the governors cleared her throat noisily.

'Getting back to the topic in hand,' she said, 'We can't just give up on dissidents. If we allow rebellion to grow unchecked, there will be chaos.'

Nesh glowered at them. 'The whole point of this meeting is to correct the injustices that cause rebellion. We need to solve the problem, not just react to it.'

'Rebellion will always exist, though,' said Kerrig thoughtfully. 'No matter what solutions we come up with, there will always be some people who are unhappy about them. We'll need a system in place to deal with that, including a way to contain those who insist on making trouble.'

'You can't seriously want to keep Camp Freedom,' said Sanwe, billowing her robes out dramatically.

'Of course not,' said Kerrig. 'I was thinking that a portion of the Great Sanctuary could be sectioned off to house the more violent and disruptive types. Not Earthers, though; they'd have to be kept elsewhere. Perhaps out at sea.'

Nesh smiled. 'I never thought I'd hear you admit to the possibility of Earthers ever being violent or disruptive,' she said.

Kerrig shrugged. 'Not *true* Earthers, naturally.'

There was a moment of tense silence before Ash caught the look in Kerrig's eye and laughed.

Not all the discussions went so smoothly. The Fire Plains would likely remain hotly disputed territory for generations, and opening up the Sidrax Academy to non-Sidrax was going to take some serious thought; most of the study programs were designed around learning new forms. And then there was the matter of spreading, and enforcing, all these new rules.

After two weeks of consultations, Kerrig found he actually missed the sunshine. Strange, considering that he'd been nearly ten years old before he saw the sky. The council chamber was suffocating in a way that no cave or seam could ever be, and he couldn't wait to get back to real life again.

But where was his life now? On the Island? With the Caravan? In the newly liberated Great Sanctuary? He'd changed so much in the last year that he hardly knew himself. He was still Kerrig, but Kerrig of where?

He considered his options for someone to talk this over with. Ash didn't seem to have a place he called home, and it was a touchy subject for Nesh. Maddie was too young, and Volnar - well, home for Volnar was the Citadel, in all its stuffy glory. He'd probably advise Kerrig to stay put and start a business selling rocks or something.

After weighing his options carefully, Kerrig sought out Erben. He didn't know the man particularly well, but he at least had experience of leaving home and facing the unexpected. After a bit of searching, Kerrig found the Air Walker sitting outside a local brewer's shop.

Erben was boisterously pleased to see him, and Kerrig wondered just how long he'd been sitting there, trying different brews.

'Great news about the promotion, eh? Seven governors, there's going to be, and my Sanwe's one of them. And you too, of course. If you stay. You're staying, aren't you? You wouldn't leave us in the lurch, eh, Kerrig? Course not.'

The bewildered Earther beat a hasty retreat to the council chamber and asked, rather desperately, what was going on. He was told that the representatives had the option of staying on the council and becoming permanent members, or of nominating a suitable replacement.

'Will you stay on, Kerrig?' asked Ash. 'I know Sanwe wants to, and I'm thinking about accepting, too.'

'I... I don't know,' said Kerrig. 'When do you want a decision?' he asked the assembled governors and representatives.'

'There's no rush, Mr. Kerrig,' said one of the Avlem governors. 'Take your time and think it over.'

◆◆◆

Kerrig was still thinking it over the next day, when Nesh came looking for him.

'Have you decided yet?' she said, by way of a greeting.

Kerrig groaned and rubbed his temples. 'No,' he admitted. 'I'm trying to do right by everyone, but I've got too many responsibilities. I feel that I'll be letting people down no matter what I choose.'

'Never mind all that for a moment.' Nesh came and sat on the window seat beside him. 'What do *you* want to do?'

'I *want* to do my duty and fulfil my responsibilities,' Kerrig told her. Nesh conceded the point, but pressed on.

'Well then, where do you want to be? Do you want to live here, in the Citadel?'

Kerrig actually flinched. 'No,' he said. 'I don't like it here, it's too... it's the wrong kind of busy. I really want to start up the caravan again, and work my way back towards the Great Sanctuary. I'm an Earther, and I specialise in working with stone. And there's a lifetime of repair work needed there.'

'So why don't you?' said Nesh.

'Why don't I what?'

'Go. Gather up the caravan, and head northward. Sally forth into the noonday sun, hero, your work here is done.'

Kerrig laughed, then grew grave. 'Is it, though? People still need so much.'

'And they always will,' said Nesh. 'You're allowed to be a little selfish sometimes, you know.'

Kerrig was silent for a long moment, then he nodded. 'I'll head out when my ribs have healed properly,' he declared. 'After all, I need to visit Traegl's family again; and I did promise Maddie I'd take her home one day. What about you? Have you decided to stay on as "Governor Nesh"?'

'I... no, I haven't decided yet. There's a lot to consider. Right now, I'm not even sure what I want.'

Kerrig watched his friend's face become lined with worry and uncertainty.

'Let's think about it tomorrow,' he suggested, and turned to look out of the window. Volnar had shed his business attire for the day and was leading a crowd of smaller children in some sort of game. Ash was sitting in the shade, talking with a few of the Citadel's soldiers. The sun was shining. And, for now, the Land was at peace.

-- The End --

Acknowledgements

This book had its start in 2013, and has grown a lot along the way. Big thanks to Ella Barnard, Megan Barnhard, Deanne Adams, and everyone from the Arvon week in April 2016. Yes, I've finally finished this one!

Thanks also to my mam and sister for their support in all things. Thanks for being my first readers, and first fans.

Thanks to my writer friends, for the practical help, and to my non-writer friends for your infinite patience.

Thanks to everyone who listened while I rambled on about this idea, and encouraged me to get it written. And thanks to you, for reading.

Read the next fragment...

At 17 years old, Brinesha Tynnar is young, privileged, and determined to get justice for the down-trodden Elementals of the Land.

But things are seldom as straightforward as they seem, and trusting the wrong people leaves Brinesha facing some serious consequences...

The Avlem Burden
Coming 2022

Printed in Great Britain
by Amazon

62269936R00166